DIVERGING CADENCE

KATIE HAMSTEAD

DIVERGING CADENCE

book 2

Cover design by Ashley Ruggirello

ISBN: 978-1-942111-24-5

This is a work of fiction. Names, characters, places and incidents are either the product of the author's imagination or are used fictitiously, and any resemblance to actual persons, living or dead, business establishments, events or locals is entirely coincidental.

REUTS Publications
www.REUTS.com

As always, for my wonderful husband, Landon, and all the 1986ers out there.

part one:

changes

Chapter One

The plane shuddered as it touched down on the runway. After five hours in the air, I was more than ready to get out and into the sunny West Coast heat.

During the flight, I'd wished I had James by my side. The pain in his eyes and the ache in his kiss lingered with me. I sucked my lip, glancing at the woman beside me while we taxied toward a gate. After being together for more than three years, being apart from him felt strange. Had I done the right thing?

The seatbelt light blinked off, and the plane filled with clicking and murmurs as the other passengers prepared to disembark. I sighed, pulling my bag out from under the seat. Although eager to get off the plane, I wasn't in a hurry—check-in at the student accommodations ran all day, and classes didn't start for almost a week. After opening the bag to replace my Discman and novel, I noticed a little wrapped package had fallen to the bottom. I pulled it out, staring at the mystery gift.

The lady beside me filed into the aisle with the other passengers, leaving me alone. I unwrapped the gift and a silver charm bracelet fell into my hand. I found a note in the wrapping:

Cadence—

The bracelet is just something I hope will help you remember me. The basketball is the closest I could get to a netball, so I put it next to the soccer ball to help you remember our crazy winter Saturdays, and because you're an insane sports nut. Then there's a musical note to go with your name, and a wing because you're my angel and I hope you will fly back to me.

I love you,

James

My heart melted as tears blurred my vision. Taking a deep breath, I clipped the bracelet around my wrist and stood to join the last of the people disembarking.

Although years had passed in this new timeline, returning to the place that had changed my life made the memories of my first vibrant again. Austin, Melody, our friends and family, they all waited for me, but I'd also left family and friends behind. Geri, Harper, Dusty, and especially James hadn't been in my life the last time I'd done this, or at least, not like now. Harper and Dusty might be my siblings, but this time around, they were my friends too. And Geri and Dusty . . . their secret stolen kiss over New Year's had me excited about the possibilities between my best friend and brother.

I hurried through the airport to collect my bags. I'd become so accustomed to the Perth airport in the first timeline that I didn't bat an eye as I found a taxi for the half-hour journey to my student accommodations.

In the cab, I turned on my phone. Three texts popped up immediately—one from Dad, another from Geri, and of course, one from James—all asking me to check in with them once I'd arrived safely.

I typed out quick messages to each, taking a little longer to work on James's and to make sure I thanked him for the bracelet. I missed him already. I imagined how obnoxious he would have been on the flight over, and again I doubted leaving him behind. But I had to do this. I had to know what could happen with Austin, if I could get back the life I'd had ripped from me. The whole point of reliving this part of my life was to save him and Melody—to get my family back.

The taxi pulled up at the student accommodations. I climbed out and looked up at the dormitory where I'd lived my first year before moving into a small flat with my soon-to-be friend Lyla. The red brick buildings brought back more memories—hours of studying, hanging out with Lyla, flirting shamelessly with the guys—but despite the familiarity, everything felt so new. A rush of adrenaline pulsed through me. Like high school, I'd do university better this time around.

As I dragged my suitcases behind me, I gazed around at the familiar faces of people I didn't know yet. It felt exciting and nerve-racking all at once. If Geri were with me, she'd comment on all the guys, telling me I was lucky I didn't have to worry about them because I had James, who, according to her, was perfect for me.

"Cadence Anderson." The woman at the check-in desk scanned a list. "A Sydney girl, huh?"

I nodded. "I wanted to try something new."

"Hopefully we can make your wish come true." She gave me a winning smile. "Your room is on the top floor. Turn left, and you'll find it about halfway down."

I shuffled along toward the stairwell and dodged a football after I heard, "Heads up!"

A guy with dirty blond hair, who I remembered would develop a major crush on me, grabbed one of my suitcases. "Hey, need some help? Where are we going?"

I didn't want to encourage him. I tried to protest, but he charged ahead of me.

"Just take it up to the top floor and I'll be fine from there." I met him at the third floor and took my bag from him. "Thanks."

"No worries. I'll be seein' ya 'round, unless you're one of those hermit types." He winked at me. *Oh, good heavens.*

I hurried to my room and shut the door firmly behind me to block out all the noise. The room looked exactly how I remembered it, with a bed by the wall, a small desk with shelves built over it, and a wardrobe with mirrored sliding doors.

Exhausted, I kicked my bags against the wall, then lifted one onto the desk to unpack. I made my bed, put my clothes in the closet, and finally pulled out my scrapbook. Setting it on the desk, I ran my finger over the black cover.

When I opened it, the picture of Austin and Melody rested on the title page for 2005. I smiled, excited by the prospect of seeing Austin soon. We could start all over again, fall in love again, have Melody, and more . . .

Except . . .

Moving the picture of them, I found the picture I'd taken of me and James underneath. I still loved James so much. Closing my eyes, I took a deep breath. How would I handle that? Our relationship wasn't supposed to last this long. I was fifteen when we started dating! How many fifteen-year-olds date the same guy for more than three years?

And he wanted to marry me.

Grabbing my jewelry box from my suitcase, I set it on the desk and opened it. Inside sat the necklace he'd given me for our first anniversary, the sapphire ring he gave me for our second, and the engagement ring he gave me for our third. I had other jewelry too, but those three items stood out. They were a testament to James's love—our love.

I lifted the engagement ring and turned it in my fingers. The diamonds glittered in the sunlight coming through the window. Missing him more than ever, I slid it on my right hand. I had a year before Austin came along, so putting off losing James seemed like the best thing. I didn't want to lose him, ever, but so much could change in a year.

Flicking through the pages of the scrapbook, I remembered struggling with homesickness for the first few months. Since I had left so much behind this time, especially compared to last, I set my mind to avoiding the longing.

Grabbing my handbag, I set out for the campus. First things first: student services.

Unlike the first time, I didn't feel overwhelmed and confused. I headed directly for the office and jumped in the line for my student ID. No drama, all done in minutes. I remembered it being far more complicated.

Once "official," I signed up for the netball team and the gym. Being involved and busy always kept the homesickness at bay. Then I checked the notice board and found my job from the first timeline advertised as open. I grabbed the details for the local supermarket twice, since Lyla would also need the information once we met. It would be a good job with reasonable pay and flexible hours; the owner had kids of his own in university and high school.

Since it was getting dark as I left the campus, I stopped for a sub. Once back at the dorm, I headed straight for the stairs.

"Hey!"

I glanced back at the male voice. The blond guy from earlier trotted over to me. "Are you coming in for dinner?"

"Ahh . . ." I raised the bag with my sub. "Not today."

He tilted his head, his eyes gleaming. "Bring it in with you."

I glanced toward the stairs. "I'm kind of tired. I had a long flight, and I came in from the East Coast, so . . ."

"Ah, okay. A few hours out."

"Yeah, time zones."

He thumbed toward the dining hall. "Next time, then."

I just smiled and headed toward the stairs. There was no way I'd consider him. Plus, I had James, who outshone him in my eyes. I didn't want to lead on the poor guy.

Back in my room, I called Geri while I ate. She screamed as her "hello," nearly deafening me. We talked about my flight and my room, and she dodged my questions about Dusty.

Next, I called home. "Cadence, sweetheart," Dad answered.

"Hey, Dad," I said, grinning. "Just letting you know I'm safe."

"Great. Is the security like the website explained?"

I rolled my eyes. "Yeah."

"Good. Make sure you lock your door and window."

"*Dad.*" I shook my head.

"I just want you to be safe," he said gently. "I can't be there to watch over you, so I worry. There's no boys nearby, are there?"

"The boys are in a separate building."

"Good, good."

"You wouldn't be the only one upset if we shared a building. I think James would have a thing or two to say about it."

"James has no room to complain," Dad mumbled. "He came here after you left."

"Oh yeah?" I grinned, lying back on my bed.

"Yeah. He and Dusty spent the day together. They went out and Dusty came back battered and bruised, so I don't know if I'll let that happen again."

I chuckled. "Dusty can hold his own. He's not a kid anymore."

"He's sixteen! Of course he's a kid."

"Dad." I smirked. "Chances are Dusty brought it on himself."

"Your boyfriend is a bad influence on him," Dad grumbled.

"Anyway," I said, redirecting our conversation. "I went down and picked up my student ID . . ."

Dad and I talked for a while. He let Mum talk to me for a few minutes before he snatched the phone back to warn me about the dangers of university boys. I told him not to worry because I had James. He responded by pointing out that James was one of them too.

When we finally said goodbye, my eyelids drooped. In Sydney it was 10:00 p.m., even if my clock showed 8:00 p.m. local time. I'd had a long day, and a long flight, but I needed to make one more call.

"Hey, beautiful," James said.

I sighed, smiling. "Hey, James. Would it be pathetic of me to say I miss you already?"

"Pathetic, yes, but completely understandable. I *am* a stud."

I chuckled. "Do you miss me?"

"I dunno," he said with a sigh. "There were these girls at the airport today—I think their names were Geri and Harper?—and they were hugging me and basically all over me."

I groaned, rubbing my forehead. "Oh my gosh."

"They were pretty hot."

"Uh-huh."

"You don't think your sister and best friend are hot?"

"You're not going to make me jealous," I said, smirking.

He laughed. "I can try."

I shook my head, curling up in bed. "I'm in bed right now."

"That's so hot. Are you naked?"

"James!"

"What? I can fantasize."

"Anyway," I said with a grin, "Dad said you hung out with Dusty today."

"You called your dad first? I'm offended."

"James." I rolled my eyes. "I wanted to be able to talk to you for however long I wanted."

"Oh, I guess that's okay then."

"So, you went out with Dusty?" I said, trying to get him to be serious for a moment.

"Yeah. The kid's psycho. He's probably worse than you."

I smirked. "What did you two do?"

"I thought it would be fun to go to the raceway, you know, to drive the go-karts. But he has that insane competitive streak too! He tried to force me off the track any time I came near him."

I laughed.

"It's not funny! You two are way too similar at times. It borders on creepy. No wonder he has a thing for Geri and loves me so much."

"Did he mention Geri at all?" I grinned as I climbed out of bed to change my clothes.

"Um, yeah. Did you know he kissed her over New Year's?"

I giggled.

"Of course you did. But he says she's avoiding him now."

My heart sank. I loved the idea of Geri and Dusty together. Even though he was two years younger than her, I could see them working. Dusty had never settled down in the first timeline. In fact, I couldn't remember him seriously dating anyone. "Should I talk to her?"

"*No*," James said sharply. "Dusty needs time. He knows he's got a steep hill to climb—he doesn't need her best friend getting involved."

"But I—"

"Trust me. Dusty talks to me about *everything*. Sometimes it's kind of annoying, but he's a cool kid. He's got a lot of game for a sixteen-year-old."

"Okay, I'll leave it." I pulled a baggy t-shirt over my head. "So if you were go-karting, how did Dusty get all beaten up?"

James laughed. "Because he's an idiot. Somehow he managed to flip his. I have no idea how he did it, because those suckers grip to the ground. The staff guy was pretty pissed off, but luckily the kart wasn't damaged, just Dusty's face and shoulder."

"What did he do?"

"His helmet knocked his jaw around, and his shoulder got all grazed up, but he *still* wanted to take me on. Come to think of it, I definitely think he's worse than you."

I chuckled.

"But it was fun. A great distraction." He sighed. "I wish you were there too. Seeing you leave . . ."

"I'm sorry," I said softly as I sank back onto the bed.

"It's okay," he said with a trembling voice. "You said you need this, so I'm going to go along with it. I trust you, and I love you. We'll get through this."

I snuggled my pillow, wishing it was James. After sleeping by his side for more than a month, I missed his warm presence, his arm draped lazily over my waist. "I wish you were here."

"Cadence," he said gently. "I'll call you every day, or at least, I'll try. Work and uni might get in the way for both of us, but I'll do everything I can. Don't worry about a thing. I'll always be right here for you."

I yawned, closing my eyes. "That means so much to me."

"You should go to bed," he said. "Goodnight, beautiful."

"I love you," I muttered.

He hung up, leaving me drifting in a contented haze. My family and friends, despite the distance, were still close to me. And James wasn't going anywhere.

Chapter Two

When I awoke, I felt for James in the bed, but he wasn't there. My heart sank. It felt like a month had passed since I woke beside him the previous morning. But I refused to cry. He stayed strong for me at the airport, so I needed to stay strong too.

I climbed off the bed and turned on a light to check the time. Breakfast had started already, but the dining hall would be pretty empty. I cleaned up, dressed, and hurried down to the dining hall. As expected, because of the early hour and lack of commitments, the line for food was nonexistent.

I filled my tray and looked around at my soon-to-be friends scattering the room. I sat in the vacant chair opposite my future roommate, Lyla. She glanced up at me, flicking her straight black hair over her shoulder. She wore heavy black eyeliner, but with her olive complexion, she looked far from Goth. In contrast to her hair and makeup, she wore an indigo Billabong t-shirt and a shell necklace, both displaying her love for surfing. I had every intention of being friends with her as soon as possible to fill the void left by Geri not being around. I needed someone to hang out with regularly, and since her room was down the hall from mine, we'd end up spending many hours together.

I smiled at her as I started eating, and she smiled back. Finally, I cleared my throat and said, "I'm Cadence."

She stretched out her hand. "You have an equally obnoxious name as me. I'm Lyla."

"I think Lyla is pretty."

She scoffed. "If I was from Texas, maybe."

I hurried to change the topic, knowing how easily set off she was about her name. "What are you studying?"

She swallowed her mouthful. "Aboriginal health. I'm from the sticks, so I wanna go back and help out my community."

I nodded. I'd always been impressed by her nobility. "That's awesome."

"Yeah, you're just humoring me. I know it's boring."

"No, not at all! Aboriginal mortality rates are generally higher than similar demographics, so I think that's a very noble cause."

She stared at me, gaping. "Wow, you're the smartest blonde chick I've ever met." She leaned forward, suddenly interested in me. "So, what are you studying?"

I dodged her gaze. "Nothing anywhere near as selfless as you. I'm studying sports science."

She looked me over with a crooked smile. "I can see that. You have that sports girl look about you. Not too thin, not too fat, nicely toned, but not over the top. But your rack is considerably larger than the standard B-cup. What are you, a D?"

I smiled at her forward manner. "Yeah, a D."

"I bet guys like to come to your comps just to watch you bounce."

I covered my mouth to hold in my food as I burst out laughing. She grinned, obviously liking me. "Hey, we should hang out. I don't know anyone here, so . . ."

"I don't either," I answered. It wasn't technically lying, since physically I'd never been there before. "I'm from Sydney."

She raised her eyebrows. "Ohh, big city girl. I met a girl from Melbourne once and didn't like her at all. She turned out to be a huge snob."

"I hope I'm not like that."

A smirk spread across her face. "Well, Miss Musical Terminology, I guess we'll find out."

We finished eating and headed upstairs to retrieve our class schedules, agreeing to explore the campus to find where we needed to go. So, with maps in hand, we climbed onto the shuttle.

"I noticed you're only a few doors down from me," Lyla said as we rode along.

"Yeah. That's pretty cool." I smiled. "But I promise I won't harass you constantly. I'm pretty private, so I can respect your privacy too."

She nodded. "Sounds good." Then, with a sparkle in her eyes, she said, "You know what we should do?"

I grinned, my memories of her rushing back to me. Although reserved most of the time, she occasionally showed glimpses of a wild side.

"Check out the campus bar." She winked.

I glanced at my map. "There's a tavern here, but mostly it looks like cafés."

She chuckled evilly. "Cafés are only useful when you've had a late night at the tavern."

I let out a short laugh as we climbed off the bus.

We made our way around the campus finding our rooms, and Lyla insisted on finding the nearest bathroom and emergency exit to each as well. Although an odd combination, Lyla was quirky, and I'd missed it.

We found the tavern for lunch, and she sampled their beer while I stayed "dry." She loosened up and grew very giggly on the way back to the dorms. It made me snicker, and people on the bus gave us odd stares. We wandered the property the rest of the afternoon, and when we found a group of guys playing cricket, Lyla insisted we stop in the shade to watch.

"Hot guys," she said dreamily. "Thanks for hanging out with me today. It probably wouldn't have been anywhere near as fun on my own."

"No worries." I stared across at the game, getting irritated with the guy batting because he wasn't doing it right.

"Hey, that's a pretty bracelet." She brushed her finger over the chain. "A gift from someone special, maybe?"

I hesitated. James was incredibly special to me, but I'd had memories of Austin floating around in my mind the whole day. I couldn't tell Lyla about James when she'd eventually meet Austin and support my relationship with him.

"Cadence? You've kinda zoned out."

"Sorry." I gave her a quick smile. "It is from someone special—my best friend back in Sydney."

"Cute." She flicked the wing. "Are you missing them?"

My heart skipped. "Who?"

"Your friends and family back in Sydney, duh."

"Oh . . . yeah." I released the tension from my shoulders. "I'm pretty tight with my family, and I have friends I've been with for years. It feels strange not having them with me."

"I completely understand. Except I don't really have friends, and my family and I aren't close." She scowled, tapping her toes together.

"Maybe you can start fresh here."

A wide smile grew across her face. "Yeah."

Back at my room, I collapsed onto the bed. *What a day!* I clasped my heart and grinned like an idiot. Everything was back on track. With Lyla back in my life—and when classes started, Tara would be too—I'd have a blast leading up to meeting Austin. They'd given me back my faith in friends the first time, so this time I wanted to give them my friendship wholeheartedly. No broken Cadence, just fun, happy Cadence.

My phone rang. Rolling onto my belly, I answered with a grin. "Geraldine."

"Ugh, *why* would you call me *that?*" Geri's beautiful voice came through loud and clear, and after my day out and about, hearing my best friend in the world made it all complete.

"It's your name, isn't it?"

"Technically, but not the point."

I laughed. "So . . ."

"Yeah, so how is it so far?"

"You know, introductions, exploring in advance so I don't get lost . . ."

"Yeah, same here. My only complaint is the serious lack of guys in my course. Oh, especially straight guys. Can you believe that stereotype is true?"

I laughed.

"Seriously, how am I ever going to meet anyone?"

"I'm sure you'll do just fine." I smirked at the memory of her and Dusty kissing on New Year's.

"Oh no. I don't like that tone."

"What tone?" My smirk grew.

"That whole 'I know so much' tone. Nope, I'm *not* dating your brother."

"I didn't say anything about Dusty." I bit my lip to stop from laughing.

"Good, because he's, like, a dorky kid. Ew! No, I'm going to find a sophisticated pre-med guy, preferably *older*."

I giggled. "Go for it, then."

"You're so stuck on me being with your brother! Cut it out!"

I laughed again. *Talk about oversensitive.* "I didn't say anything like that."

"Yes, but your *tone*. It's there. I can feel it."

"Geri." I shook my head. I couldn't believe how much she liked Dusty! So much denial on her part. "Just have fun, okay? And be safe. I miss you."

She sighed. "Aw, Cay. It's all your fault."

"I know."

We talked for more than an hour, catching up on how things had gone for our first days and social lives so far. I told her about Lyla, and she made me swear not to like her more. I laughed, claiming that was impossible.

My phone beeped. Looking at it, I saw James calling through and I grinned. "Geri, James is calling."

She sighed dramatically. "Of course, ditch me for your boyfriend."

"I can ignore it?"

"Please don't." She snorted. "Did you know he was at your parents' house all day today? Talk about desperate."

"And *how* do you know that?" I smirked again.

"Just answer him!" And she hung up.

I laughed as I answered James. "Hey."

"You're in a good mood." His voice lifted my spirits even higher. "What's so funny?"

"Geri." I flopped onto my back. "Has she visited Dusty?"

He let out an evil laugh. "Oh yeah."

"This is awesome." I stretched, grinning. "By the way, what's with you hanging out at the house?"

"Your dad loves me. I think he's considering trading Harper for me."

"You're so weird."

"But you love me," he said gently.

"I do."

A brief pause followed. "I miss you."

"James." I sighed, tears welling in my eyes. After spending almost every day with him for so long, his absence left a noticeable hole in my life. I curled up with my blanket again, missing having him to do the same.

"I'm making you cry."

I snorted. "You wish."

"I totally am." He chuckled.

"How's your course going?" I asked, wiping my eyes.

"Nice segue."

Like always, our conversation flowed easily. We talked for so long I missed dinner, but I didn't care. Getting a cab to get fast food seemed more than worth it to hear James's excitement about how well everything was going for him, and to tell him all about my new friend. He even stayed on the line as I ordered my meal, teasing me for choosing the "wrong" burger.

Finally, on the way back to the dorm, he realized how late it was there, being two hours ahead. He said goodbye, and I made my way back to my room with a deep contentment.

As I reached my floor, Lyla waited by my door holding a paper bag with food. Although I wasn't hungry, I was touched by her thoughtfulness. With so many good people around me, I'd never been happier. I had months before Austin would step into my life, so I pushed the fear of losing James far from my mind. I'd deal with that when I came to it.

I smiled as Lyla handed me the bag. For now, I'd make sure this part of my second timeline worked out perfectly. With my family united, and Geri and James with me, nothing could possibly go wrong.

Chapter Three

Attending my first year classes again felt bizarre, just as bizarre as when I'd gone back to being fourteen. I eagerly took it all in, making sure I took down notes for what would be needed in exams and assignments.

I slipped into my first biology tutorial and sat next to Tara. Tara went to high school with Austin, so I wanted to make sure we were just as good of friends as the first time. She glanced at me as I sat, flicking her straight, strawberry blonde hair away from her face. Petite in build, only barely reaching my shoulder in height, she had a face full of freckles and resembled some kind of doll. She wore a floral dress with straps, the skirt barely reaching her knees. She was super girly, despite her sporty preferences.

I smiled at her, and she smiled back, stretching out her hand. "Tara."

"Cadence," I replied, shaking her hand.

"I hope you're smart."

"Why?" I cocked my head, already knowing her answer.

"Because we'll be working in pairs, and I *so* don't want to fail."

"I don't either." I pulled my giant textbook from my bag. "I've traveled a long way to be here, so I'll take this very seriously."

She tilted her head. "Huh. Where are you from?"

"Sydney. Western Sydney, to be exact."

Her eyes sparkled. She'd always loved that I came from Sydney, the *big* city. She compared it to London and New York, even though that never made sense to me. "That's interesting. I grew up just down at Fremantle. You know, *so* unexciting. Tell me about Sydney. What's the shopping like?"

"I guess it's good."

Her eyes widened. "Come on! You have the Queen Victoria building, that giant—"

Our tutor spoke loudly to grab everyone's attention.

We worked hard through the tutorial, making the perfect fit as a team, just like before. When class ended, she invited me to join her for lunch. We sat together in the cafeteria, and as we ate, she asked, "So why did you come out here?"

"The sports science program is just what I wanted," I replied, while munching my sandwich. "I want to work with an AFL team. You know, watching half-naked men run around a football field . . ."

She chuckled. "Oh yeah, I can see the draw to that. Me? I want to be a teacher. It's not exciting or anything, but I want to keep playing sports my whole life."

Several of her girlfriends joined us. I smiled as they introduced themselves, and we all had lunch together. Scanning the room, I wondered if Austin was anywhere nearby. I wouldn't have noticed him before since I didn't know him my first year, but he was nowhere in sight.

I did see someone of interest, though. In the far corner by the window sat Lyla, her nose buried in a textbook as she munched on a salad. Launching to my feet, I weaved my way over to her. I desperately wanted both my girlfriends back in my life as fast as possible.

Lyla looked up as I stood beside her and stopped chewing. "Miss Musical Terminology."

I grinned. "Girl from Texas."

She snorted. "You're cruel."

"Come sit with me."

She raised an eyebrow. "With your peppy, jock-chick friends? No thanks."

"Come on." I closed her textbook. "I promise we won't bite."

She glanced around me and locked her gaze on Tara, who was staring at us. "Wow, that girl is *short*."

"Tara? Yeah, you'll get over it." I plucked up her book. "I'll take this hostage if I have to."

Her eyes narrowed as she stood. "You're way too confident. It's that horrible city air, right? No other reasonable explanation."

Well, aside from knowing that you'll be one of my bridesmaids alongside Tara? I smiled. "Come on."

She followed me back over and slid in beside me. Tara leaned across, grinning. "Hey! You're friends with Cadence?"

"Ah, I guess." Lyla glanced at me.

"We live in the same building," I replied.

"Awesome. Do you like parties?"

Lyla stared at the table. "I don't drink. It makes people act like idiots."

I snorted. The day before, she'd gotten herself tipsy at lunch, but she did have a point. James definitely had moments of utter humiliation while drunk.

My heart froze. James . . .

I didn't want to think about him—I'd only miss him. I spent every night curled up with my blankets wishing he could hold me and wake me up with his snoring or potent farts. The strange things you miss when someone is gone . . .

"Parties aren't just about drinking. I go to have fun and meet hot guys." Tara wiggled her eyebrows.

"Guys, huh?" Lyla scanned the room. "It *has* been a while since I had a date."

"Perfect." Tara offered her hand and Lyla took it. "Tara."

"Lyla."

"Well, how about we all go out this Saturday? Cadence?"

I grinned, excited about my old life being renewed. "Sounds fun."

Lyla and I sat on the grass, watching several guys playing AFL. With our textbooks open, we did a good job pretending we weren't watching. Several weeks had passed, and I'd settled into a groove. Although I missed home, everyone—especially James—called me regularly, and I kept busy to battle the homesickness. Lyla and I had started working at the supermarket, and when I had down time, I took to the campus library and gym to keep occupied.

"That guy is smoking hot," Lyla said, pointing to the guy who just kicked the ball.

"He has terrible form." I scowled as the ball veered off course.

"I think he has *great* form."

I glanced at her and laughed. "Go talk to him then."

"In the middle of their game? *So* not happening." She waved at her face. "I like to keep this thing pretty."

I smirked as I leaned over my book.

"How can you focus on that when we have *this* to watch?"

I highlighted a line of text. "It's not like any of them are any good. It's a sloppy game."

She punched my shoulder. "You're gay, aren't you?"

I stared at her, surprised. "No. Why would you say that?"

She waved at the football field.

"Oh." I stared out. I hadn't noticed any other guys in so long—James still held my attention completely. As I glanced up, the blond guy from the stairs gave me a subtle wave. I looked back at my textbook. I had to give Lyla some reason why these guys, as hot as they were, weren't grabbing my focus. "They probably all have girlfriends."

"All? Not likely." She raised an eyebrow. "Are you one of those girls who has really weird tastes?"

"What?" I laughed.

She shrugged, looking out. "Well, if you're not game, *I* am. Be my wingman." She motioned to the game. "Go out there and make that one guy come over here."

"Uh . . ." I stared out at the field, having no desire to talk to any of them, especially with the blond stealing glances in my direction.

"You're the sports freak. Go kick some butt. Emasculate them enough that they end their game."

"You think emasculating them will win you points?" I rolled my eyes, smirking.

"Not if *I* do it."

My phone buzzed. I opened it, finding a text from Melanie. CAN U CALL JAMES? I THINK SOMETHINGS WRONG.

I scowled. "Sorry, Lyla. I have to make a call."

"Sure, abandon me in my time of need."

I packed my bag and gave her a quick hug. "Here's a tip: sit somewhere so the ball will come toward you, then save the day by catching it before it goes too far."

I gave her a wink as I hurried back toward the dorm. On my way up the stairs, I called James.

"Hey." He lacked his usual excited tone. "I'm the worst person ever."

"Why?" I asked as I unlocked my door.

"Because Cane hates me."

I dumped my bag, confused how his insanely adorable fluff-ball of a pup could hate him.

He let out a loud moan. "He got his balls chopped off."

I giggled. "That's the responsible thing to do."

"The whole time he was in there today I was thinking, 'how could I do that to him?' How would I feel if someone knocked me out and cut off my balls? It's humiliating! He's been avoiding me all evening."

"He's probably just drugged up—" A knock on the door made me start. "Hang on, James."

I rushed to the door. Pulling it open, I found no one there. "Huh."

"What?" James said.

"Knock and"—a rose had been taped to the door—"run. James? Did you send me a rose?"

"Someone sent you a rose?"

"I guess not." I scowled, running my finger over the petals. Then I remembered: the guy from the stairs. He must have noticed me leave and decided to make his move. Last time, this was how it all started. A rose here, a box of chocolates in a week or so . . . I definitely didn't want to encourage that. "I'll just leave it where it is."

"Someone sent you a rose?" James repeated.

"Mmm. I'll just ignore it."

"Oh no." He snorted. "Your ignoring isn't effective. Trust me. I'm a pretty good example of ignoring your . . . ignoring."

"James." I laughed as I shut the door. "Are you jealous?"

He grunted. "Why should I be jealous? You're way over there, and I'm way over here. It's not like high school when they trembled at my incredible good looks."

I chuckled.

"No, you're all alone. Maybe you could wear the ring?"

I sighed, flicking open my jewelry box to look at the engagement ring he gave me. The five Princess cut diamonds glittered in the dim sunlight. Wearing the ring would simplify things, but what if Tara asked about it? She could tell Austin, which would change everything.

"Maybe," I responded flatly.

"You don't have to." He let out a long breath, and I could just see him ruffling his hair. "What matters is that you love me. You love me, right?"

"Yeah." I smiled, setting the ring back in the box.

"And you know I love you."

I chuckled. "Yeah."

"Good, because you're insanely beautiful and guys over there *will* notice. Just remember what we have, and I know we'll be okay."

"I will." I slid open my top drawer to look at our photo. James didn't want to take the shot, so he scowled into the camera while I poked his cheek to try and make him smile. I loved it, but underneath that photo rested my scrapbook, with the photo of Austin and Melody. I needed to remember them too.

"Cane's crying," James said, his voice heavy. "I should go console the poor guy. He's going to hate me for life."

"He doesn't hate you," I replied gently. "He's just uncomfortable. You did the right thing."

"Did I? I stole his manhood."

I chuckled. "He'll get over it, I promise."

"Yeah, I guess." Canis's howling grew louder. "Poor little guy."

"Give him a hug for me."

"What about me?" he asked seductively.

"Goodbye, James. Tend to your pathetic dog."

Being local, Tara showed Lyla and me all the best places. Her friends took to us quickly, although I still wouldn't meet Austin for a while. That didn't bother me—I wanted to meet him at the right time, just like before—so I happily settled in with Tara and Lyla. I'd even introduced Lyla to Geri over the phone, and she'd liked her. How perfectly things were coming together!

When Tara took us to a fantastic surfing beach one Saturday, Lyla was particularly impressed with her new friend.

"Just watch out for sharks!" Tara teased.

Tara and I sat on the beach together, watching Lyla paddle out to wait for her wave, neither of us wanting to venture into the mid-autumn water. I'd always loved the beach, and the West Coast beaches were no different, except for the sun setting over the ocean. That would take some getting used to . . . again.

Further out, beyond view, was where I'd spent countless hours with Austin on Rottnest Island. Taking a deep breath, I reveled in those happy memories, aching to relive them. Soon, so soon.

"So, Cadence," Tara said, startling me from my reminiscing. "You're a bit of a mystery to me. You rarely mention your family, or friends, or boys. All I know about you is that you're from Sydney."

"I'm sure I've mentioned my family at some point," I replied.

She shook her head, waiting for me to elaborate.

"Well," I leaned back onto my elbows, "There's my mum and dad, still together, and then I have an older sister named Harper, who's twenty, and a younger brother, Dusty, who's sixteen."

"Do you have any photos?"

"Ah . . ." I dug into my handbag. In my wallet I found Dusty's recent school picture and a photo of Harper with Daniel climbing the Harbor Bridge for Valentine's. I smiled at the pictures as I handed them over.

She examined the photos closely. "Wow, your sister is so different, but you and your brother look almost the same."

I shrugged. "Dusty and I *are* almost the same. We both love sports, have the same favorite foods, and"—I paused for effect—"my best friend is the girl he likes."

"No way!" She sat forward. "Is she like a younger best friend?"

I shook my head. "She's our age, which is why she's holding back. She's known him since he was ten and we were twelve, so I think the whole thing weirds her out a bit."

"I can understand that." A mischievous grin swept across her face. "Cadence, you've been holding out on me! You have some interesting stories to tell. So, what about boys, eh?"

I froze. As the person destined to introduce me to Austin, I did *not* want to tell her about James. She sensed my hesitation and leaned closer to me. "Come on, Cadence. You're pretty. Surely you had some boyfriends in high school."

I flushed. "I did, yes—"

"Hey, losers!" Lyla ran over and tossed her board on the sand in front of us. "I'm hungry. How about you?"

Relieved by the diversion, I jumped to my feet. "I'm starving."

Lyla grinned. She peeled off her wet suit before wrapping her towel around her waist and pulling a sweater over her bikini. "Come on then. There's that awesome fish and chips place just around the corner."

Tara didn't bring up the subject again, but seemed satisfied to listen to me talk about Geri and Dusty. While we ate, we chatted away in a manner that made me miss Geri, Harper, and even Melanie. The way Lyla and Tara spoke to each other was so much like Geri and Melanie's interactions that I felt a pang of homesickness. But I refused to let it beat me. Brushing the thoughts aside, I focused on the moment and the two friends I had loved so much in the first timeline.

After I returned to my room, my phone rang. I grabbed it and saw it was Harper. "Hey—"

"Oh my gosh, Cadence!" she screeched. "I'm engaged!"

I pulled the phone away from my ear as she screamed with excitement.

"It happened last night when he took me out. We went to this fancy place on the harbor for dinner, and he spent a hundred dollars on the meal. It was insane! Then we went for a walk and ended up behind the Opera House facing out onto the harbor. It was so beautiful with all the lights, and the boats on the water, and the Harbor Bridge over-head. And then, right then, he knelt down and proposed!

"He told me he'd asked for permission and Dad said yes! Can you believe it? Dad actually *agreed*. Anyway, I said yes without hesitation. Oh Cadence, I love Daniel so much, and you've got to be my maid of honor. When are you off for summer?"

"Ah . . . I'm not sure, but I'll definitely have January," I answered.

"January will be perfect!"

"But you want me as your maid of honor? You don't want Loz?" Making it into the bridal party the first time around had been Mum's idea. I'd ended up at the edge of all the pictures, so maid of honor seemed like a drastic jump.

"No! Geez, Cadence, you're my sister. Why would I choose her over you?"

I smiled, grateful for her love. "Thanks, Harper. I'd love to do that for you."

"Good. Send me your measurements so we can get the dress shopping started. And don't you dare lose or put on weight once you've sent me your measurements, or I'll kick your butt!"

I laughed. "Okay, Harper, and congrats. I know how much you love Daniel, so I know you'll be happy."

"Thanks, Cay. I love you."

"I love you, too."

I hung up. I was happy things were turning out well for her, and that she wanted me to be part of it. Being her maid of honor was proof of how I'd done things better, except now I wished I could be there with her.

Chapter Four

Sitting outside the dorms, I basked in the warm, late-autumn sun. A group of guys played basketball nearby while I flicked through my textbook. I had to get my notes straight for the upcoming exams. I really wanted to ace them this time, and with James back home, I wasn't distracted by hot males.

He called me the night before, fretting over his own exams. I didn't know why he dragged me through the same conversation every time.

"I'm too stupid," he said with a growl. "These exams are getting harder and harder. Why did you talk me into going to uni?"

I sighed, letting him vent all his steam.

"I'm not like you, Miss . . . Smarty-Pants."

"We're not three," I muttered.

"I heard that. Just because you're a super brain doesn't mean you can be condescending to us lower life-forms."

I groaned, rubbing my temple. "Is there a point to this? I have to study too."

"Yes!" he yelled, making me jerk the phone from my ear. "You're supposed to be *here*, kicking my butt to make me study harder so I'm not such an idiot."

"Consider this a butt-kicking," I replied, flicking through my bio book.

"So you do think I'm an idiot! I knew it."

I rolled my eyes. "I don't. Why are you picking a fight with me?"

A long pause followed. "Sorry."

"It's fine, but what's going on?"

He let out a long sigh. "I'm not used to doing this alone. You've always been here to help me study."

My heart melted. "Oh, James."

"I miss you more than ever. It's been months."

"I know, but it's only a few weeks until I visit."

"A few ridiculously long weeks."

"I miss you too." I smiled as I hung up, brushing my finger over his name in my phone.

A wind whipped up, snapping me to attention. I slapped my hand on the textbook to keep my page open, then scrambled to catch my pen and pencil before they rolled off the wooden table.

"Need some help?" The dirty blond guy sat opposite me, catching my highlighter. He gave me a wide smile.

I dropped my gaze. He'd left all kinds of gifts at my door over the weeks, but I ignored them. Apparently, like James had said, my ignoring really didn't get the point across.

"I'm Peter." He set the highlighter in front of me. "I've noticed you around. You're quite withdrawn."

"I like to focus," I said, gesturing to my textbook.

"I can see that." His fingers brushed over mine.

I pulled back, clearing my throat. Could he be more obvious? Could I? *Probably.*

"I'm sorry, but I'm not interested in dating."

He blinked, his smile faltering slightly, but he persisted. "I'm not saying you should date, I'm just inviting you to come hang out some time. A group of us are going out on Saturday night, if you want to join?"

"I really need to get my notes sorted." I closed my textbook and opened my bag.

"Wait." He caught my wrist.

I stared at him, startled by his audacity.

"If you don't want to be with a big group, why don't you and I just do something?"

This guy seriously doesn't get it. I slipped my free hand into my bag, rummaging around for the photo of me and

James. "Look, you seem nice, but I really do need to get my work done, and"—I found the photo between some notes and slipped it out, setting it on the table—"my boyfriend wouldn't be impressed if I was hanging out with some guy."

"Oh." He ran his hand through his hair as he stared at the picture. "I didn't know. I never see you with anyone."

"He's in Sydney." I returned the picture back to my folder. "I'm sorry. Maybe your persistence will pay off in the future."

"Yeah." He looked into my face as he stood, his slight frown reflecting his disappointment. "Could I at least get your name?"

I smiled at him, pulling my bag onto my shoulder. "It's probably better if I don't. Goodbye, Peter."

As I turned away, he said, "Goodbye, Cadence."

I hesitated, glancing back at him. *Poor guy.* I turned to him, deciding to play matchmaker to help him get past his bump in the road. "Look, there are three girls on my level who have this list of hot guys they'd love to date. I've seen the list and the pictures, and you're on it."

He raised an eyebrow. "What?"

"Yeah. Here." I slid out a pen and wrote their names and room numbers on a scrap of paper. "They're nice girls. Look them up."

"Ah, thanks." He took the paper, staring at it.

"And I'm sorry, again. Really." I hurried away, not wanting to drag out the awkward situation further.

A few days later, as I returned to my room, I saw him with the girls, all laughing and chatting away. He glanced across at me and gave me a nod.

I grinned as I slipped into my room, glad to have helped someone.

As I flopped onto my bed, my phone rang. I snatched it up and heard the familiar, "Hey, beautiful."

"Hey, James." Then, grinning like an idiot, I told him all about what had happened.

I sat at the bar beside Lyla as Tara flirted shamelessly with some random guy. In the first timeline, I'd always been closer to Tara—we'd both flirted and been crazy together—but this time, I drifted more toward Lyla. Maybe it had something to do with having more shame, or because I wasn't interested in snagging random guys. Either way, I enjoyed Lyla's slightly more reserved nature and got to know her differently.

"Incoming," Lyla muttered as she sipped her drink.

I glanced up at two guys approaching us. Lowering my gaze, I swiveled to the bar and ordered a drink, hoping they'd gravitate more toward Lyla if I shut down. But no, one stood beside me and the other beside Lyla, sandwiching us in.

"Hey," the guy beside Lyla said.

She smiled brightly, turning to face him. "Hi."

The guy beside me rested his hand on my back. "What are you drinking?"

"Umm . . ." I tensed, wriggling free of his hand. "I don't know. What are you drinking?"

Lyla stood. My head snapped around to see the other guy leading her toward the dance floor. *Good job, Ly. Now, to shed this guy.*

He sat beside me, pressing his shoulder against mine. Last time, I would have given him a chance. He was nice-looking—brown hair, dark eyes, easy smile—but I had better than *nice* waiting for me. I had Austin in my future, and James now.

"I've had a few VBs," he said, smiling eagerly at me. "Looks like you prefer the cocktails though."

"Yeah." I stirred my drink. "Look, you seem nice, but I'm just here with my girlfriends to let off some steam after exams."

"I can help you with that." His arm slid around my waist.

I drew back. "I have a boyfriend."

"Is he here?" He glanced around, smirking. "You look unattended."

My eyes narrowed. "I'm trying to let you down nicely. Please go find someone else."

"Come on." He stood and grabbed my arm. "You need to loosen up."

I glared at him. "Let me go."

"Just a dance, hot stuff."

"I said, let me go." I punched him in the throat. He released me, gagging.

I shot to my feet, grabbed my drink—since I'd already paid for it and didn't want to throw good money down the drain—and hurried away. But with Lyla and Tara both preoccupied with guys, I didn't know where to go. I headed to Tara's car to check my phone in peace.

As I passed through the door, my phone started to ring. I slipped it from my purse, smiling at seeing James's name.

"Hey—"

He laughed loudly. *Great, he's drunk.*

"Did you really just drunk dial me?" I asked.

"Cay, babe, oh man." He laughed again. "I just met this girl, and she looks so much like you."

My insides turned cold, and I froze mid-step. "What?"

"She's got the hair, the boobs . . ." He laughed again. "I miss your boobs."

"James!" My cheeks burned.

"Here, say hi to her."

"Hi," a girl's voice came through.

I could hardly breathe. He had a girl with him, while he was drunk . . . . But maybe this was a good thing. Maybe this was the beginning of the end so I could be with Austin.

But then, why did I feel sick about it?

"Cadence, you have a rockin' body," James said.

"My name's not Cadence," the girl responded.

"Just pretend for me." He laughed again.

"James!" My rage boiled over as tears rolled down my cheeks. "What are you doing?"

"I just miss you so much," he whispered loudly into the phone. "Do you have any idea how lonely I am without you? And then you tell me some guy has been making moves on you, and you blow it off like it means nothing."

"James—"

"It doesn't mean nothing, does it, Cadence?"

My breath caught in my chest.

"My name's not Cadence," I heard the girl say again, annoyed.

"Don't get all pissy with me! You left!"

My stomach flipped. *He's talking to her, but he obviously means me.* "James—"

"You're crazy. You might be hot, but I'm out," the girl said.

"That's right, run away."

"James!" I yelled.

"What?" he yelled back.

"You're usually a happy drunk," I said cautiously. "What's going on? Why would you bring some random girl into this?"

"Because you *left* me!" he snarled, and then burst into tears. "Cadence . . ."

"James." I rubbed my eyes, fighting back my own tears at the sound of his pain.

A new voice came on the line. "Cadence?"

"Tom?"

"Oh, geez. James, get up."

The voices fell quiet as shuffling sounds came down the line. I leaned back against the wall, my heart aching. My throat clenched as I struggled to stop crying. I'd broken James. I'd hurt him because I was selfish. Maybe I should just transfer back. I'd have to wait to finish the year, but still . . .

"Cadence?" Tom said gently.

I struggled to speak. "Yeah?"

"Whatever James said, just forget it. I've never seen him this drunk. He's completely out of it."

I sniffed, wiping a tear from my cheek. "I did this to him."

"Don't do that. He's an adult. He makes his own choices."

"Yes, but—"

"Cadence!" James moaned in the background. "Where'd she go?"

"Hey, man. Just relax," Tom said.

"Why did she leave me?" James sobbed. "I just want to be with her. There's no one like her. I love her so much it hurts."

"I know. Just take deep breaths and keep drinking that water."

I covered my mouth as I sobbed too. "Tom?"

"One sec," he said to me. "James, stay in the car."

"Cadence was here a moment ago. I have to find her."

"No, that was someone else. Now sit down and relax. Cadence is still in Perth, remember?"

"With guys hitting on her!" James yelled. "I'll kill 'em!"

"Talk to him," Tom said to me quickly.

I hesitated, but assumed he'd given the phone to James. "James?"

"Cadence!" His tone brightened. "Aw, babe, how are you?"

"I'm gonna be there soon, remember? Less than two weeks." I tried to smile so I sounded optimistic for him.

A long pause followed. "You're still in Perth?"

"Yeah. Just finished exams."

Another pause, then he whispered, "I think I squeezed someone else's boobs."

My stomach hit my throat.

"And we're done with this conversation," Tom said, coming back on the line. "Cadence, he's confused."

My chin quivered as my tears flowed freely. "How bad is he?"

"Really drunk, but nothing a good night's sleep and a ton of coffee won't fix."

"No, I mean . . ." My hands trembled. "He always sounds like he's doing well. I mean, he says he misses me all the time, but he never . . . . Tell me the truth. How bad is he?"

Tom sighed as James's slurred jabbering filled the background. "Honestly, he's a lot quieter than he used to be. He spends more time alone in his room, and he only jokes around when he's with Dusty. But he could be worse. We've talked about it, and he knows he has to let you be you. He doesn't want to suffocate you. But since you mentioned that guy hitting on you, he's gotten agitated, as you can tell."

"That guy meant nothing to me," I said quickly. "I shed him as fast as I could. I told James because I didn't want to hide anything from him."

"He knows that. It just bothers him." He paused for a moment. "When you get here, do everything you can to reassure him, okay? I have to go. He's crying again. I need to get him home."

We hung up. I stood, shaking against the wall.

What have I done?

A couple walked by me, laughing. I needed to go somewhere private to cry. Rushing back inside, I headed straight for the bathroom. With the music pounding through the walls, no one would hear me, and I'd be able to clean up easily afterward.

I burst into the cubicle. The second I locked the door, I broke into sobs. I'd crushed James. And for what? For someone I hadn't met yet, for someone I had memories of, but didn't feel anything for. How could I do this to James when I loved him so much? I couldn't remember if I loved Austin as much as I did James. Maybe I was making a huge mistake and driving James mad for no reason.

I clung to my shoulders as I whispered, "Angel?"

The music cut short. I peered through the gap in the door. My angel appeared by the sinks. "Cadence."

I opened the door, staring at him.

He smiled gently, scanning the room. "This is fairly disgusting."

"Angel." I burst into tears again. "Tell me I'm doing the right thing. I'm destroying James."

"You know I can't do that." He touched my chin, lifting my face so I'd meet his brown eyes. "You are the one who needs to decide what the right choices are for your life."

"But James . . . and Austin . . ." I pressed the heels of my hands against my eyes.

He grasped my wrists, drawing my hands away from my face. "You still haven't met Austin yet."

"I know. But I don't know if I can let that life go. I mean, we had Melody. What about her?"

"No matter which life you choose, you will always have Melody."

That didn't make sense. She was Austin's daughter. How could I have her without Austin? "But—"

"Look." He gestured toward the sinks. Ghostly shapes formed and solidified. James sat by a bar, his hair long, his face unshaven, wearing baggy jeans and a blue Bond chesty. Robbie sat beside him, laughing his head off.

"I don't want to see this," I said, looking up at the angel. "I already know James led this life and how it turned out."

"Just watch."

A girl about my age approached James. He grinned, looking her over. He licked his lips as she stopped in front of him. As they talked, Robbie smirked, chuckled, and ordered another drink.

My heart ripped open. "Please, I know where this is going. Don't make me see it."

The girl leaned in, whispering in James's ear. As she did, her hand wandered over his crotch. He grabbed her around the waist and dragged her away.

Robbie lifted his glass after them. "Go for it, son. You always get the hot ones."

I swung to the angel, tears streaming down my face. "What's the point in showing me that? Do you want to hurt me more than I already am? That's not him now. I don't want to know about . . . all that."

He pursed his lips and waved his hand. The sinks shifted, turning into the back seat of a car. James formed on the seat, the car taking shape around him. Tom stood by the car door.

"Come on, mate. Get some more water into you."

"I cheated on Cadence. I'm such an idiot."

My heart lurched as I rushed forward. "James."

"It's an echo, Cadence," the angel said. "From only moments ago, but an echo all the same."

"You didn't cheat," Tom said, squeezing his shoulder.

"I grabbed that girl's boobs."

"You thought she was Cadence."

James growled, tugging at his hair. "I've blown it. Cadence has options—plenty of other options—and I go and do *that*. She's so smart and beautiful, any guy would want her. She already ran away from me, and now she has a perfect reason not to come back."

Tom sighed, coaxing a water bottle to James's lips. "She'll forgive you."

I reached to clasp James's face, but my hands went through him. My chin trembled as I looked to the angel. "Make it stop."

He waved his hand and the image drifted away like smoke. "Do you understand why I showed you these moments?"

I shook my head, gazing down at the floor as tears rolled down my cheeks.

"You were right when you said James isn't the same this time. In the first timeline, James would sleep with any girl without even knowing her name, but this time he's all about one woman."

"Me," I said weakly.

"He still loves you, and you love him."

I nodded. "But—"

"Do you want to give that up?"

"It's not that simple. It's . . ." The music faded back in. Looking up, I saw he'd gone.

"Why do you do that?" I muttered, turning to the sink. I splashed my face, and carefully wiped away the mascara streaks. My relationship with James had fractured, and I'd done it. He thought I'd run from him, when in reality, I'd gone in search of a dream, or at least, what felt like a dream.

Maybe I needed to reevaluate my position. I could stay with James, marry him, and be perfectly happy. I'd just arrange a transfer for the next year. I was sure I could work something out. The University of Western Sydney had given me a great offer, and I'd be there with Geri too. I could live with James and see Geri regularly. Austin wouldn't know the difference.

Except there was still one problem: I couldn't forget Melody.

Chapter Five

I stayed with my family the first week of winter break, spending most the time planning for Harper's wedding. My dress was fitted, I helped Harper decide on one of three dresses for her, we ordered flowers, and I went along with her and Daniel to pick and book a venue. Everything went exactly as before, except this time, I was involved. It made me so happy.

By the second week, I found myself standing outside James's townhouse. No one was home, so I entered on my own. I'd called him the morning after the drunk-dialing incident, and he'd begged me to forgive him. I did, no problem, but I was still nervous about seeing him again. After so long, and all the strain, I needed this. We both did.

Canis barked at me from the backyard. He'd obviously recovered from his ever-so-traumatic experience of being neutered. I couldn't believe how much he had grown. He still looked like a puppy, but he'd more than doubled in size.

I entered the kitchen and gasped in horror. Every inch of space was completely trashed. I scraped together all the food scraps and, to Canis's delight, gave them to him. We instantly became friends again. I let him run around and clean up the food left lying around. It took an hour, but I cleaned the kitchen, dining, and living rooms. Since most of the mess turned out to be trash and food, Canis proved quite helpful.

I ventured upstairs with Canis at my side and entered James's room. I groaned in disgust, and then picked up all his dirty laundry, sorting it into piles in the hallway. Canis sniffed around and found the moldy, rotten food for me.

When I opened the bathroom door, the smell made me sick. I slammed the door shut. Canis looked at me and cocked his head.

"James is doing that one," I muttered to him and scratched his ears.

By the time the front door opened, I had a load of laundry in the wash and was sitting on the bed reading one of James's novels. I set the book down to listen as three male voices entered.

"And then he was all . . ." Sam's voice trailed off. "Have we been robbed?"

"Ah . . . no, the TV's still here," Tom answered.

"What day is it?" James asked in an excited voice.

"It's Monday—"

But James didn't give Tom a chance to finish. He bounded up the stairs and the bedroom door burst open. He stared at me as I jumped to my feet.

"James."

"Guys! I'm gonna need a few!" he called down the stairs. He shut the door and locked it.

He rushed at me and clasped my face, kissing me passionately. He had me undressed and back on the bed in minutes.

"Cadence, I'm so glad you came back," he said between kisses.

"Of course I did," I said breathlessly as his lips wandered down my neck.

We made love with such intensity I thought my heart would explode. I'd missed him so much—the smell of him, his touch, his warm body wrapped around mine—everything about him filled my senses, and I let go of all my anxiety. I had him, and nothing else mattered at that moment.

Afterward, we lay in each other's arms. I breathed in his scent, having missed it more than anything. His fingers stroked my back, making me shudder.

"Hello, beautiful," he said gently.

I smiled and nuzzled into him. "Hello, handsome."

He chuckled. "It's nice to have you back. You have no idea how much I've missed you."

I looked into his eyes and my heart melted. I caressed his jaw, feeling his rough-shaved skin, and brushed my fingers over his sideburns. I took in every inch of his face, his thick, chestnut hair, his bright gray-blue eyes, his amused smile as he watched me examine him. My hand drifted over his Adam's apple and followed down to his lean, sculpted chest and arms.

"Do you like what you see?"

I nodded, examining his pectorals.

"So I take it you missed me too?"

My gaze lifted and met his. I smiled. "Very much. But by the state of this place when I arrived, I think you missed me more."

He laughed and tickled me. When I finally wrestled him into stopping, I gazed down at him, searching his eyes.

His chest rose and fell. "I love you."

"I know you do." I softly kissed his lips. "I don't want you to worry about what happened, but maybe avoid getting so drunk in the future."

He smirked, running his hand through my hair. "So I can't get drunk, but I can grope boobs?"

I slapped his chest. "You know what I mean."

He pulled me down to kiss me, and then rolled me underneath him. "Cadence," he whispered, our noses brushing as he looked into my eyes. "I feel so guilty for doing that."

"You don't need to—"

"But I do." He stroked my hair. "I've missed you so much."

"I'm here now." Wrapping my arms around his neck, I kissed him.

My three weeks with James flew by. I wore the engagement ring on my right hand, but after helping Harper prepare her wedding, I seriously considered switching which hand I wore it on. It didn't go unnoticed by James, and he often stroked it with a gleam in his eyes while we held hands.

James was perfect the whole time. He took me out hiking, shopping, sightseeing, and anything else he could dream up so not a single moment together was wasted. When the time came for me to leave, I found it even harder to let him go than it had been the first time.

"I have to go," I said, breaking away from his kiss but still clutching his shirt. "Maybe . . . maybe I could look into transferring back here."

He grinned, pulling me in to kiss him again.

I whimpered as I forced myself away. "I'm going to miss my flight."

He caught my hand and kissed the ring. "Be safe."

As I sat on my five-hour flight, it dawned on me that letting go of James would be impossible. I didn't want to end it with him, and began to consider marrying him instead of Austin.

The second semester had just begun and already I managed to be late for my tutorial. I hurried down the hallway in a jog, my handbag resting in the crook of my elbow and my arms overflowing with my textbooks and folders.

As I rounded the corner, my phone rang.

"Ugh!" I tried digging into my bag to answer it and dropped everything in the middle of the corridor. I huffed, knelt down, and answered my phone. "Not good timing, Geri!"

"Oh, sorry . . . I just got out of a lecture, so I thought I'd give ya a call."

"I'm running late for a tutorial."

"Okay, sorry. Call me back when you're done?"

"No worries."

"'Kay. Bye, love ya."

I dropped my phone back in my bag and reached for my notes that were now strewn everywhere, but a pair of hands already worked at gathering them up. I followed the arms up and saw Austin. My heart jumped into my throat and I froze. His dark brown eyes were down as he gathered my notes, and his thick, almost-black hair made my fingers itch to touch it.

I couldn't meet him yet—it wasn't supposed to happen for another six months!

His gaze lifted to meet mine. "Hey, are you okay?" He smiled at me with his crooked smile that had always made me melt.

"I, ah . . . no. I'm really late." I looked down and grabbed my notes and books. He handed me what he'd gathered and our hands touched for a moment. My cheeks burned.

"You're really flustered. Do you need any help?"

"No," I answered far too quickly. I jumped to my feet, and he hurried to stand in front of me. "I've gotta go."

"Okay, well, it was nice meeting you."

I forced a smile. "Thanks for your help."

I rushed away without daring to slow down until I rounded the corner. I pinned myself against the wall to catch my breath, ignoring all the strange looks people gave me. I glanced back down the hallway. He stood outside a tutorial room, his arm around a pretty girl with auburn hair.

I bit my lip. She was his girlfriend before me. They did the same course, and they'd dated for about seven months. I watched them as they talked together, but when he gave her a quick kiss before heading into his tutorial, my jealousy burned hot within me.

I turned back around to compose myself. He didn't even know me yet, and since I was still with James, I had no reason or right to be jealous. But to see him, real and in person, had stirred up my feelings, making my mind foggy. I shut my eyes and breathed. I then panicked, realizing I had only made myself later, and dashed off to class.

I made a lame excuse about getting lost before sitting with Tara. She raised her eyebrow at me. "It's not like you to be late, Cadence."

"I know, I got distracted."

"By what? Or maybe I should say who?" She grinned.

My cheeks burned. "Geri called me and I dropped everything. It was quite embarrassing."

She giggled. "I wish I could've seen that."

We turned our focus onto our lesson, but I couldn't stop thinking about Austin. Now that our paths would cross, I knew I'd stare at him every time, and would have to fight myself not to lose my mind.

That weekend, Tara invited Lyla and me to hang out at her place with her new fling. After lunch, we headed down to the beach.

We stopped at a news agency so Tara and Lyla could argue about something on the front cover of a magazine. I'd stopped listening. Austin was making his way down the opposite side of the street with his best friend, Aaron. By the gear slung over their shoulders, they were about to head out to Rottnest. Austin looked amazing, all broad shoulders and dark hair—

"Cadence!"

I jumped, swinging around. "What?"

"What are you looking at?" Tara asked.

"Ahh . . ." I scanned the area as Austin disappeared around the corner. "A pelican."

"A pelican?" She scowled, raising an eyebrow behind her large glasses. "I'm pretty sure they have those in Sydney."

"Yeah." I shrugged. "I thought it had something caught on its leg, but I was wrong."

"Sometimes you're so blonde." Lyla patted my back. "Let's go."

That night, James called me. Something about him seemed . . . different.

"You sound happier than you have been lately."

"That's because I am." The sound of him typing came down the line. "I've been thinking about what you said about transferring back, so I did some research. It's totally doable. Here, I'll email you a link."

I opened my laptop and saw the email waiting for me, but after two encounters with Austin, I had doubts about moving back. I opened the email anyway.

"This is just for Macquarie, and none of these are my course."

"I know. But they're close to the same, and you'd be here with me."

Oh no. I'd given him hope. I groaned, rubbing my forehead.

"Fine, it doesn't have to be Macquarie." He started typing again. "You get pretty good grades, so you could try UNSW with Harper?"

"James . . ."

"Or UWS with Geri? She'd love that."

"James, I've just started the semester. I'm not ready to think about that yet."

He hesitated. "You've changed your mind."

"No, I just—"

"If you want to transfer, you have to start preparing now."

"I just . . ." I growled. "Can we not talk about this? I need to settle in first. I don't want my head filled with transferring and transcripts while I need to focus on studying."

"Okay," he said softly.

I stuck out my lip. "Please don't be disappointed."

"I'm . . ." He sighed. "I thought you wanted to come back. You were so happy to see me, and we spent so much time together. You wore the ring every day."

"I know, and I was." I flopped back onto my pillow, shutting my eyes. "I'm just here without you, and I'm basically on my own, fending for myself for the first time. I get pretty stressed out."

"I can tell."

I let out a gush of air, twisting my hair off my neck. "This is hard, being long distance."

Pause. Finally, he said in a gravelly voice, "Yeah."

Tears burned my eyes. I was losing James. I covered my face and mouth to smother the sound of my crying. I wasn't ready to lose him. I didn't even know if I was doing the right thing, hoping to reunite with Austin.

"Please don't cry," James said softly.

I gasped, struggling not to sob. "How did you know?"

"Because I know you better than anyone." He let out a long sigh. "I love you, Cadence, so don't worry about me going anywhere. It's hard right now, but . . ."

I waited, afraid of how he might end that sentence.

"I'm here."

I buried my face into my pillow to cry.

"When you're ready, we'll look into transferring together. I want to help you, and I want you to be happy. Please, Cadence, please don't cry."

"I want you to be happy too, James." I tilted my head away from the pillow. "But I don't think I make you happy anymore."

His tone turned cold. "Don't you dare say that."

"It's true. Me being over here . . . . I know you're miserable." I curled up with my blanket. "Tom told me you're quieter, and you don't joke around anymore."

"Tom can shut his fat gob," he said harshly.

"But you're not you. I've broken you."

He drew a sharp breath. "Don't you dare dump me."

"That's not what—"

"Because yeah, this is hard, but I refuse to give up. We've gone through worse and made it out stronger. That's all this is."

My chin quivered as I wiped my eyes. "I'm not dumping you."

He groaned. "Okay, yeah, I've been struggling. I just hoped . . . well, I thought we'd be a bit more permanent by now, more along the lines of Harper and Daniel. I'm taking it a bit hard, but I'll be fine."

"I'm so sorry," I replied, grabbing a tissue to get the snot off my face.

"No, I get it. I've talked a lot with your dad about it—"

"You what?" I cracked a grin.

"Your dad's a pretty cool guy. Well, sometimes anyway. If he thinks I've slept with you he kinda gets grumpy, but you know."

I giggled.

"That's a beautiful sound." He sighed. "Who could have thought bringing your dad into the conversation would lighten the mood? The number of times he's made me almost piss my pants . . ."

I laughed.

He chuckled. "You're beautiful, Cadence. I love you."

"I love you too."

We hung up soon after that, it being quite late in Sydney by then. I stared at the unopened emails from him, with the links for transferring. Taking a deep breath, I shut my laptop. I wished I could find some way to know what to do.

Slipping out the scrapbook from my drawer, I stared at the picture of Austin and Melody. The memories of seeing him that week melded with the memories the photo brought on, and my heart fluttered.

Chapter Six

The next week, I scanned for Austin as I made my way to class. I knew I shouldn't, but the temptation was too strong. When I saw him standing by the wall, looking at his notebook, my heart skipped a beat. Thankfully, he didn't see me, but I smiled as I rushed around the corner.

My parents came to visit that weekend. They met me outside the accommodations as I returned from a late tutorial. I gasped when I saw them and rushed over.

Mum wrapped me in her arms. "We thought we'd surprise you."

"You have!" I squeezed her tighter. "Where are you staying? How long will you be here?"

Dad rested his hand on my head. "Just the weekend. We found a hotel up the road."

"I can't believe you're here." I released Mum to hug Dad. They hadn't come the first time around until after I was engaged, so this, *this* was amazing. "Come see my room."

I led them upstairs. Lyla stood by my door, kicking at the carpet. I grinned, eager for them to meet her. She glanced up, opened her mouth, then shut it again as she stared behind me.

"These are my parents," I said, waving at them. "They came to surprise me. Isn't it great?"

She stared at Dad warily. "Yeah."

I wrapped my arm around his. "This is Lyla. Geri's probably mentioned her, or should I say, complained about her." I chuckled.

"Hello, Lyla." Mum offered her hand.

Lyla shifted her books onto her left arm. "It's nice to meet you. Cadence only ever says nice things about you guys."

Dad kissed my head, and I grinned up at him.

"Oh, you're a daddy's girl." Lyla rolled her eyes as she smirked. "That explains so much."

"Shut up." I stepped to my door. "Do you wanna come hang out with us?"

She shrugged. "No, I have this strange thing called an assignment to work on. I just stopped by to see if you wanted to head down to dinner with me, but it looks like you'll be having something better than bulk spaghetti and cheap chopped salad."

I opened my door. "Seriously, you can come with us."

"No, this is your time with your parents. Go, enjoy it." She turned to my parents. "It was nice to meet you."

As she walked away, I let my parents into my room.

"It's not much, but it's what I call home." I set my bag on the bed and placed my books on my desk. "It's pretty safe with the security, and guys aren't allowed in here . . . well, technically anyway. I see girls sneaking guys in all the time." I shrugged, grinning. "But they leave me alone. And Lyla's right down the hall, so—"

"That's not what James said," Dad said, plucking up a photo from my desk.

"Ah, about what?" I asked, leaning over to see the picture of me and James in his hand.

"Guys leaving you alone." He raised an eyebrow as he turned the picture to face me.

I groaned. "James told you about that? It really wasn't a big deal. He just left a gift here and there. When he actually talked to me, I made it clear I had a boyfriend and directed him to some other girls."

"I don't like it." Dad scowled as he scanned the room.

"You didn't like James either." I took the photo from him. "Anyway, this is where I live. Lyla and I are talking about getting a flat together next year—"

"Next year?" Dad's gaze shot to me. "I thought you were transferring."

I slumped. "James has a big mouth."

Mum rested her hands on my shoulders. "We'd like you to come back. You're so far away. We all miss you."

I rubbed my temple. "This is why you came out here."

She glanced at Dad. "We'd like to help make the transition smoother. We can help with talking to someone about moving your transcripts, applying for a university in Sydney, whatever you need."

I sank onto my bed. That explained why they came this time and not last. "How many people has James told?"

"He's excited," Mum said as she sat beside me. "You can't blame him for being eager to have you come home."

I looked into her eyes. "I don't know if I'm going to transfer."

She gazed into my eyes, her brows furrowing.

I sighed. "It's just a possibility. I haven't decided yet. I'm established here, with this course, and I could lose units if I transfer. I might have to take a year off. There's a lot I have to think about before making that decision."

Dad scowled, resting his hands on his hips. "It sounded like a sure thing to me."

Slumping, I rubbed my eyes. "Oh, *James*. I told him I was just thinking about it. Seeing him again over the break made me realize how much I missed him, so I said I'd think about it. He's blown it out of proportion."

Mum brushed my hair back. "He misses you."

"I know." I lowered my hands. "I miss him too, but I need this." I looked up at Dad. "I'm just me out here. You wanted me to be sure. Out here, I'm learning who I am and how to be independent. This way, I can know for sure whether marrying James is the right thing or not, because I'm having the chance to be an adult. I'm not a daddy's girl, or Harper and Dusty's sister, or Geri's best friend, or James's girlfriend. I'm just . . . me."

His gaze softened as he sat beside me. "I understand. Like always, you're levelheaded about this." He stroked my hair. "I'd love for you to come back, but if this is what you need, then I trust you. Whatever you decide, we'll support and help you however you want us to."

I wrapped my arms around him. "Thanks, Dad."

On Sunday night, after spending a pleasant evening with my parents, James called. He growled into the phone. "You're not serious."

"I'm sorry," I said, pacing my room. "It's just not practical for me to transfer."

"Practical?" He'd never sounded so angry. I sank onto my bed, clutching my pillow as he growled again. "You know what's not practical? You going out there in the first place. It just doesn't make sense. You could have done what you're doing right *here*."

"You know why I had to do this," I said, my voice trembling.

"Yeah, because I freaked you out." He let out a long breath. "Is that why you don't want to come back? Am I pushing too hard again?"

"No." I rubbed my brow. "I want to come back because of you, but . . ."

"But what?" he said softly, with a hint of desperation.

"But I'm tied in now. Some of my classes aren't transferable, and that would be a waste of time and money."

"So you'll have to do some extra classes. Isn't that worth it to be back here with your family, and me?"

I couldn't answer that. I did want to be back there with him and my family, but after seeing Austin so much, and with the time fast approaching when I'd meet him, officially, I doubted every path I had before me.

James sighed. "Cadence, I hate fighting with you. Please, just come home."

A tear ran down my face. "I can't. I'm sorry."

"All right," he said softly. "All right."

"I'm so sorry. I'm not running from you. *Please* understand that."

"I should go," he said flatly. "It's late."

"Okay." I wiped my eyes. "I love you."

He sighed. "I love you too."

We hung up, but I couldn't shake my heavy heart.

In the morning, Mum and Dad stopped in to say goodbye. Dad noticed I looked down, so after a brief explanation, he promised he'd talk with James.

I headed to a tutorial and glanced over to see Austin talking with some guys. When he laughed, I thought I would faint, my sadness over James evaporating. And then Austin's gaze lifted and met mine. He smiled. I caught my breath and hurried on. *He smiled at me!*

Austin, Austin, *Austin*!

In class, I daydreamed of our future. Tara smacked my forehead with her pen. "Where is your head today?"

"Oh, ah . . ." I had no answer. My future husband *smiled* at me!

"Wow, you're acting really weird." She smirked. "Did you meet someone?"

"What?" My face burned, and my heavy heart returned. With my relationship with James strained, I felt guilty for letting my feelings for Austin bloom. "No!"

"Denial! Oh, wow, *such* strong denial." She drummed her feet on the floor. "Details."

"There aren't any." I tried to focus on my work.

"Uh-huh. Well, whenever you're ready, I expect to be the first person informed. I told you about Cameron, and no one knows about him yet."

Cameron? *Oh, she told me about him yesterday.* He'd be gone in a week, maybe two if he was a good kisser.

I wondered how much longer it would be before I couldn't hold a single conversation with James without breaking into an argument. It made me feel worse for hurting him so much.

Tara yelled out as I stood on the football field doing a practical lesson. My heart stopped as I looked in the direction she was waving. Austin strolled by with several of his friends, but paused to wave at Tara.

I backed away, hoping he wouldn't notice me.

While he and Tara chatted, I watched. How could one guy be so gorgeous? Yes, James was crazy hot, but Austin . . . how could I forget how strong and masculine he always looked? I knew every inch of him intimately—five years of marriage and carrying his child would do that. I stepped closer, chewing my lip as he laughed with Tara.

Then a ball smacked me in the head.

I stumbled, grasping at the injury. "Ouch."

One of the guys rushed over. "I'm sorry! Are you okay?"

He grabbed my elbow to help me stand.

"I'm okay," I said, smiling as I slid the hair tie from my hair.

"Cadence!" Tara shoved in front of me. "Are you hurt?"

"I'm fine, seriously."

She grabbed my head, pulling it down to her. "Do you need ice?"

"It was just a football."

"You're not usually that clumsy." She met my gaze, frowning. "What happened?"

"I wasn't paying attention," I muttered, nodding to the guy as he left.

She squinted. "That's not like you, either."

"Yeah." I rubbed my head. "I guess I didn't sleep well last night."

"If you say so."

As we turned back to focus on our class, I glanced over to see Austin walk into the building.

After the spring break, with my thoughts on transcripts and hesitating to follow through with transferring, my mind was completely off avoiding Austin. I stepped into the corridor, seeing him among a group of guys. As I passed by, his gaze followed me. I couldn't help the flush that burned in my cheeks.

In class, I sat beside Tara. She tilted her head. "Your face is red."

"What?" I touched my cheeks.

"There's something going on with you lately. This is, like, the millionth time you've come in here all flustered." She winked. "Is it a guy?"

"No," I replied sharply. "I was running late, that's all."

"Uh-huh."

That night, I flicked through my scrapbook. Although I'd dated in the first timeline, usually as a double for Tara, I never mentioned Austin in my journal entries. My memories of how we first met were right, and I hadn't noticed him before then. I wondered what had changed.

Sighing, I set the scrapbook aside to stare at the pictures of Austin and Melody, and me with James. How could I choose between these two lives? As sad as it made me, things with James had changed. He called less frequently, and when we did talk, we grew upset with each other. Although we always made up, it wore me down emotionally.

The next week, when I rounded the corner to class, someone ran into me, knocking all my books and notes out of my arms. I glared at him as he walked on without even apologizing, and when I turned back around, I found someone squatting in front of me. I knew the legs in those dark jeans too well, but I didn't dare look up.

"Hey, need some help?" Austin's voice rang in my ears like a songbird on a spring afternoon.

"I'm . . . I'm okay," I stammered, as I focused on gathering my things.

He deliberately went for the same notes as me and touched my hand. Electricity shot up my arm, and I pulled away.

"I'm Austin, by the way."

No, no, no! We aren't supposed to meet yet! I refused to look up at him. "Hi."

"And you are?"

I snatched my things from him. "Late for class." I hurried down the corridor as my heart pounded in my throat. *That was too close.* From then on, I took a different route.

That night, James called me. I answered warily, afraid of getting blasted again. "James."

"Hey," he said flatly.

We fell silent.

He groaned. "Your dad talked to me. He gave me a real earful. Thanks a bunch."

My cheeks burned as I shut my notebook and laptop.

"So you're not coming back? And that's it?"

My heart ached. "James . . ."

"I can't . . ." He let out a long breath. "Don't give me hope when you don't intend to follow through."

Ouch. "I didn't mean to. I want to go back, but it's not . . ." I hung my head. "Practical."

"You should have just stayed here in the first place."

A tear rolled down my cheek at his bitter tone. "I'm sorry."

Another long pause followed, ripping my heart out.

"Cadence . . ." His voice filled with emotion. "Your dad said you're finding yourself out there. He said you need this, and I understand, I do. I'm just . . . I'm . . ."

"I know," I whispered.

"I wish I could be there with you."

I wiped my eyes. "Me too."

"I just love you so much. I don't . . ." He took a deep breath. James's emotions rarely got the better of him, and right then, I could hear it in his voice. I never wanted to be the one to torture him like that.

"James, I wish I could hold your hand and tell you everything will be okay. Please, I never meant to hurt you."

"Babe, I know." He sighed, reigning in his emotions. "Promise you'll stay with me when you come back for Harper's wedding?"

"I promise."

"Good. I need that time."

"Then you'll get it."

We said goodbye, but I ached all over. I couldn't help feeling like we were falling apart.

Chapter Seven

Tara and I attempted to enter the water, but the ocean was still far too cold for our taste. We retreated back onto the sand and watched Lyla surf.

"So, when exactly are you heading back to Sydney?" Tara asked.

"Well, I can't get too much time off work since I took four weeks during July, so I'm going to go for the two weeks around Harper's wedding. I'm leaving on the sixth of January."

She grinned. "Perfect! You can come to a Christmas party with me tonight. All my school friends will be there, and there are some hotties you might like." She nudged me in the ribs.

I giggled. "I don't feel like picking up."

"Fine, then let one of them pick *you* up."

I laughed and remembered that this was the party where I first saw Austin. He would be there, but I couldn't talk to him. That wasn't supposed to happen until the new school year. With everything that had happened already, I felt nervous. What if he approached me? I didn't want our relationship to be altered; I wanted it to play out the same way.

And James. Things were strained between us, to the point of near collapse. I doubted he could handle another year with me gone. I needed to be fair to him by ending us before . . .

But the prospect of ending us hurt so much.

Brushing the thoughts aside, I decided to focus on enjoying the evening with my friends. I carefully chose my outfit so I looked tidy—but not pretty in any way— in dark jeans and a blue, fitted t-shirt. I put on a small amount of makeup, determined not to stand out. After all the close calls I'd had with Austin, I didn't want to draw his attention before the right time.

Tara picked up Lyla and me right on time, and we headed to the house. As we entered, just like the first time, I saw Austin standing by the bar in the kitchen with a few of his guy friends. I paused at the sight of him and caught my breath. He looked magnificent. He was an average height, but his arms and shoulders made up for it in sheer muscular bulk. He had gelled his hair and had facial hair growing on his solid jawline, which only enhanced his masculine appearance. He looked so perfect it took my breath away. There he was, my husband—alive, vibrant, and just as I remembered.

Tara nudged me. "Hey, Cadence, are you okay?"

I forced myself to think and said, "Who's that?"

Her eyes twinkled up at me. "That's Austin Jones. Why?"

"Is . . . is he single?" I asked. Even though I already knew the answer, I wanted to keep everything the same.

"I believe so, yes."

I met her gaze. "Is he straight?"

She giggled. "Yes. Do you want me to introduce you?"

Yes! I screamed in my mind, but kept my cool. "He wouldn't wanna talk to me. If we meet, then we meet. I won't force it."

She rolled her eyes. "Suit yourself."

I watched him out of the corner of my eye as we passed and saw him do a double-take on me. He leaned forward to see me clearer before I walked through the door to the backyard.

A table with food and drinks sat on the porch, and chairs stood in a circle on the lawn with bug repellent lanterns burning to keep the mosquitos away. I sat with Lyla while Tara introduced us to some of her friends.

I had a great time, forgetting about Austin until he stepped outside while Tara refilled her plate and grabbed a drink. He shuffled up beside her and spoke. She nodded and touched his arm before they turned and headed down to join us together.

As he turned, his gaze locked on me. *Shoot!* I averted my gaze and tried to engross myself in a conversation with Lyla. Then, where Tara had sat beside me, he sank down; she pulled up a chair on the other side of him. I turned slightly, hoping to avoid contact with him. When he cleared his throat, my nerves got the better of me and I leapt to my feet to rush inside.

"Cadence? Where are you going?" Tara asked.

I rushed into the bathroom and sat on the toilet seat, struggling not to hyperventilate. I didn't want it to be different. I wanted everything with him to be the same. Just the same. Our relationship had been wonderful, and I didn't want to screw around with it.

I needed to talk to someone.

"Hello, beautiful. You realize it's midnight here, right?"

I smiled, and my heart calmed at the sound of James's voice. "Not like you'd be sleeping anyway."

He chuckled. By the sound of things, he was out drinking. "Yeah, I'm out. How are you?"

"I'm at a party right now."

"Oh . . . then why are you on the phone with me? Not that I'm complaining."

"I just . . . everyone's hooking up, and a guy started hitting on me, so I needed to hide and talk to you."

He hesitated, and I remembered how badly he'd reacted the last time I told him a guy hit on me. I doubted I'd made the right call. "Do I need to catch a red eye and beat him up for you?"

I smiled at his attempt to sound chill about it. "No, your voice is reassurance enough."

"Well, I'm glad." I heard Tom talking with his girlfriend Nicki in the background before James said, "Hey, I gotta go. I love you, and I'll see ya in two weeks."

"You too, James. I miss you."

I smiled as I hung up the phone. James had soothed my nerves, and I felt calm again. I flushed the toilet and washed my hands as a cover, then stepped out.

Austin stood in the family room with a direct line of sight to the bathroom. His gaze locked on me; I knew he had waited for me. Tara appeared beside me and grabbed my arm so I couldn't escape as he approached. I tugged, trying to free myself.

"No! I'm not ready to meet him!" I said in a hushed voice.

"Not ready?" Her eyes narrowed. "Cadence, he *wants* to meet you."

"But I'm . . . not yet . . ."

"Hi."

My heart hit my stomach, and all the calming influence James just had on me flew out the window. I stared at Austin as he smiled cautiously down at me.

"Cadence, isn't it?"

My cheeks burned. I felt fourteen. *Again.*

Tara nudged me and released my arm so I could shake his outstretched hand. But once free, I balked and made a dash for the front door.

"Cadence!" she called after me, with clear frustration in her voice. Then I heard her say, "Go after her!"

And to my surprise, he did. He caught my arm by the front door and electricity shot through me. I turned to face him, gasping with surprise, before getting lost in his eyes.

"Cadence, you keep running from me."

"Mmm." I bit my lip and dropped my gaze. *Not yet, oh please, not yet.*

"Have I done something to offend you?"

"No!" My gaze shot back up and my hand lifted to rest on his chest, but I caught myself and pulled away.

The gesture didn't go unnoticed. He caught my hand and placed it on his chest. "Are you afraid of me?"

I couldn't help my eyes falling onto his lips as I responded, breathlessly, "A little, yes."

"Why?"

I tried to pull my hand away, but he held tightly to it. "I'm . . . I'm just not ready to meet you yet."

He raised his eyebrow. "What does that mean?"

"I just . . . I'm . . ." My fingers wandered over his chest. Even after all that time, it still looked familiar, the place I'd rested for comfort. He shifted closer to me, and his free hand pressed against my waist. I looked up and we gazed deeply into each other's eyes. I'd begged him to come back to life, and here he was—so alive.

I whimpered and pulled away.

"Hey, I don't get it," he said gently. "You're obviously just as attracted to me as I am to you."

"That's . . ." My face burned. I covered my face and slipped out from under his arms.

"Cadence!" he called after me as I rushed out the door.

I hurried down the street and hid behind a bush. An assault of memories and feelings slammed into my brain, as if a dam had broken open right on top of me. Austin's eyes gazing into mine as he asked me to marry him, as we said our vows, as I gave birth, as he loved me endlessly.

I fell to my knees as the image of him stretched out dead in the morgue overwhelmed me. My Austin. My wonderful, devoted Austin.

"Angel!" I screamed.

He appeared in front of me. He bent over, his expression cold. "What is it?"

I pulled back, startled by his lack of warmth. "Why am I suddenly remembering everything so clearly?"

He hesitated, his eyes narrowing. "All your memories are coming back?"

"Yes! Austin touched me, and a moment later, *bam*! The most vivid image is his dead body. How can I face him with that burned into my mind?"

He straightened and folded his arms, but his expression softened. "Stand up, Cadence."

I hurried to obey. He looked me over slowly and sighed. He reached out and touched my shoulder. The image faded back into that of a mere dream. I rubbed my eyes as his hand fell, and I fought to compose myself. "Thank you."

"You're very welcome. Now, what are you going to do?"

I slumped. "It's too early to talk to him. I want everything to be the same. Our relationship was so wonderful that I don't want to change a thing."

"But a great deal has already changed."

My gaze shot up to meet his. "Oh no . . ."

He smiled. "Cadence, this is a second chance. What if, like everything else, you can make it so much better?"

I dropped my head and stared at my hands. "What could be better than perfect?"

His breath brushed against my cheek as he whispered to me, "Nothing is perfect."

He vanished.

I stopped breathing. What did he mean? Had I done something wrong with Austin the first time around? I thought we had loved each other so completely, despite our fights over dishes, money, and other petty domestic disputes.

"Cadence!"

I jumped at Tara's voice and took a sharp breath. She ran up in front of me and paused to catch her breath with her hands on her hips. "What was that?"

"What?"

She waved her hands in the air. "You just ran out on him!" she said slowly and precisely. "What's *wrong* with you? I thought you thought he's hot!"

"I . . . I do," I stuttered. "It's just, I didn't expect that."

"What? A guy hitting on you?"

I nodded.

Her expression softened, and she grabbed my hand. "But *you're* hot. Surely guys have hit on you before."

I scoffed. "It's been a while."

"What do you mean?"

I met her gaze. James had done a fantastic job at keeping other guys away from me. He had a threatening presence, being so tall and strong, and his former bad boy reputation still lingered around him. I'd never minded either—I was happy with him.

I sighed. *James*. Here I was again, conflicted.

I squeezed Tara's hand. "I dated a guy from my ninth grade year onward. No one ever hit on me because of that. He was too *scary*."

A smile crept across her face. "Oh, I get it. That's why you never talk about guys. A boyfriend for that long makes it hard to move on."

I nodded.

She wrapped her arm through mine. "Come on. I'll explain to him to give you some space for a bit, huh? Because seriously, when I saw you two together, it *worked,* and I'm not just saying that."

I smiled. She had no idea.

Back in the house, she walked me back to Lyla before she disappeared. A few moments later, I saw her through the kitchen window talking to Austin. He listened closely, nodding every so often. When she finished, he rubbed the hair on his chin and spoke. I wished I was a fly on the wall.

She responded. He nodded and glanced out the window. I looked away, hoping he hadn't noticed me. When I glanced back, they had both gone.

Tara returned to sit beside me. She waited for Lyla to talk to someone else before she said quietly, "I told him to take it easy on you."

"What do you mean?"

"He kinda thought you were a bit nuts, so I explained what you told me and he understood. He's a great guy, Cadence. I think you'd really like him if you gave him a chance."

I huffed. I'd almost blown it. Thank goodness for Tara saving the day. "He really thought I was crazy?"

She grinned sheepishly. "Well, you did act pretty weird. If I didn't know you, I'd think you were too."

I slapped my forehead. "I'm such an idiot."

She giggled. "Don't worry. He understands. Maybe after the holidays, when we go back to school, you'll have had enough time to cool off, and you'll let him approach you without acting like a fourteen-year-old."

"Maybe."

He passed by the back door and my gaze followed him. Tara nudged me with a grin.

Chapter Eight

I sat with Lyla in the common room, searching for housing links and emailing them to her. She wasn't going home for the holidays. Instead, she would line up a flat for the both of us, so when I returned after the wedding, I could move straight in.

"It's been the New Year in Sydney for almost two hours," she muttered.

"Mmm." I wasn't paying much attention. I instant-messaged James as I searched. I could tell by the increased number of typos that he was growing tired—the time in Sydney was almost 2:00 a.m.—but he stayed up, determined to wait for me to cross into the New Year before going to sleep.

"It's about to start," Lyla said nonchalantly.

The TV hosts spoke excitedly. I looked up and saw the countdown begin. Ten, nine, eight . . .

I stared at James's picture on the messenger and my heart sank. It had been years since we hadn't been together over New Year's. It felt strange to not have him with me for the midnight kiss.

"Three, two, one . . ."

Freeze.

I remained seated and stared at the computer screen.

"Hello, sweet Cadence."

"Hello, Angel," I replied, completely fixed on James's face.

He stepped up behind me and touched my shoulder. This time, since the memories of Austin were already restored, the memories that flashed into my mind were of Melody. I smiled as her innocent face entered my thoughts. Her giggles echoed in my ears, and that warm, new baby smell filled my nostrils.

But then she was dead.

I shuddered and fought back tears. "Everything's changing. Even things I didn't mean to change."

"Other people have their choices too," he said.

"Is that why things are different with Austin? Whose choice changed that?"

He came around in front of me. I set the laptop aside as he stretched out his hand. "Let's review the year."

I took his hand and, as I stood, the scene around us shifted. To my left I saw the first timeline, and to my right the second. In both, I rushed down a corridor in the university, late for class.

Austin stood by his classroom, and as I rounded the corner, he looked up. He watched me as I walked, letting out a long breath. In the first timeline, I hurried on, but in the second, my phone rang.

I saw myself drop everything, and Austin came over to help me. He looked me over as I talked on the phone, completely unaware of his presence as he gathered my papers.

"There it is," the angel said to me. "Geri's choice changed everything. She called you, and that was the only difference you needed."

I watched as I blushed like an idiot and fumbled over myself before hurrying away. He watched me go, a dazed grin across his face, before his girlfriend called to him. He hurried over, and the scene changed to three weeks later.

He looked up in both timelines and saw me. In the first, he watched me pass by while I rushed on without looking, but in the second, I looked across at him and he smiled. I blushed and rushed away.

As I disappeared, he stepped out and watched me go. "Wow."

A few weeks skipped, and we stood outside just after the spring break. I saw him among a group of guys. In the first timeline he glanced at me, but barely reacted;

but as I passed by in the second, his gaze followed me. I glanced across at him and turned bright red as I kept walking. He grinned and rubbed the back of his neck as he watched me go.

From then on, he barely paid any attention to me in the first timeline as I hurried by. But in the second timeline, he arrived early the next week and pulled a few of his friends aside.

"Hey, so there's this girl," he said. "She passes by every week, and she's gorgeous. We always exchange looks, but I'm pretty sure she's shy because she blushes and hurries away before I have a chance to do anything. I need to get her to stop."

His friends grinned, and one said, "What do you want us to do?"

He pointed to the corner. "At about five 'til, she'll come rushing around there. One of you needs to run into her so she drops everything and I can do the whole 'saving the damsel in distress' thing."

They chuckled, and the one who had spoken watched the corner. "I'll do it."

A few minutes later, I appeared around the corner.

"There she is!" Austin said. "The blonde! Go!"

The guy hurried right at me and landed a firm knock on my shoulder, sending everything in my arms flying.

"Perfect," Austin said, hurrying over to help me.

"That was planned?" I gasped.

The man in white chuckled.

Austin rushed over, and I turned bright red. He smiled, apparently enjoying my discomfort.

"I'm Austin, by the way. And you are?"

I snatched my notes from him. "Late for class."

He watched me with a strange, lost look in his eyes and a slight smile as I hurried away.

His friend returned and asked, "Did it work?"

Austin grinned. "Yeah, I think so."

The next week he watched out for me again, but I didn't come. He looked disappointed, but didn't let it bother him. It wasn't until the third week that he became discouraged. He asked his friend, "Have you seen that girl pass by recently?"

His friend shook his head. "Sorry, mate."

Austin grabbed his hair. "I freaked her out, I just know it."

"Hey, dude, she'll show up. She goes here, so just be patient."

The scene changed and we stood at the party. I felt a rush of anticipation to see his perspective on what happened.

In the first timeline, I entered and saw him. He didn't notice me at first, but glanced up as I walked by, his gaze following me. But with no reaction from me whatsoever, he didn't bother pursuing.

As I walked by in the second, he saw me and paid attention. Once I'd disappeared out the back, he grabbed his friend Aaron's arm. "Dude, that was her with Tara."

"What, the girl you've being ogling in the hallway?" Aaron responded carelessly.

"Yeah. I've got to meet her."

"Well, go find Tara and have her introduce you."

"I will."

He waited for Tara to approach the table before he took a deep breath and rushed at her. "Tara."

She looked up at him. "Austin."

"Who's your friend?"

Tara didn't even glance back. "Which one?"

"The blonde."

A wicked smile swept across her face. "Why? Are you checkin' her out?"

"Yeah, actually. I've seen her around campus."

Tara giggled. "She's noticed you, too."

A hopeful light shone in his eyes. "Really?"

"Yeah."

She waited for him to make the request for an introduction, and when he did, she grinned. "Of course! I'd be delighted. Cadence is awesome. She's sweet and a lot of fun. But I'd recommend being on her team when it comes to sports. Phew, she's scary!"

"Her name is Cadence?" he asked overenthusiastically.

She nodded. "Cadence Anderson, from Western Sydney."

She grasped his elbow. He caught me looking at him just before I turned away. He grinned. "Do you think she'll like me?"

"She definitely likes the *look* of you. The rest of you will be easy after that."

She gestured for him to sit beside me. He stared at me as I turned away, trying to engage elsewhere. He glanced at Tara for help. She waved her hand and mouthed, "*Just talk to her.*"

He cleared his throat to speak, and I rushed away. He stared after me, his jaw hanging. He turned to Tara. "Is she avoiding me?"

Tara huffed. "I don't think she's real good with guys. She never talks about them, and whenever we go out anywhere she's a ruddy wallflower."

He raised an eyebrow. "Are you sure she's straight then?"

Tara grinned. "Yes! She definitely eyed you off as we came in. She was freaking breath-taken for goodness' sake! Come on, let's find her."

They searched the house and, as they passed the bathroom, Tara paused. "She's on the phone in there. We'll wait."

When I came out, Tara rushed me. Austin advanced, but I dashed away, frightened. Tara ordered him to follow—not that he needed to be told, he shot after me before she finished saying the words. I watched as I let him move closer to me, and then I ran away.

"Cadence!" he called in frustration.

Tara rushed up beside him. "What happened?"

"She's a weirdo, isn't she?" He scowled. "She has a screw loose or something. She obviously has no desire for me to hit on her."

Tara growled. "What's wrong with her? She's not normally like this."

"I dunno, Tara, you tell me. She may be gorgeous, but I don't want a fruitcake."

Tara's gaze flashed to him angrily. "Cadence isn't crazy! Something's wrong, that's all. Let me talk to her."

She rushed out the door after me.

Time fast-forwarded and we stood in front of Tara and Austin talking in the kitchen.

"She dated some guy through most of high school," she said, "so having guys hit on her isn't something she's used to. Add into that how long a ninth through twelfth grade relationship is, and how much she probably laid on the line for that guy, and she's probably a little nervous about dating again.

"I think you should stick to it and be patient until she's ready. I swear to you, what you saw tonight was a crazy Cadence, not the real Cadence. She's awesome, Austin, and I really think you'll like her if you give her a chance."

He nodded, rubbing his chin. "Did she say how long it's been since she broke up with that guy?"

Tara shook her head. "I didn't want to push for those details."

He sighed. "I guess I'll play it by ear then."

The scene froze, and the man in white stepped over and looked down at Tara. "She's a good friend."

I smiled. "She is. I'm very lucky."

"So, did that answer your question?"

I nodded. "I always thought I noticed him and made him pay attention to me, but he noticed me all along. He noticed me first, but *I* wasn't paying attention."

He chuckled. "You didn't pay attention to much in the first timeline, did you?"

I pouted. "Apparently not."

He covered my eyes. "But you still have another path open to you."

When he removed his hands, we stood in James's room in his townhouse. James worked at his computer, clicking around on websites. His school work sat on his desk, and browser tabs for his classes were open in the background, but he was focused on several university sites—on how to transfer.

"He wants you to come back to him," the man said, staring down at James. "He has looked into every scenario he can think of. Despite the tension between you, all he wants is to be with you."

I slumped, stepping up beside him as he read through a course description at UWS. "This is so hard. I don't want to let him go, but Austin is my future. I know that. We were so happy."

"And you're not happy with James?"

"Yes, but . . ." I look up at the man. "I'm meant to be with Austin."

He raised an eyebrow. "Our destiny is what we choose it to be. Either path can be yours. Both paths will bring you family and love. Destiny isn't one set future, otherwise, where would choice fit in?"

I chewed on my lip. *Why does everything have to be so confusing?*

We returned to the common room through the door. Lyla stared heavy-eyed at the TV screen. I walked over to her and touched her hair. "I made amazing friends here. Tara and Lyla stayed with me from here on, even after we graduated and moved on. Do you think Geri will like them, too?"

"I cannot tell you the future, sweet Cadence. Only you can discover that answer."

"My sister made me maid of honor. That's incredible. Her wedding is in a week, and this time I'm excited for it. This is how I should be feeling. I'm doing things right, aren't I?"

"If you are happier, then yes."

I returned to my chair and placed the laptop back on my lap. "This year, I'm gonna trust my judgment. I've done well so far, so I need to let things happen as they happen." I looked down at James's face on the screen and my heart sank. "Including losing James."

"Are you sure you want to lose him?" the man asked as he stepped in front of me.

"Yes, and no. I don't know. Things have been hard between us."

"Just because things are hard doesn't mean you should give up."

"I know that, which complicates things more." I slumped. "But I can't be with both of them. It wouldn't be fair."

I looked up to find him gone. As my gaze dropped back onto the computer screen, the TV erupted with noise again and a message came through from James that read, *Happy New Year, beautiful. I'm going to bed. I love you.*

Chapter Nine

James waited for me at the airport. My heart skipped a beat at the sight of him. He stood, texting, standing with one hand in the pocket of his gray dress pants for work. He'd found a job at a medical lab, and would be given a full-time position once he graduated at the end of the year.

He looked amazing in those pants and pale blue dress shirt.

A moment later, my phone beeped. His head shot up and he grinned when he saw me approaching. I threw my arms around his neck and he lifted me into the air as we kissed.

He pushed my face away as he caressed it. "Let me look at you."

I smiled and bit my lip as his eyes took in my face.

"How could you be more beautiful than I remember?"

"You're getting old, so Alzheimer's is setting in."

"You're funny," he responded sarcastically.

I giggled.

His fingers ran over the ends of my hair. "Come on, let's get home."

I monopolized the conversation the whole way home, telling him about Tara and Lyla and all the fun and crazy things we did together. He listened patiently and laughed at our antics. Once we pulled up at the townhouse, I leaned over and kissed his cheek. "You're wonderful, you know that?"

He grinned. "I did know that, yes."

I giggled and kissed his cheek again.

He sighed, touching my chin. "It's good to have you back."

I looked into his eyes, enjoying the warmth and comfort they gave me. "It's good to be back."

He kissed me on the lips, and then climbed out of the car. "Let's get you settled in. Your family wants you tonight, so I need some time with you first."

We dragged my suitcases inside, and I almost died of shock. "It's . . . it's *clean!*"

James laughed. "I thought it would be a nice surprise for you."

I nodded, unable to speak. He led me up the stairs. As we entered the bedroom, a chocolate ball of fur charged us. Canis looked full grown and had to have reached the maximum size allowed for their townhouse's contract. He resembled a Labrador, just smaller and leaner.

"Look at you!" I knelt down to scratch his ears.

"Yeah, he's a right little terror." James grinned as he picked him up and tossed him out the door. "Get outside, you!"

Canis raced down the stairs as James shut the door.

James's gaze turned to me and looked me over, slowly, carefully absorbing every inch of me. "Six months, Cadence. It's been six months since we were last together. I haven't gone that long since . . . well, okay, our sexual encounters have always been sparse, but to not even kiss you or hold you has been torture."

He started unbuttoning his shirt as he advanced on me.

I backed toward the bed and my mind filled with doubt. *What about Austin?* I was supposed to break up with James at some point. With the strain between us, it only seemed fair, for his sanity. But as his arms wrapped around my waist and he bent down to kiss me, all those thoughts drained out of me.

I moaned under his touch, his kiss. He pulled off his shirt, and my hands found his bare skin. Goose bumps broke out all over him and our lips parted. "Cadence?"

"Yes, James?"

He shuddered as my hands drifted down toward the button on his pants. "I've been thinking."

"Okay." I unbuttoned his pants and unzipped his fly.

"I graduate at the end of this year, and . . ." He groaned as my hand slipped into his pants.

"And?"

"Forget it." He pushed me onto the bed. "It can wait."

I sat between Mum and Dusty, watching Daniel's rowdy Italian family. The middle child of seven, Daniel had three older sisters—all married with children—two younger brothers, and a younger sister. It seemed like they wanted to fulfill every stereotype possible—we had every pasta dish imaginable spread before us, all made completely from scratch and divine to eat, and his large, boisterous family spoke quickly in heavy Italian Australian accents, making them difficult to understand.

The brother immediately below Daniel, Franco, was about the same age as James, and Daniel's best man. He seemed intent on hitting on me, much to Dad's disgust. He sat across the table from me and leaned forward. "Cadence, right?"

"Right." I tried to focus on my food.

"I usually prefer ethnic girls myself, but you're cute."

I rolled my eyes. "Well, you're in luck, because this non-ethnic girl isn't interested."

"Aw, come on! As maid of honor and best man, we should be getting along."

I glanced up at him, and he winked. *Gross.*

"Hey! Back off!" Dad pointed at him.

Harper sank into the seat beside Franco. "Cadence is spoken for. She's been with her boyfriend for four years, so she's practically married to him."

I flushed. "No, I'm not."

"Whatever." Harper looked back at Franco. "Her boyfriend, James, will be at the reception, so don't even bother. It took forever to get Dad to like him, and even now, I don't think Dad's completely sold on him . . ."

I glanced across at Dad. He scowled as he resumed eating.

Harper managed to drag Franco away from us, and Dusty breathed a sigh of relief. "Seriously, Daniel's family is a bit much."

I giggled. "Well, we'll only have to see them occasionally. Harper's the one who'll have to live with them."

We looked across at Harper. She rejoined Daniel and gazed adoringly at him while he talked to his stepfather.

"She's happy, though," I said. "That's what matters."

Wedding preparations filled the week. Whenever Harper wasn't working, she dragged me around with her to finalize everything and pick up items. The few times I was home at the same time as James, we spent it focused on each other. I completely forgot about Austin.

The wedding day finally arrived, and it couldn't have been more perfect. The weather was warm and sunny, but not too hot like a typical January day. The ceremony was held in a packed Roman Catholic church. Harper hadn't been pleased with the number of guests, but after a huge argument about family traditions and not wanting to offend Aunt So-and-So, she yielded—but she still didn't like it.

I led the bridal party in on Franco's arm. As I passed the front row, James grinned at me from the other side of Mum, and next to her sat . . .

"*Geri!*" I mouthed excitedly.

Geri shrugged and mouthed, "*Dusty.*"

I stood to the side of the altar to wait and met James's gaze. He looked me over approvingly and mouthed, "*Wow!*"

I smirked.

"*Nice dress.*"

I glanced down at the teal dress and shrugged. "*Could be worse.*"

He chuckled.

The other two bridesmaids made their way up the aisle—Daniel's younger sister with Dusty, and Harper's best friend, Loz, with Daniel's other brother.

Then, Harper entered. She had her arm wrapped through Dad's and she glowed, her smile lighting up the room. She'd never looked more stunning. Her dark hair was pulled back and draped in curls around her neck. Her dress had a low waistline, so her slender curves were pronounced and elegant under the lace and beading. I'd always envied her smaller frame, and in that moment, I felt like a brick compared to her with my shorter, athletic build.

But Harper stared ahead. I followed her gaze to Daniel. By the look on his face, I saw that he'd never laid eyes on anyone more beautiful and he wondered why she chose him. I had a flash of my own wedding and remembered Austin gazing at me that same way. Tears burned in my eyes.

Harper stepped up to hand me the bouquet with tears in her own eyes. "Stop it, or you'll mess up your makeup."

I giggled softly as she smiled at me.

Dad gave her hand to Daniel. I watched Dad as he turned to sit beside Mum, and he nodded to James before all the guests took their seats.

The ceremony ran smoothly. Mum cried a steady stream of tears through the whole thing. Finally, Daniel was told to kiss his bride, and he clasped her face and kissed her deeply. Everyone cheered, and my own love for Harper swelled. She was so happy, and as their lips pulled apart, she turned to me. Without letting go of Daniel's hand, she wrapped her arm around my waist and kissed my cheek.

"Thank you, Cay. I love you."

We went to some gardens for the photos, so Dusty and I took advantage of the time to catch up. We moved to a bench under a jacaranda tree while Harper and Daniel had shots taken of just them.

"You're doing the HSC this year," I said.

"Thanks for that." He rubbed his hands together. "I'm at a point where I just want it to be over. I feel really burned out, you know?"

I nodded. "Yeah, I know."

He looked down at me with wary eyes. "I'm thinking of taking a year off."

He'd done that the first time around, so it didn't surprise me. "Sounds like a plan. You can travel a bit, build up some money, and when you're ready, go back to school."

"Hey, there you go mind reading again." He smirked and punched my shoulder.

I rubbed it. "That's going to bruise."

"Whatever."

"So . . ." I glanced around as Daniel's siblings yelled and laughed at each other, while Loz stared between them uncomfortably. "Do you spend much time with James?"

He chuckled. "Yeah, actually. We hang out at least once a week. It's kinda nice, you know, with us both only having sisters." He paused and stroked my back. "He misses you like crazy."

I flushed. "I miss him, too."

"Neither of us get it. We don't understand why you had to go so far away, or why you won't come back. We thought you were happy here."

"I am," I said, looking into his eyes. "There's just some things I need to do that I can't explain."

"James thinks it's his fault." Dusty gazed ahead. "He thinks it's because he asked you to marry him before you were ready."

I sighed. "That's not it at all. It has nothing to do with James."

Dusty turned to face me with a look of concern. "Nothing to do with James? Cadence, everything you do has *everything* to do with James. Every choice you make affects him, and sometimes, I really think you don't even know how much."

I couldn't respond; my guilt was too strong. I was already up and down about breaking up with him. One minute I'd be determined to end it, but then he'd walk in and my resolve would disappear as I fell into his arms.

"I'm torturing him." My chin quivered. "Maybe I should let him go until I finish my course and can move back—"

Dusty grabbed my shoulders and pulled me around to face him. He wore an expression of pure horror as he said in a tight voice, "What are you saying?"

I couldn't look him in the eyes. "Maybe he'd be better off without me."

Dusty slammed his hand over my mouth. "Shut up! Don't even think about that! What you just said never leaves this place, do you hear me? *Never*. And James must never know you said that."

"But I'm not being fair—"

"What's not fair is if you cut him off. He's already let you go as far as he can take. He wants to *marry* you, Cadence. That's got to tell you something. But all you seem to be doing is running away, like you always do when something you're not sure about gets in your way. You did it when he started pursuing you, you did it when you guys first had sex, and you did it when he proposed. Now, you're trying to run—*again*.

"I know you love him—we *all* know you love him— even Dad accepted him because he can see how strong your feelings are. I think you're the only person who hasn't accepted it. Yeah, I get that you think you're too young, and I respect that, but at the same time, you guys have been together for ages. People at school still talk about your epic romance and how he won you over and mended his wild ways. All the girls want their own James, and even hit on me 'cause I'm your brother and James sometimes picks me up from school so we can hang out. They think I can give them that same romance."

I giggled. "You? Romantic?"

"I know, right? They're completely bonkers." He stretched his arms out along the back of the park bench. "Cadence, don't run scared. I like James—he's like a brother to me—and he loves you."

How could I let go of James after that? Dusty was right. I did love him, and realistically speaking, I'd altered my relationship with Austin and potentially ruined it permanently. He thought I was crazy, and who would date someone who's crazy? But I did have James—wonderful, faithful James whom I loved.

I couldn't let him go.

At the reception, I sat with Harper alongside the bridesmaids. James and Geri sat with my parents and seemed content enough talking with them. We'd all been together for such a long time that they were practically family.

My phone vibrated, and I discreetly pulled it out to read the text from James. THAT GIRL NEXT TO YOU IN WHITE IS SMOKING HOT.

I giggled and set the phone on the table so Harper could read it. She scanned it, then gave James a sarcastic look. "Your boyfriend's hilarious, Cadence."

I looked across at him and saw him texting again with a smirk. Then I received: BUT THAT GIRL ON THE OTHER SIDE OF YOU . . . OH MAN, CADENCE, YOU HAVE SOME SERIOUS COMPETITION TONIGHT.

I looked up at him, and he twitched his eyebrows at me, still smirking. I rolled my eyes and he laughed.

As we progressed into the speeches, his texts increased in frequency as he pointed out the strange faces people pulled or mocked the speeches. Every time my phone vibrated, Harper grew more and more annoyed until she finally snapped during Daniel's dad's speech. "Tell your stupid boyfriend to cut it out!" she said sharply.

His next text said, TELL HARPER I HEARD THAT HA HA!

I showed her and she smoldered, throwing him a dirty look. He shrugged, smirking, and tucked his phone away.

The daddy-daughter dance came up, and Dad hurried over to take Harper's hand. She smiled up at him, and he gazed lovingly into her eyes. That moment hadn't happened in the first timeline—Harper didn't want the daddy-daughter dance then. Thankfully, this time around, she did.

"Cadence?" I looked up as James stretched out his hand for me. "Will you let me dance with the most beautiful girl in the world?"

"Harper's over there." I nodded across the dance floor.

"Shut up and dance with me."

I laughed and took his hand.

He guided me onto the dance floor and held me in a waltz position. "It seems those classes in PE where we learned line-dancing are paying off." He grinned. "Look at me box-stepping!"

I chuckled and rested my head against his chest. It rose and fell as he sighed, and he kissed the top of my head. His arm wrapped tighter around my waist, and he held me close.

"James?"

"Mmm?"

"I love you."

He pulled back and lifted my chin with our joined hands. "Cadence, I love you more than anything." He kissed me softly. "I wanted to tell you something."

"What's that?"

"When I graduate at the end of this year, I'm going to move west to be with you. The lab I work for has branches out there, so I can arrange a transfer. I want to be there for you as you finish your last year."

"James!" I lifted my hand off his shoulder and touched his face. "That would be wonderful!"

"Really? I thought you went out there to get away from me for a while, so I thought you'd be a bit more apprehensive."

I shook my head. "I wasn't running from you—I've told you that over and over. I just needed to go out and find myself, and I'm getting there. I have to be self-reliant and independent, and everyone just sees me as *me*. Not as one of the Anderson kids, or Geri's best friend—"

"Or my girlfriend," he said flatly.

I sighed. "James, I *promise* this is not about you. I love you. That's why I need to find me."

He clasped my face. "It's just so hard. We seem to fight all the time, and I hate it. Cadence, I promise I'm going to study hard so I can graduate and be with you again."

I smiled. "I'd like—"

"Okay! Can all the single ladies gather around?" the MC's voice boomed over the microphone.

James kissed my head before turning me toward a small crowd of gathering women. "Show those crazy Italians what being a psycho, sports-fanatic, white chick means."

"Ah, so that's what you call me behind my back!"

"Don't you doubt it!" He spanked me firmly across the rump.

I walked over, and Geri caught my arm. "Finally, I can talk to you! Come on, let's get into this catfight for old time's sake."

She dragged me right into the middle of the pack.

"So, you're here with Dusty, huh?" I said.

"Yeah, he needed a plus one, and I was convenient." She shrugged.

"I know he kissed you last New Year's."

She stiffened. "What?"

"Yeah, I saw it."

She blushed. "It was just a thing. You know, being New Year's and stuff."

"Geri, it's okay for you to like him."

She pursed her lips and stared ahead. "I don't like him. He's just a kid."

"No, he's not, and he likes you."

Her breath caught and she met my gaze, but before she could say anything, Harper stood in front of us and the shoving began. We both shoved back, and Geri snickered manically. The bouquet flew into the air. Geri shoved everyone nearby as the bouquet flew right at us. She pushed a girl charging at it onto the floor, and it landed gracefully into my hands without much effort. "Oh!"

Harper spun around and grinned when she saw me holding it, but the fight had only just begun. One of Daniel's cousins charged me with a roar. Geri blocked her, and they wrestled on the ground.

"Shoot!" I rushed over to the bridal table, tossed the flowers on my chair, and jumped into the fray.

There was screaming and the pulling of hair, but Geri and I fended off the four women attacking us before they realized the bouquet had gone and they were fighting over nothing. The fight ended abruptly, and Geri and I stood with huge grins as we did a knuckle bump.

"I got your back, sistah," Geri said.

"And I got yours, girlfriend."

We laughed and turned to see Mum covering her face and shaking her head. We must have put on quite the show. Dad stood with his arms folded, scowling, and Dusty and James rolled with laughter.

Next was the garter toss. James and Dusty were up in a flash, determined to beat our little show. Daniel went under Harper's skirt to get it with his teeth and we all burst out laughing, except Dad. Geri and I looked over to see him turning bright red, clenching his jaw. I rushed over and grabbed his hand. He looked down at me and I smiled. His expression softened, and he squeezed my hand.

Daniel emerged with the garter in his teeth to cheers and whoops of approval. He stood and flung it out over the heads of the guys. Dusty and James rushed in and started a tussle for the prize.

"Are all my children wild?" Dad muttered. "I thought Dusty was at least moderately sensible."

I chuckled. "Dad, Dusty's the worst one."

"Yes, and when he gets with your boy there, he only gets worse."

"Oh Dad, you love James."

He grunted.

James launched into the air and cleared the fight, waving the garter in his hand. Everyone cheered and his eyes locked on me, swiveling it around on his finger. Dusty slugged him. He spun around and the struggle began again, before James rushed to me and used me as a body shield. "Dusty, you wouldn't hit your sister!"

Dusty rushed over. "You're joking, right? She'd hit me even harder right back."

Dad pulled me out from between them. "Dusty Anderson! I think you've had enough."

His fists lowered as he glanced at Dad. "Yeah, okay." But he gave James a look to tell him it wasn't over.

The party wrapped up after that, and soon we stood watching Harper and Daniel disappear down the road for their honeymoon. James wrapped his arm around my waist and grunted.

"Dusty hit me hard! When did he get so strong? Seriously, last time I checked he was a little kid who barely reached my chest in height."

I looked up at him and saw a bruise forming on his jaw. I touched the swelling, making him wince. "Ouch, James! He did hit you hard."

I swung around to tell off Dusty, but couldn't see him anywhere. "Where is he?"

"Don't worry about it," James said.

"Oh, I will. No one hits my boyfriend like that and gets away with it!"

James smirked. "That's my crazy, competitive girl."

"Shut up."

We rushed back inside, but couldn't find him anywhere. We checked the bathrooms, the gardens, everywhere. Finally, after I checked the bridal room, we headed to the groom's room.

Just before I flung the door open, James grabbed my arm and pressed his finger against his lips. "Do you hear that?"

"Wha . . . ?"

James signaled for me to be quiet again and cracked open the door. We peeked in and saw Dusty on the couch with Geri underneath him, making out like crazy. His hands were all over her, and her hands were all over him.

James carefully pulled the door shut with a grin, and we hurried away as quietly as possible.

"I don't think we'll bother saying goodbye to them." James wrapped his arm around my waist. "But you should finish packing up so we can go home."

I nodded and rushed into the reception hall to grab my handbag. The room was abandoned except for Dad. He walked slowly around the space, running his hand over chairs and tables, and finally paused where Harper had been seated. He leaned over and plucked up a stray flower that had fallen onto the table and tucked it into his lapel. He sighed.

I moved toward him slowly, wondering at his behavior. My heels clicked on the wooden dance floor and he turned, startled. "Oh, Cadence, it's you."

I walked over and adjusted the flower in his lapel. "Are you okay?"

He nodded. "Yes, I'm just wondering where the time went. One minute she was the most beautiful little baby in my arms, and the next she's gone, married, and on her way to having her own family." He caressed my cheek as he gazed into my eyes. "And you probably aren't too far behind. My little girls are women now, and I just don't feel ready to let you go."

I wrapped my arms around him and nuzzled into his chest. "Neither do I, Daddy."

He held me tightly and kissed the top of my head. "But you are ready. That boy loves you, and I know you love him. Don't be afraid to give him your whole self, because he has fought harder for you than I ever thought possible. There's nothing more deserving than that."

I gasped and pulled away from him. He was supposed to say that about Austin. He was supposed to say *Austin* was the only person who could ever deserve me. It only made my internal conflict worse.

He caught my wrist. "Sweetheart, you don't have to be afraid—"

"Stop it, Dad. You don't understand."

Pain flooded into his face. "Then help me."

I turned away and grasped my bag. "I can't. It's . . . complicated."

"Cadence . . ."

"We're leaving. It's getting late. I love you." I hurried out the door.

James stood talking with Mum. He smiled when he saw me, and my conflict melted away. I smiled back.

We quietly drove back to the house, but it felt comfortable as his hand rested over mine. Back home, I took a shower and came out to find him lying in bed. He sat scanning the internet, wearing only a pair of . . .

"Glasses?" I climbed up beside him. "Since when do you wear glasses?"

"It's fairly recent, and just for reading and such."

I shuffled up beside him and, holding my towel, I leaned against him and ran my hand down his chest and abs. I shifted the sheet covering him and his breath caught.

"Do you want something?" His voice was thick.

"What do you think?"

He held his breath as my hand wandered downward. His hand weakly lifted and shut the laptop. I kissed his neck and he shuddered. He set the laptop aside, and when his fingers barely touched my arms, I pulled away.

He grasped his hair with a moment's frustration as I sat up in front of him. But then I removed my towel. His eyes widened as his hand and jaw fell. "I can never get over how beautiful you are naked."

I giggled, and before I knew it, his lips were on me and he had pinned me underneath him. His lips and fingers explored my body, piquing my senses.

"James!"

"Yes?"

"I need you."

"You need me?"

"Yes! James!"

He lifted himself over me to gaze into my eyes. I shuddered as he made love to me. With my senses so heightened, I screamed out in ecstasy. "James! Don't stop!"

My nails dug into his back, and he grunted, pulling back slightly. He gazed into my face as he continued. I shut my eyes, taking it all in.

He whispered, "Marry me, Cadence."

My climax hit me. "Oh, yes, James. I will."

When he finished and rolled off, he didn't let me go. We clung to each other. I gazed into his eyes as I caught my breath, and it dawned on me what I said. I sat up, startled.

He shot up beside me and ran his hand down my back. "What is it?"

"Did I just agree to marry you?"

He smiled lovingly. "Yeah, you did."

I gasped and covered my face. "No, no, no! Not now!"

"Cadence, it's not like we'll get married tomorrow."

"No. James, I can't . . . I'm not . . ."

His arms wrapped around me. "You're freaking out on me again."

"James . . ."

"Cadence, it's okay. We don't have to be engaged. Just the promise that it'll happen eventually is enough for me."

His lips pressed against my shoulder, making goose bumps break out all over me. I relaxed as his hands wandered over my collarbone and he nibbled on my ear. He lowered me onto the bed beside him, and he kissed and caressed me until I fell asleep.

part two:

austin

Chapter Ten

James handled me leaving better than ever. He kissed me without any tears and waved as I disappeared through the gate. On the flight, I couldn't stop thinking about him and the promise I'd made. It pleased me to think that in the not-so-distant future we could be married.

But once I arrived at the flat, my conflicted feelings returned. Lyla gave me the grand tour, and then showed me to my room—the room where I'd first made love to Austin and given him my virginity.

"So, what do you think?" Lyla asked. "Better than student housing, huh?"

I smiled. "I think so, although I'll need to buy a bed for that mattress."

She scoffed. "You'll be fine."

Classes resumed in late February. After collecting all our unit outlines, Lyla and I made our way to the student bookstore. What seemed like the entire student body packed into the store. We scanned the room and made a plan to collect our books, then she grabbed the back of my shirt and we charged inside.

She snatched a basket as we dashed through the door, heading for each bookshelf and scanning for our assigned reading. I grabbed the books, then passed them back to her to dump in the basket. Once we found everything, we joined the mile-long line that circumnavigated the bookstore. We fell silent after the first few minutes as we shuffled slowly toward the checkout.

"This sucks," she groaned.

"I know."

Tara popped in front of us, grinning. "Can I cut in line?"

"No," Lyla and I said in unison.

She ignored us and slipped in front of me. She glanced back past us, and then looked at me. "Okay, you need to entertain me. So, Cadence, I wanna know what's with all your family's weird names."

"Yeah," Lyla muttered. "I mean, my parents saddled me with Lyla because they had some crazy notion that it was pretty, but my siblings have normal names."

I giggled. "It's actually a family tradition."

"A family tradition to have weird names?" Lyla cocked her eyebrow.

I laughed. "No, as in the girls having musical names. Several generations ago, on my mum's side, we had the surname Handel, like Handel's *Messiah* Handel. Someone had the brilliant idea that the daughters should have musical first names to go with it. So it's been this way for a while. If you look at our family tree, I'm, like, the third Cadence, and my mum is the fifth Harmony. Harper is the first Harper though. I think my dad came up with that one."

"Harper?"

"Yeah, like someone who plays the harp."

"Oh! But what about your brother? Dusty's not a common name."

"Well, with Harper and me having unusual names, they didn't want to give him something boring like Steve. So one day, while Mum was pregnant, they heard Slim Dusty's rendition of 'Waltzing Matilda' and decided to call their son Dusty. So, in a way, Dusty's name is musical too."

"Huh. Your family is weird," Tara said, glancing over my shoulder.

I laughed. "My family is awesome."

We shuffled closer to the checkout, the conversation helping to pass the time.

"You haven't told me much about the wedding," Lyla said, giving Tara an odd look as she looked behind us again.

I shrugged. "I've told you the important parts. Harper was stunning, Daniel was awestruck, Mum cried, Dusty and Geri hooked up, and my Dad nearly lost it about twenty times."

"But what did you get up to? Did you get wasted or hook up?"

I shrugged. "Not really, no. As maid of honor, I kept it all under control."

"Come on, you didn't even hook up with one of the groomsmen?"

I scrunched my face, poking out my tongue. "Gross, no. Daniel's brothers and my brother? Urgh."

Tara glanced back again. "Did you at least join in the bouquet toss?"

"Yeah." I chuckled uncomfortably. "Harper told everyone I had to catch it, so it was fixed."

She burst out laughing just as the cashier called us to the checkout. I didn't think my story was that funny. I turned to see if something else caught her attention, but she patted my cheek hard, stopping me. "Naw, you're gonna get *married*."

"Ouch." I rubbed my cheek. "That's just a stupid superstition."

The three of us set down our books and asked for separate receipts.

"So you caught the bouquet, huh?" Lyla nudged me in the ribs.

"Yeah."

"But you're not even seeing anyone. Does she have someone in mind for you or something?"

Tara glanced at me.

"Ah . . ."

The cashier read out our amounts, and we hurried to pay and grab our bags. We turned to leave and came face-to-face with Austin. I gasped—since he'd been right behind us, he must have heard our entire conversation. *No wonder Tara was acting so weird.*

He smiled as our eyes met. My cheeks could have melted metal as I hurried out the door.

"Cadence, wait up!" Lyla called. She caught my arm as I exited the bookstore. "What was that about?"

Tara trotted up beside her, giggling.

"You knew he was there, didn't you?" I pointed at Tara. "He totally heard *everything*."

"So?" She pulled us to a halt, and my cheeks heated up again.

"He thinks I'm a nut case."

She put her hands on her hips. "I need to talk to him."

She marched away before I could stop her. I hurried after her, but when he stepped out of the store, she made a beeline for him. I ducked behind a corner, and Lyla crashed into me.

"You're into someone?" Lyla asked, pushing off from me. "Since when?"

"Hey," I heard Tara say in a cheerful voice.

"Hi, Tara," Austin answered, making butterflies fill my stomach.

"Cadence?" Lyla hissed, her eyes sparkling.

"What do you think of Cadence?" Tara asked.

"Ah, she's . . ." I bit my lip, pressing my forehead against the wall. "Has she said something about me?"

Tara chuckled. "Maybe. Why? Because she thinks *you* think she's crazy."

"Ah . . ." He laughed uncomfortably. "No, I don't think she's crazy."

"Okay, good."

There was a break in the conversation, and then he said, "Hey, wait!"

Tara appeared around the corner a moment before Austin. My eyes jumped up to his as he stared at me. I started backing away, but Tara caught my arm and brought me forward.

"Cadence and Lyla here are flatmates, and we totally hang out all the time. You should join us sometime."

His eyes never broke contact with mine as he answered, "I'd like that."

My cheeks flared again, and he smiled.

"So, you guys are in the same course?" he asked, motioning to me and Lyla. "Tara told me that's how she met you, Cadence."

Lyla looked at me to answer. I stared at my feet, trying to force my blush to fade away.

"*We're* in the same course," Tara replied, pointing to me. "But Lyla is doing something else. What was it again?"

Lyla opened her mouth to answer, but Tara continued. "Cadence is brilliant. I've never had a better partner. Hey, Cadence?"

I nodded and chewed on my lip. "I have to go."

With a sharp yank, I pulled myself free and hurried away.

"And there she goes again," Tara said.

Lyla rushed up beside me. "What was that about?"

"It was that guy," I muttered. "We've been having this thing going on where we exchange looks and he always smiles at me, but he totally heard our entire conversation because he was right behind us in the line."

"Whoa, whoa! Rewind!" She stopped me as we stepped through the doors to the parking lot. "This is news to me."

I kicked at the footpath. "I thought you noticed at the Christmas party we went to with Tara."

"Uh-uh. You guys were ogling then?"

My face burned. "He started making moves on me, and I freaked out. Now he thinks I'm a nut case."

She glanced back. "I definitely didn't get that impression."

I hurried on. "It doesn't matter. I can't do this."

"Why not?"

"It's complicated."

She didn't follow as I headed toward my next class. I thought about James and the promise I'd made to him. What was I *doing?* When I was in Sydney with James, he was the obvious choice, but now, back in Perth with Austin, *he* felt like the obvious choice. I needed to do something, but I had no idea what.

James called as I walked home from the bus stop. I shifted my bag onto my other shoulder and answered.

"You sound out of breath," he said.

"I just want to get home before it gets dark," I replied.

"Where's your friend? Lyla, right? I thought you bought a car together."

"She has a late lecture, so I caught the bus."

I rounded the corner and a rat about the length of my forearm scurried into the storm drain. I screamed.

"What?" James's voice became panicked. "Cadence, are you hurt?"

I rested my hand over my racing heart. "I did *not* know rats got that big."

"A rat?" He burst out laughing. "You scream bloody murder over a *rat?*"

"Shut up. It was huge." I started walking again. "Don't you have something with Melanie tonight? Shouldn't you be there?"

"The guy's a douchebag," James mumbled.

I rolled my eyes. "You're only saying that because he's dating your sister."

"Mum and Dad are totally in love with him." He snorted, apparently disgusted. "He's just Brian all over again."

"I doubt that." I reached into my bag for my keys as I approached the flat.

"Uh-huh. You haven't seen him. He kinda looks similar, and he oozes sleaze."

I unlocked the door. "Obviously, she has a certain taste in appearance, but I think you're being too quick to judge. Brian wasn't sleazy, just kind of . . . confused."

"Don't stand up for him," he said as I pushed the door open. "He was into you—"

A mouse scurried across the living room, and I screamed again.

"What, *what*?"

"A freaking *mouse*! You've got to be kidding me!"

He laughed again.

"Stop laughing. It's one thing to see vermin in the street, but in here, it's something else entirely."

"Just kill it."

"Ew."

"Stop being such a girl."

"I *am* a girl." I darted into the kitchen, shuddering. "What do I do?"

"Get traps or poison."

"That's so disgusting."

"It's better than having them in your place."

I scowled, imagining waking up to a mouse in my bed. "How do I have a mouse and you don't?"

"Canis."

"Good point." I moaned, scanning the kitchen for more little demons. "What do I do?"

"Just go to the store and get some traps."

"But then I'll have to get rid of the bodies. That's so gross."

"Cadence, stop being a baby."

I pouted. "Shut up."

He chuckled. "Just keep me on the phone while you go."

I headed to the end of the street and caught a taxi. On the way, I had him fill me in on the details of his evening meeting Melanie's boyfriend. From what Melanie and Geri had told me, he was a really nice guy, but James made him out to be a huge jerk.

As I headed into the store, he ranted about how he'd apparently given James a suspicious look.

"A suspicious look?" I asked, finding the aisle for insect repellants and pest control. "What do you mean?"

"He was sort of staring at me, like he was daring me to take him on."

"Um, okay." I found the traps on a lower shelf. "How do I know what to use?"

"Huh?"

"Mousetrap."

"Oh, just a spring one will do. They're usually a couple of bucks. A cheap one is fine."

"I can't believe I'm doing this," I said, grabbing a box of three.

"Anyway, he's going to need a serious talking to. There's no way I'm letting another Brian into her life."

"It could be worse. It could be another Robbie." *I probably shouldn't have said that . . .*

"That's it! She's breaking up with him."

"James." I pressed my hand against my hip. "You sound like my dad."

"Maybe your dad is onto something. Guys are scumbags."

I shook my head. "James."

"Melanie obviously has terrible taste, and I need to protect her."

"She doesn't need you protecting her," I said firmly. "I've talked to her and Geri about him, and I really think you're overreacting."

"Overreacting?" He snickered. "She's my sister, and she's proven she can't pick 'em. He's bad news, I just know it."

"You weren't exactly squeaky clean. I took a huge risk on you."

He hesitated. "I can't believe you went there."

I groaned, rubbing my brows. "Just let it go. She's a big girl. She can make her own decisions, good or bad."

"I can't believe you're taking her side."

"James—"

"Well, I'm not standing for it. I can't believe you'd turn against me on this."

"James—"

"I have to go deal with him. Bye."

He hung up.

"Ugh." I typed out a quick text to Melanie to warn her, and then headed to the checkout.

At home, Melanie called me. I answered, putting it on speaker as I struggled to set up the mousetraps.

"Cadence, talk to your stupid boyfriend. He's trying to ruin my life."

"I am *not* ruining your life!" James yelled in the background.

I sighed as the two argued and hung up after a few minutes.

I glued a chocolate chip onto the trap with peanut butter, because according to the Internet, mice like chocolate. *Go figure.* The mouse peered out from behind the fridge as I worked. I glared at it, and it ducked away.

"You're dead," I muttered, setting down the trap near where it had disappeared.

My phone rang again. It was James.

"Tell Mel she's being stupid," he said.

"Absolutely not," I replied, leaning back against the counter.

"I can't *believe* you!" Melanie yelled in the background.

"Cadence, a little support," James said shortly.

"I'm sorry."

"Are you insane?" he yelled. "She'll get pregnant again, or worse!"

"Don't talk to her like that!" Melanie interjected. "No wonder she went all the way over there to get away from you."

I winced as the line fell silent.

"Low blow," James said softly.

"James, I'm sorry," Melanie pleaded.

"I should go. Bye, Cadence."

"James, wait—" But he hung up.

I groaned, heading to my bedroom to change. As I pulled on my pajama pants, I heard a snap. I stumbled to the kitchen, tying my pants along the way. The trap had flipped over as the mouse's leg twitched underneath.

"Eww!" I grabbed a plastic bag. Cringing, I carefully scooped the dead mouse and the trap into the bag and carried it outside to the trash. When I returned back inside, I mopped the floor, then scrubbed my hands and arms to my elbows.

I texted James: MOUSE DEAD. PLEASE DON'T BE MAD AT ME.

He didn't respond.

Chapter Eleven

"We're going out tonight for my birthday," Tara said quietly during a lecture. "No arguments."

I glanced at her while still writing. "I wasn't arguing."

"Good." She looked me over. "And dress cute this time. You looked kinda dumpy at the Christmas party."

I looked up from my notes. "I wasn't trying to look cute."

"Well, you should. You're pretty."

"So are you."

She scoffed. "Maybe, but at least you're not five foot nothing with a freckle face. What guy wants to kneel just to make out?"

I stifled a laugh.

"Yeah, see? You know it's true."

"You'll just have to find a short guy, won't you?"

She grinned. "I love the way you think. We'll leave at eight."

When I arrived home, Lyla had already raided both our wardrobes and set out three different outfits for me. I looked them over. "I don't like miniskirts."

She raised an eyebrow. "Then why do you have them?"

Because James likes them.

"I don't know." I rushed to my wardrobe and pulled out a pair of dark jeans. "I could wear this with my pink halter top."

"As long as you still wear those boots," she said.

"Deal."

We showered, dressed, straightened our hair, and put on our makeup. Lyla hovered the whole time, telling me my jewelry was wrong or that she could see my bra. She snatched the straightener to fix something I missed and even switched out my eyeshadow.

"What's up with you?" I asked.

"I need a hot wingman, don't I?" She grinned and twitched her eyebrows.

I rolled my eyes and put on my lip gloss.

Tara arrived spot on at eight. She looked at my pants and rolled her eyes. "Cadence . . ."

Lyla came up behind me and slapped my butt. "Don't worry, her butt looks incredible in these."

Tara huffed and adjusted her short, tight black dress. "Whatever."

We climbed into Tara's car. She slid into the driver's seat, maneuvering her dress to somehow not flash me as I sat in the front passenger seat.

"By the way," Tara began as we drove away. "I invited a few other friends, like, for example, Austin."

My stomach flipped, and I bit my lip.

"You should talk to him," Lyla said with a grin. "He's pretty cute. Not my type, but I can see him being yours."

I turned to Tara. "Why didn't you warn me?"

She smirked. "Because you'd dress dumpy if you knew."

"Seriously, Cadence." Lyla leaned forward. "Why else would I care what you look like, Barbie doll?"

"I sense a conspiracy," I muttered, staring out the window.

Tara poked my shoulder. "For the last year, you've watched us hook up while you hid in the corner. It's time you loosened up a bit. Austin is awesome, and you're totally into him. Don't deny it."

I couldn't, so I pursed my lips as I continued to stare out the window.

We pulled into the car park, and I thought I would be sick. I sat in the car, unable to move as Tara and Lyla climbed out. I kept thinking about James, then Austin, then James . . .

The door flung open and Tara climbed over me—probably flashing everyone behind her—to unbuckle me. "Get out, Cadence!"

She grabbed my arm and gave it a sharp tug. Lyla grabbed my other arm to help her. They dragged me over to the short line waiting to get past the bouncer and wrapped their arms through mine to prevent me from running. It only took a few minutes before we were allowed inside. We walked through a dark hallway, and I started to hyperventilate.

"Geez, Cadence!" Tara hissed. "Anyone would think you went to a Catholic girls' school or something!"

We stepped through the door, my mind flipping between James and Austin. James, Austin, James, Austin . . .

And then there he was, sitting by the bar with his friends. Three girls hovered nearby and chatted to him occasionally, making his wide, easy smile spread across his face. He looked incredible. He wore a dark blue dress shirt that hung open to reveal the white Bond chesty underneath. The tight top enhanced his muscular form, and I couldn't help lingering over his pecs and abs. He wore dark jeans and black shoes, giving him a casual appearance, yet incredibly sexy all at once. He rubbed the scruff on his face, which seemed to serve as a symbol of his masculinity.

Tara elbowed me and giggled. "Stop staring."

My cheeks warmed. "Sorry."

"Really, Cadence, you should let him in. You're *so* into him, and he's only holding off because he thinks you want him to."

I glanced back over and saw the three girls surrounding him as he leaned back onto his elbows. Images of him stepping out of the shower when we were married flashed into my mind. An inferno blazed in my cheeks and I shook off the thoughts. "It doesn't look like he's holding off for me."

"Cadence . . ."

I hurried away onto the dance floor with Lyla in tow. We danced together, but I soon noticed that Tara hadn't joined us. Scanning the room, I saw her talking to Austin. He smiled. I turned my attention back to Lyla.

Lyla noticed. "That's him, right?"

"Ah . . ." Then it dawned on me. This was the night Austin and I got together in the first timeline. If I wanted to know what would happen between us, this was the moment. "Yeah."

"You should talk to him."

I winced. "Oh no, I don't think I could."

"Cadence, you look smoking hot tonight. It's the perfect time to get his attention."

"I, ah . . ." I ran my fingers through my hair hanging loose over my shoulder. "I want to, but he's surrounded by girls. I can't compete with that."

She sighed. "Okay, Cadence."

A short while later, she excused herself to go to the bathroom. Then, she did exactly what she'd done in the first timeline: she made her way over to Austin. She stood beside Tara and wrapped her arm through hers as they both talked to him. After a brief exchange, he straightened, his attention piqued. He glanced over to me, and I let our eyes connect.

He smiled, and I smiled back. He moved toward me, so I spun to dance as sexy as I could. I had no idea what I was doing. I was still with James, but the memories of my marriage with Austin and all the wonderful, happy times we shared overwhelmed me.

Sensing his presence behind me, I raised my arms up and ran my hands through my hair and over my curves. As my hands reached my hips, his hands rested over them. I paused, then slipped my hands out from under his and turned to face him.

His hands rested on my waist as our eyes met. He smiled. My cheeks rushed with heat, but I didn't look away.

"So . . . ah . . ." His right hand came up and he offered it to me. "I was wondering if you'd be okay if I introduced myself to you. Austin Jones."

I slid my hand into his and electricity shot through my arm. Squeezing his hand, I responded, "Cadence Anderson."

His smile widened as our hands broke apart. The hand he kept on my waist crept around to the small of my back, and he shifted closer to me.

I rested mine on his chest as I admired his masculine beauty.

"Do you wanna dance?"

My gaze pulled away from his chest to meet his eyes. "I would like that."

With his arm still around me, he guided me away from my friends, losing us in the crowd. Once we were alone, he pulled me against him. My hands were far more troublesome than his as they explored his chest, shoulders, and arms. But he didn't protest. He kept his eyes firmly locked with mine as I explored his new, yet familiar, body.

"So, Cadence Anderson," he said as I ran my hand down his bicep. "I know you do sports science, and I know everyone in your family has musical names."

"That's right." *His arm is so beautiful.*

"And you're from Sydney, right?"

"The best city on earth." I lifted my gaze to meet his and grinned.

"She says to a born and raised Perth boy."

I giggled, which made his smile grow.

"What brought you out here?"

I shrugged. "I needed a change of pace."

"You needed a quieter city, huh?"

"Pretty much."

"How are you finding it so far?"

My hand returned to his chest. "The scenery is very nice."

He laughed. "This is a very different girl to the blushing blur I've been watching over the last few months."

His fingers found the bare skin on my back. I gasped and gazed into his eyes.

"Well, Cadence, tell me more about yourself."

"You won't tell me about you?"

"I know all about me. I'm interested in knowing about you." His fingers ran up my spine, making me shudder.

"You're driving me wild," I said, barely loud enough to hear over the music.

He leaned closer. "That's my goal," he said in my ear. "I don't want you to run away again."

He kissed my ear. He knew exactly what he was doing. He'd always known how to get under my skin. My arms automatically wrapped around his neck as his fingers ran up my back and through my hair.

Austin was so alive again. My wish came true.

We danced pressed together as he whispered questions in my ear. I responded by whispering back into his. His body rubbed against mine, making my hormones surge and pulse through me. When his fingers found sensitive places on my back, I gasped, and he'd pause and run his fingers over them again.

I completely forgot about James as I became intoxicated and completely engrossed in Austin. He was exactly how I remembered him: sweet, charming, gentle, and patient.

It started to get late, and since I had work in the morning, I forced myself away from him. "I have to go."

He ran his fingers through my hair as he examined my face. "Let me take you."

I bit my lip as I smiled, knowing what would happen. "Okay."

He walked me to his car, my hand in his, and he opened the door for me. We had an easy conversation on the ride home as he finally let me ask about him. I knew everything already, but I loved hearing it all over again as his eyes gleamed with excitement from my interest.

We pulled up outside my flat, and he dashed around to get the door. He offered me his hand to help me out and shut the door behind me. I paused and leaned against the car, my hands resting on his waist.

"Well, Austin Jones, it was very nice meeting you."

"Finally."

I giggled. "I know. I've been holding back. You're just so . . ."

I ran my hand over his chest again.

He wrapped his hands around the back of my neck and kissed me. A rush surged through me from his lips. I wrapped my arms around his waist, pulling him up against me. After so long, I could kiss my husband again—even if he wasn't technically my husband—but I could barely believe it.

His hand fell from my face and found the handle for the back door. He opened it and lowered me onto the backseat, closing it behind us.

It played out just how I remembered. He climbed on top of me and kissed me firmly, openmouthed, our tongues entwined. His facial hair tickled my nose, and his hands tangled in my hair.

In return, I slipped my hands under his shirt to feel the muscles in his torso flex and twitch under my touch. My head spun with excitement. I broke away from the kiss as his lips wandered down my neck. I stroked the line of hair down the center of his chest. "Your body is incredible."

His breath tickled my neck as he chuckled. "I think yours is pretty good too."

I moaned, wanting more, but knowing it was too early, and then a flash of James's face crossed my mind.

Crap! What am I doing?

I pushed his hands off and encouraged him to sit up. "I need to go."

"Just a little longer." He pressed his lips against mine again and stroked my neck.

I kissed him back, having missed him more than anything. He was alive—so very alive—and he was mine again. But I had to pull away. I was still with James. I'd made him a promise. As much as my heart pulled me to

Austin, the part of me that loved James told me I needed to stop.

As our lips broke apart, he followed me, not wanting it to end.

"Austin?"

"Yes?"

"Goodnight." I pushed open the door behind me and climbed out of the car.

He shot out and cut off my path to the flat as I dug for my keys. Our eyes met. He clasped my face and kissed me again. It felt electric, exciting, and so perfect. He pulled back first, but only an inch so I could still feel his breath on my lips. "Goodnight, sweet Cadence."

I smiled at his pet name for me. "Bye."

I moved away from him as his hand slid down my shoulder and arm, and I glanced back as our fingertips broke apart.

Inside, I flopped onto my bed, my heart all atwitter. My Austin was back, and I was lost in him. I stripped down to my underwear as I ran through the night in my head. Then, I removed my scrapbook from the drawer.

The night had played out almost exactly the same, except I hadn't started it acting like a bashful idiot last time. Our eyes met, he approached—apparently because Tara was pushing him to notice me—and when he'd held me close, both of us had fallen fast. I'd even noted that he'd opened all the doors for me like a true gentleman. He'd done it again that night.

I sighed, holding the scrapbook to my chest. I couldn't wait to fall in love with him all over again.

Chapter Twelve

A knock on the flat's door woke me. I groaned and rolled over to see the time: 6:30 a.m. I refused to get up.

The knocking came again. I heard Lyla groan and rush to the door. She stumbled back to my room. "It's for you. Please make it stop."

I grunted and reached for my bathrobe. As I plodded to the door, the knocking came again. "I'm coming!"

I threw the door open and stared.

Austin stood in front of me, smiling sheepishly. "I hope I'm not being presumptuous, but I just couldn't stop thinking about you."

My jaw dropped. It was exactly how I remembered. I should have read the next page of my scrapbook to be prepared. "Really?"

"Yeah. You're just so beautiful. I really wanna get to know you better."

I bit my lip and pulled my robe tighter around me. His gaze fell onto my lips as I released the bite. I smiled at his obvious attraction. "Do you wanna take me out?"

His gaze met mine. "That's why I'm here."

I stepped back to let him in. "Watch some TV or something while I get ready."

He entered and sat. I hurried into Lyla's room and jumped onto her bed. "Lyla!"

She groaned. "What?"

"I'm calling in sick today."

"I don't care."

I shook her shoulder. "Lyla! Austin wants to take me out!"

"Tell me again in about two hours, when I actually have to be up and will care."

But a slight smile curled her lips, as one of her eyes flickered open.

I squeezed her shoulder, then dashed across into my room. I knew exactly where he planned to take me, so I picked out comfortable jeans, a t-shirt, a light jacket, and slipped on my thongs. I rushed into the bathroom, washed my face, and rolled on deodorant. After some quick primping, I tied my hair back in a high ponytail, took a deep breath, and stepped out.

His gaze took me in slowly as I walked into the living room. He shot to his feet and rubbed the back of his neck as I approached. "Wow."

I shrugged, averting my gaze. "It's nothing special."

He came around and took my hand. "It's very special."

I beamed as he wove his fingers into mine.

He drove us to a port in Fremantle, and led me through several rows of boats.

"My parents are letting me take this today," he said. "This is very rare. My stepdad is crazy about his boat, so we've got to be very careful with it."

"A boat?" I grinned excitedly.

He paused and we looked down at a motor boat. "Yeah. It's his baby. I think it cost more than his car."

He climbed in and set down the bag and cooler he'd brought from the car, then offered me his hand to help me in.

He gestured for me to sit as he started the engine and backed out. Once in clear water, he picked up speed and headed toward Rottnest Island. I stood beside him and he smiled. "Wanna steer?"

"Ah . . ." I shook my head. "I'll probably crash."

He laughed. "Into what? Come on, I'll be right here."

He took one hand off the steering wheel and pulled me in front of him. His arms wrapped around me and rested over mine on the wheel. Chills shot up my arms as every inch of me tingled with his warmth.

My Austin.

"See?" he said into my ear. "No worries."

I smiled as he helped me steer. "So, you have a boat license?"

"Oh yeah. The day I could get it, I did. I'm studying marine science, so out here, this is my thing."

"I can see that."

His arm released from around me. "We'll be coming up on the island soon, and I don't want the water rats pulling me over."

I stepped out from his arms and stood beside him again.

We made our way around the south of the island to a small, abandoned bay. He cut the engine, and then lowered the anchor. He sat beside me and pulled out a bottle of water for each of us. He nodded toward the beach. "It's beautiful, isn't it?"

"I love how secluded it feels."

He grinned and leaned back. "Right here is where I saw my first whale. I was ten, and my stepdad brought Mum and me out here for some fishing and swimming. Then, out of nowhere, these humpback whales came right up to the boat. I swear I could have reached out and touched one. There were two of them, and a young one.

It was probably one of the most amazing experiences of my life."

I'd always loved that story. His mother would tell me it frightened her that the whales came so close, because they could tip the boat, but Austin had been spellbound. He wanted to jump right in the water with them, but his stepfather warned him against it.

"That's amazing," I said softly. "Have you been that close to any since?"

He shook his head. "Unfortunately not. I've seen them around, but never that close." He shuffled closer and ran his fingers down my arm. "I've seen all kinds of interesting things around this island, sea turtles, ship-wrecks, the coral . . ." His hand moved up and rested on the back of my neck. "This place inspired me to study marine science. It's so beautiful. I'd do anything to keep it this way. I think I've snorkeled and dived every inch of the surrounding beaches and bays, and it still looks new and wonderful.

"I've been saving for a while to go to the Great Barrier Reef. I'd love to dive there and see all the different species of coral and fish." He pulled his hand back. "But you probably didn't need to know that."

I caught his hand. "I think that's a wonderful goal. Maybe if you teach me how to dive, we could do it together."

His face lit up. "I think I could do that." He leaned forward for a kiss and paused an inch away from me. "When would you like me to start?"

"Whenever you want," I replied breathlessly. I touched his cheek and closed the gap between us.

Making out with him felt so right. He'd always been an amazing kisser, so he swept me off my feet again. I fell head over heels, madly, crazy in love with him.

When he pulled away, I grabbed onto his shirt so he would stay close to me. He smiled and clasped my face. "I think this might mean we're a couple now."

I nodded as I bit my lip and gazed into his eyes, completely lost in him.

"Wow," he said breathlessly. "Your eyes are the same color as the ocean. They're so beautiful."

I dropped my gaze, grinning like a love-struck fool. He ran his fingers through my hair, then stood to turn the engine back on. He took us to an isolated beach and pulled up just outside the break.

"Let's go for a swim."

"But it's not warm enough," I said, shuddering at the thought. I'd forgotten that he wanted to swim. *I really should have checked the scrapbook.* "And I don't have a swimsuit."

His eyes twinkled, reminding me where this was going. "No one's around. Just swim in your underwear."

He whipped off his shirt and jeans, standing in front of me in his black boxers. It took all my effort to keep from staring at his junk.

He peeled my jacket back, then fingered at the button on my jeans. "Come on, Cadence."

I bit my lip, nervous because so much time had passed since he'd seen my body. Since his was so amazing, I felt self-conscious of my own. But he held my gaze, a flirtatious smile spreading across his face. I impulsively pulled off my shirt as he removed my jeans.

He stood back up slowly, taking in my body with his eyes and hands. "Wow, you're gorgeous."

My cheeks burned, and I wrapped my arms around myself. "No, I have terrible legs, and my boobs are too big."

"I think they're perfect." He rested his hands on my bare waist. Their warmth, in stark contrast to the autumn sea breeze, sent shivers all over me.

"Let's swim." He jumped right in.

I screeched as the cold water splashed me, and rushed to grab my clothes.

"Cadence!" He laughed as he broke the surface.

"You're insane! It's way too cold!"

"What, are Sydney girls a bunch of wimps? Can't take a bit of cold?"

My blood boiled. *Stupid competitive streak.* I swung on him. "*What* did you say to me?"

"You're a wimpy city girl!"

"Oh! Wimpy, huh?" I leaned over the edge of the boat. "Well, Mr. Jones, you're going to regret you said that."

He scoffed. "What are you going to do?"

"Wouldn't you like to know?"

"Yeah, I would."

I growled and climbed up on the side of the boat, but the sight of the cold water made me hesitate.

"You don't have the guts."

I glared at him. "You're going down."

I jumped in. The cold water jarred my senses. I broke the surface and gasped for air.

He laughed at me. "Wow, you actually got in! I'm impressed."

My teeth chattered. "Shut up."

He swam toward me, but when he touched me, I splashed him in the face. "You don't get to touch me."

"Why not?" He chuckled as he moved in again.

I grabbed his arm, glaring at him as I shivered. "Because I said so."

He smirked and scooped me up into his arms. We struggled as he held tightly to me, and I tried to push him off, but he dunked us both under the water. When we resurfaced, I gasped for air, clinging to his neck. "It's . . . so . . . cold . . ."

His arms tightened around me. "We better warm you up then."

He carried me to the beach and laid me on the sand. He sat beside me and looked me over as his hand wandered over my belly. "Cadence?"

"Yes?" His eyes had me mesmerized as they looked into mine.

"Are you enjoying yourself?"

I giggled. "Yes."

My hand lifted and ran over his abdominals. They flexed under my touch. He let out a long breath, then leaned down over me. He brushed my wet hair back from my face. "I've never seen anyone as beautiful as you."

My heart skipped a beat and I bit my lip. "Austin . . ."

But before I could say more, he leaned down and kissed me. I clasped onto his face, kissing him back with as much passion as I could muster. Being able to fall in love with him all over again felt like a miracle.

His hand on my face drifted down my neck, over my body, and found its way between my legs. He rubbed me over my underwear. James flashed into my mind, and the night of Harper's wedding when he'd made such passionate love to me. My legs clamped shut, and I pushed Austin off. "No, no, it's too soon."

"Okay." He touched my cheek and smiled. "I'm happy to go at your pace."

"Thank you," I said with a sigh.

He shifted over and helped me sit up. He pressed his forehead against mine and closed his eyes. "I want to see where this can go."

I caressed his face and pulled back to look into his eyes. "So do I."

His hand wrapped around the back of my neck and he kissed me again. We alternated between making out and whispered conversation on the beach for more than an hour.

He leaned back on his elbows and sighed. "We should get back. My dad needs his boat back."

"I thought it was your stepdad's boat," I said, knowing what he meant, but wanting him to know he could tell me anything.

"Yeah, it is, but I usually call my stepdad 'Dad.' My real dad disappeared when I was five, and we haven't heard from him since." He looked up at me, sitting beside him, waiting for him to continue. "But you don't need to know that. I'm sorry."

"No." I leaned over and stroked his chest up to his neck. He gazed into my eyes as I smiled reassuringly. "I want to know. You can tell me anything. Come on, I told you about my best friend hooking up with my seventeen-year-old brother, and my dad's insane rants when boys even glance at me. What could be more embarrassing than that?"

He chuckled. "Okay, yeah, I think if I was around when you were fourteen, your dad would have freaked me out."

"See?" I laughed. "So tell me anything you want."

He rested his hand over mine on his neck. "Well, my dad just disappeared, which hasn't ever really bothered me because I was so young, but my brother Malcolm was fifteen, and he's never been able to cope with it well. When Mum married George two years later, he couldn't accept it and ran away. He's tried to find our father on and off over the years, but hasn't been successful. I'm convinced he doesn't want to be found."

He paused and his gaze fell. "George is my dad now, and I think my brother resents me for it. But George did everything for me, and raised me like his own son, so he *is* my dad, you know?"

"I know what you mean. Just because he's not your father by blood doesn't mean he's not your father in here." I dropped my hand over his heart.

With his hand still over mine, he stared at them on his chest and a smile crept onto his face. "I can't believe how easy it is to talk to you. It's like I've known you forever."

"I feel the same."

He turned onto his side to face me. "I'm so glad you're more than just a pretty face. I've dated some girls, and that's all they were, but you . . ." He trailed off, stroking my cheek, then sighed. "We need to get back."

"Okay."

He took my hand and helped me to my feet. He held onto my hand as we swam back out to the boat, then climbed the ladder on the side for diving. He hurried to wrap a towel around me, then pulled up the anchor, slipped on his jeans, and started the engine. About halfway back, he told me to get dressed.

At the boatyard, a tall, ginger man waited for us. He had his arms folded and pointed at his watch as we pulled in. "Austin, I told you to be here half an hour ago."

"I know. Sorry," Austin said, tossing him a rope.

The man's gaze fell on me. "Is this the elusive Cadence?"

Austin grinned and climbed off the boat. "It sure is."

Austin gave me his hand and pulled me up beside him.

I knew exactly who the man was. George had always liked me, and supported Austin and I every step of the way, but I had to pretend that I'd never met him before as he offered me his hand. "It's nice to meet you, Cadence. I'm Austin's dad, but you can call me George."

"Hello," I answered and shook his hand.

"I hope he didn't get you into too much trouble out there," he said teasingly. "Austin plays around at that island like it's his personal backyard."

Austin laughed. "I learned from the best."

George grinned at him. "Touché. Well, go find your mother. She went to buy lunch a few minutes ago."

"Oh, lunch." Austin squeezed my hand. "Do you think she'll buy us something?"

George pretended to consider his question. "I don't know. Maybe if you did something for her, like introducing your new friend here, she might consider it."

"Done." Austin gave my hand a sharp tug as we hurried toward the town. There were several restaurants nearby, but he headed straight for a fish and chips place. His mother sat inside, looking at a newspaper while she waited for her order.

A small, plump woman, Austin resembled her a great deal, with the same dark hair and eyes. I'd always believed she felt grateful her younger son looked more like her than his father, because I'd always seen a hint of pain in her eyes when she looked at Malcolm, who resembled their father.

As we rushed in, her gaze lifted, and she smiled as Austin shuffled in beside her. "Mum, I'm hungry."

"You have money, Austin, buy it yourself." But then she saw me. She peeked around him and smiled. "Who is this?"

"I'll only introduce you if you buy me food."

She slapped his shoulder, but said, "Fine."

Austin wrapped his arm around my waist. "This is Cadence. Cadence, my mum, Linda."

Her whole face glowed as she squeezed my hand. "It's nice to meet you. You're just as pretty as he said."

His arm tightened around my waist as my cheeks warmed. "I . . . well . . . ah . . . thank you."

She chuckled. "All right. What do you want to eat?"

We had lunch with his parents, and I found them as delightful as I remembered. I wondered for the first time what they had felt and done when they heard Austin and Melody died. I'd never seen them in the hospital, but they wouldn't have been too far. They almost certainly would have visited me while I was unconscious.

I shook off the memories and thoughts as Linda wrapped her arm through mine. "We must go. It's been wonderful meeting you, Cadence. Don't be a stranger."

"Thank you for lunch," I said.

"You're welcome." She grabbed Austin's elbow and kissed his cheek. "We'll see you later."

We waved to them as we parted ways to head back to Austin's car. Everything felt right as Austin rested his arm over my shoulders. He was alive, strong, and as vibrant as ever, and his family had accepted me as easily as they had the first time.

"Cadence!" Tara rushed at me. She smirked as she glanced at Austin. "I saw you guys leave together last night. Things are going pretty well, eh?"

"Ahh . . ." I stared at my feet. I didn't remember her approaching us in the first timeline.

Austin squeezed my shoulder. "Yeah, I couldn't stop thinking about her, so I picked her up this morning."

Tara let out a tiny squeal as she danced on the spot. "Just so you know, Cadence is *so* much better than Lena."

Austin rolled his eyes, smiling. "I haven't see Lena since we graduated. But don't worry, I know I've upgraded."

Tara winked at me. "Lena's his ex, but nothing to worry about."

"I'm not worried." I glanced up at Austin and found him smiling at me. *Definitely not worried.* He never made me feel like any of his exes would get in our way. Even now, starting fresh again, I felt safe with him.

"Oh my gosh!" She pinched our cheeks. "You're so stinking cute together."

Austin scrunched his nose, pushing her hand away.

"Austin." His friend Aaron stepped out from the post office. "I thought you were busy today." He glanced at me. "Oh, you are."

Tara shoved him. "Let's leave these two alone."

Aaron held his ground, ignoring Tara. "It's nice to meet you, Cadence. I'm Aaron, by the way."

"Hi." My memories of Aaron burst to the surface. An image of him raising a toast as best man at our wedding flashed through my mind, then him at our house for "guys' night," and him coming over drunk and needing consoling when his fiancée dumped him. I chewed on my tongue as I fought to control the shock of the onslaught. He had to have come to the hospital too, along with Tara and Lyla. Why had I never considered that?

"I'm not going on a date with you," Tara said, as I came back to the present.

"You know Cadence, and since she's dating my man here, I need to have a chance to get to know her too," Aaron responded.

"*Your* man?" Tara rolled her eyes. "Your bromance is getting a touch creepy. Keep your hands off Austin. He's Cadence's now."

"Our bromance is awesome."

"We should go," Austin said, coaxing me forward.

"Wait, wait, wait." Tara caught my wrist. "Okay, we should go on a date, but not a double." She shot a glare at Aaron. "A triple. I get my own date. He goes with Lyla."

Aaron raised an eyebrow, grinning. "Who's Lyla?"

Aaron and Lyla never really got along. I opened my mouth to stop the arrangement, but Tara beat me to the punch. "Our friend. She's way hot. You probably don't deserve to go on a date with her, but oh well."

"That was harsh," Austin said.

Aaron threw his hands in the air. "Why did I agree to hang out with you today?"

"Because your *boyfriend* ditched you." Tara flicked her hair over her shoulder, then looked at me. "We'll make the arrangements. You guys go have fun."

Austin and I waved goodbye. He hurried me away. "Let's get out of here before they really get stuck into each other."

I giggled. Although Aaron and Tara were good friends, they were well-practiced at pushing each other's buttons.

Back at the flat, Lyla had left for work, so Austin and I hung out and watched a movie together. We made out again, then decided to make dinner. When Lyla arrived home, she entered the kitchen with a grin. "Wow, how many hours has it been since you arrived here, and you're still together?"

Austin looked at his watch. "Twelve."

He touched my waist and kissed my cheek.

Lyla chuckled. "Well, Cadence, thank goodness you finally let him in, huh?"

I laughed. "I know."

I looked up at him, and he smiled.

Lyla cleared her throat. "Let me know when you're done."

By the time Austin left, it was almost nine, and he gave me a long kiss goodbye.

I retreated to my room, pulled out my scrapbook, and opened it to find entries from Austin's journal appearing. A photo showed him in his car with his eyes shut and a smile across his face. His entry simply said: *I just had the best day of my life with the most amazing girl I've ever met.*

My heart fluttered as I ran my fingers over his face on the picture. "I love you so much, Austin. I'm not going to let you die again."

I closed the scrapbook and headed into the bathroom to shower off the saltwater and sweat from the day. When I returned to my room, my phone was ringing. I shut the door, hoping for Austin, and rushed to answer it without looking at the caller ID.

"Hello?"

"Hello, beautiful."

Chapter Thirteen

Struggling to compose myself, I responded. "James! What a surprise."

"Not really. I call you every Saturday, except you've been exceptionally hard to get a hold of today. Where have you been?"

Guilt consumed me. *Out with someone else. I'm a dirty, filthy cheater!*

"I went out to Rottnest Island and left my phone here."

"That sounds like fun."

I slapped my forehead. "Yeah, it was."

"What did you do?"

Made out with another guy mostly . . .

"Went boating, swam briefly but it was too cold, had some lunch. You know, just generally had fun in this new city."

"It's good to know I'll have a guide when I arrive at the end of the year."

Shoot! I'd forgotten about that. I'd forgotten about James, my feelings for him, everything. *What am I doing?* Despite our recent fighting, he was still amazing. But so was Austin.

"Yeah, I don't know if I'd say that."

He laughed. "You'll be practically local after almost two years there."

"Yeah, I guess."

He paused. "Hey, are you okay?"

Curse him knowing me so well! "I'm a bit worn out."

"I can tell. You sound pretty out of it."

"That obvious, huh?"

"Cadence, I know you better than anyone."

I officially won the prize for the worst person in the world. A sob wrenched from me, and I smothered my face into the pillow.

"Cadence, babe, what's wrong?"

"I'm a terrible person," I said in a hushed voice.

"No, you're not! Why would you say that?"

"Because . . ." Could I tell him? Could I break up with him over the phone? No, he deserved better than that, and truthfully, now that I was talking to him, I couldn't bring myself to let him go. I still loved him so much. I was so selfish. "Because I came out here away from you, and I miss you."

He sighed. "Oh, Cadence. I miss you, too. But please don't beat yourself up over it. I understand, I do, and I can see how much it has helped you grow. When I saw you at the wedding, you were so confident, and it was wonderful to see you so happy and coming into your own. I'm really sorry I've been so touchy about it all, but I'm glad you made this choice, because it's only made you more beautiful and wonderful."

Tears streamed down my face as I fought to suppress my sobs. "I love you, James."

"Aw, Cadence. I love you, too. It's getting late here, so I should go. I just wanted to catch you before I went to bed."

"I'm sorry I didn't answer sooner."

"You're fine. Just cheer up, okay? I love you."

"I love you, too."

I hung up and buried my face into my pillow to smother my sobs. *What am I doing?* I couldn't continue my relationship with James, but when he spoke to me, my feelings for him returned and I couldn't let him go.

I curled up under my blankets and cried myself to sleep. I had frightening dreams of James and Austin ripping each other apart with their hands and teeth, fighting for my heart resting on a silver platter.

My phone vibrated. Tara glanced at me, but continued listening to the lecture. Cautiously, I slipped the phone out and read the text under my table.

ARE YOU ON CAMPUS RIGHT NOW?

A stupid grin swept across my face as I replied. I'M IN A LECTURE.

It only took a moment to get my response. MEET ME AFTERWARD AT PRESCOTT COURT.

Butterflies filled my stomach as I agreed.

Tara glanced over my shoulder and nudged me. "Austin?"

My stupid grin grew wider. "Yeah."

She squeezed my arm excitedly. "I knew it! You guys are the cutest couple."

Guilt swelled as Geri came to mind, saying the same thing about me and James. I needed to end it with James—what I was doing wasn't fair to him. But ending it would be so hard. I still loved him, and after more than four years together, I needed to do it in person, especially after my promise to marry him. I wanted to be with Austin. I wanted to save him and have Melody again. Over the last week, we'd seen each other every day, and when I was with him, he brought me to life like he always had. His presence encompassed my consciousness.

"Are we still on for Saturday?" Tara asked.

I twisted my lips. "Are you sure about this? Lyla can be . . . picky."

"We're doing this for you guys, so she'll get over it."

"If you say so." *It so won't happen.*

After the lecture, I made my way to Prescott Court—a grassy area on campus with plenty of trees for shade— where Austin sat on a blanket in the grass. He leaned over a textbook and notepad, taking notes with his glasses resting low on his nose. Clutching tightly to my folder, I slowly approached as my excitement pulsed through me. It never ceased to amaze me that someone as incredible as him would fall in love with me.

His head turned, and he jumped to his feet. "Cadence."

His arm wrapped around my waist as he kissed my cheek.

My heart fluttered. "Hey, Austin."

"I bought you lunch." He took my hand to help me sit, then knelt down, handing me a sandwich and a bottle of juice. "I hope it's okay."

I took them and gave him a kiss on the lips. "It's just what I wanted."

He pulled out a second sandwich for himself and leaned back to eat it. "I have the rest of the day off, so depending on your schedule, I'd really like to spend it with you."

"I have a tutorial in an hour," I responded. "And that goes for an hour, but after that, I'm free."

He sat up and opened his notepad to the back and wrote something down. "And how long was your lecture this morning?"

"Two hours." I leaned forward to see what he wrote. "Are you taking notes on my class schedule?"

"I sure am."

"Why?"

"So I know when you're free."

I laughed and opened my folder. "Here, take this." I handed him my schedule. "I know it now, and I have a copy back at the flat anyway."

"How about your work hours?"

"I get my roster every two weeks. It's always changing."

He slipped my schedule into his notepad. "Let me know when you're working whenever you find out."

I giggled. "I guess I could handle that."

"Good." He leaned forward and kissed me. "So, Tara tells me you're a bit of a brainiac."

"She does, does she?" I chuckled.

"Mmm. She says you seem to know most of what's being taught *while* it's being taught."

"I read the notes before class. It's all online."

"Wow, nerd. Who does that?"

I shoved his shoulder, making him laugh.

"So, Saturday . . ." He raised an eyebrow.

I groaned. "Lyla's so not a blind date person."

"Aaron's cool." He took a huge bite of his sandwich. "That's not the problem."

He softly kissed my cheek. "It'll be fine."

Saturday. Lyla scowled when I let Austin and Aaron into the flat. From first sight she didn't like him, but I smiled brightly, motioning to him. "Lyla, meet Austin's best friend, Aaron."

She folded her arms as he stretched out his hand to her. "Just so you know, I'm not sleeping with you."

"Ah . . ." He glanced at Austin. "I'm not expecting you to."

"Good. Let's go." She marched out the door.

Austin smirked as we hurried after her.

In the car, Aaron tried to talk to Lyla as he drove, but she blew him off. I felt bad for him. Just like the first time-line, he tried so hard, but Lyla had no interest. I leaned closer to Austin to whisper in his ear. "Poor Aaron."

"Yeah, Lyla's not usually this . . . uptight." He turned his head to look into my eyes, but instead gave me a kiss.

"I can see you in the mirror," Aaron said.

I giggled, pulling away, but Austin wrapped his hand around the back of my neck and kissed me again.

"I just cleaned in here," Aaron said sharply. "I don't need the seats soiled."

"Austin." I pushed him back, grinning.

"You're just so irresistible." He tried to pull me in again.

"Get a room," Lyla grumbled.

I pushed Austin back, biting my lip. He'd always been very eager, especially early on. Our first year of marriage—even when we argued—it was near impossible to keep his hands off me. Some things never change.

We parked, and I dropped back a few paces to talk to Lyla. Austin winked to me as he walked ahead with Aaron. I slipped my arm through Lyla's. "Please be nice. He's Austin's best friend."

She scowled. "He's not even hot."

"He's not unattractive," I said, staring at the back of his blond head. "And he is nice. I'm not asking you to date him, just be friendly."

"You know *friendly* isn't part of my vocabulary."

"Lyla." I looked up at her with big eyes. "For me? Please?"

She groaned. "You're killing me, Cadence. Fine. I'll try."

As we approached the door, Tara burst out, shoved between Austin and Aaron, and threw herself at Lyla and me.

"Tara!" Aaron and Austin turned away as Tara's skirt flew up.

"I can't wait for you guys to meet Gareth. He's seriously the hottest guy ever."

Gareth? Which "hottest guy ever" was he? There were just so many, I couldn't recall him.

"At least your date is hot," Lyla mumbled.

"Aaron's hot," I said.

"To you, maybe."

Tara slapped her shoulder. "Don't be rude to Aaron. I've known those two for a long time, and they don't need Miss Surly Sourpuss. Now, slap on a smile and at least pretend you're having fun."

I glanced between them. They reminded me an awful lot of Geri and Melanie. It seemed I gravitated to certain kinds of people.

"Are we good?" Austin's arms slid around my waist.

After a brief struggle, Lyla forced a smile. "Dandy."

He raised an eyebrow. "Okay. Let's go, I'm hungry."

Gareth sat by a table, waiting for us. He greeted Tara with a kiss, pulling her seat out for her. To my surprise, the other two guys did the same thing. I grinned at Austin, remembering how much I loved his chivalry.

"It's not sexist at all," I remember him telling me once when I complained about it. "I'm showing you that I respect you."

Seeing the guys being respectful to my best friends made me warm inside. Even poor Aaron, facing a cold shoulder, still did his best.

"So, Cadence," Aaron said, giving up on talking to Lyla. "I want to know all about you."

"There's not really much to say," I answered, shrugging. "I grew up in Sydney, and now I'm here studying sports science."

Tara rolled her eyes. "You're so boring. I guess *I'll* have to tell you all about her. We'll start with the abseiling incident."

Lyla snorted.

"No, he doesn't need to know that." I glared at her.

"What abseiling incident?" Austin asked, stroking my back.

"You haven't told him either?" Tara grinned. "Well—"

"It's really not worth mentioning." My cheeks burned as I sipped at my water.

"Cadence, as you may or may not know, has a disgusting competitive streak."

Austin nodded. "I knew that."

I elbowed him in the ribs.

"So, while we were learning our knots, she noticed one of the guys doing it faster than all of us. She made it her personal vendetta to bring him down."

"I wouldn't call it a vendetta," I grumbled.

"The problem was, they ended up being partnered for our camping trip. So not only did they have to carry canoes, light fires, do first aid and so forth together, they had to abseil together."

I groaned, covering my face.

"The tension was insane." Tara chuckled deviously. "When their turn came to abseil with their group, the competition reached its peak. They raced to tie their own knots, and he refused to let her check his. The problem was, he'd been so concerned about beating her that he didn't tie the rope right."

I covered my face.

"No!" Aaron said.

"Yup. He didn't give himself enough rope *and* he tied his anchor wrong. When he'd reached about three meters from the bottom, he was more concerned about beating Cadence than safety, so he yanked at his rope. The knot popped out and *wham*."

The guys laughed with a sense of sympathetic pain.

"He broke his arm," Tara said with a sigh, "and his pride. I think he got a concussion too, right, Cadence?"

I groaned, covering my eyes. "Yeah. But at least he beat me."

Everyone laughed. I hadn't meant that to be funny. I felt pretty bad about it. I remembered rushing down to the wailing guy to try to help, but he wouldn't let me near him.

Austin squeezed my shoulder. "I'm sure you didn't mean for him to get hurt. You probably tried to help him, right?"

I smiled, my heart swelling with how well Austin already knew me. I brushed my fingers over his cheek, my thumb stroking the hair on his chin. He returned my smile as his eyes gleamed. My insides turned to mush.

"You guys are making me wanna barf," Lyla said.

I pulled away, my cheeks flushing.

"Shut up." Tara slapped her shoulder.

Glancing across the table, I caught Aaron smirking.

The conversation moved along as we ate. Every now and then, Austin would whisper in my ear and make me quiver. That always earned me a gorgeous grin from him.

My phone vibrated in my bag. I opened it and saw James calling. Drawing a sharp breath, I hit decline. I hoped Austin hadn't seen; he laughed, too busy talking to Aaron. But I stared at my phone, too guilty to re-engage with the others. I excused myself to go to the bathroom. I hated how much I was avoiding James's calls, but I had to break up with him, and I couldn't do it over the phone.

In the bathroom, I sat in the cubicle and typed James a text. I'M SORRY, I'M OUT TO DINNER WITH FRIENDS. CAN'T TALK.

He replied immediately. YOU CAN'T TALK A LOT RECENTLY. WHAT'S GOING ON?

My hand trembled as I stared at the phone. This was why I didn't want to talk to him. I was getting my old life back, with my friends, and Austin, but my life with James still tugged at my heart. Taking a deep breath, I typed out: I'VE JUST BEEN REALLY BUSY. I'M SORRY.

Barely seconds after I hit send, my phone vibrated with a call from him. I covered my face, more frustrated with myself than ever, and answered. "I can't talk right now."

"Cadence, I just need a minute."

"I'm sorry. I'm out with some friends, and I don't—"

"Let me say hi to them," he said firmly. "You talk about them all the time, but I've never—"

"No. I have to go."

"Are you upset with me?" The tension in his voice rose. "What have I done?"

I tugged my hair. I couldn't tell him we needed to break up over the phone. "You haven't done anything."

"Cadence?"

I flinched, hitting mute on my phone. "Lyla?"

"I wanted to check on you." Her feet appeared under the door. "You left abruptly and looked kinda upset."

I glanced at the phone as James kept talking. "Yeah, cramps. I didn't want to worry anyone."

"Oh, fair enough." She stepped away from the door. "When you're ready."

"Cadence?" James said.

"Thanks, Lyla," I said, waiting for her to leave.

"Cadence, are you listening?"

"No problem," Lyla said. "Hey, we're getting dessert. Do you want anything?"

"Chocolate and ice cream," I said hurriedly as James practically yelled at me.

Lyla finally left and I unmuted the phone. "Yes, I'm listening."

"No, you're not." I could see him ruffling his hair. With his irritation mounting, my guilt piled up along with it. "What's going on with you?"

"James . . ." I rubbed my eyebrow. "I really can't talk about this right now."

"I'm worried about you."

I sighed, tears threatening to push free. "Don't worry about me. I killed a mouse all on my own, remember?"

"Cadence." By his tone, he had to be scowling.

"I'll call you later, okay? But I really have to go."

"No. I'm tired of you blocking me out."

"I'm sorry. Bye."

"Cadence, don't you dare—"

I hung up. My heart raced, rattling in my rib cage. I had to compose myself before returning to Austin.

My phone lit up again with James's name, and I turned it off.

After several minutes, I pulled myself together enough to head back out. Austin slid his arm around me as I sat. I smiled at him as I reached for a fork. He brushed a kiss on my neck, and then his lips caressed my ear as he asked, "Are you okay?"

My skin tingled. Meeting his gaze, I felt breathless. I'd gazed into those eyes so many times. Those eyes that lit up when I told him I was pregnant, those eyes that flashed with irritation when I told him to put out the trash, those eyes that stared lovingly at me as we made love the night he died.

I kissed him, and he caressed my cheek, kissing me back.

"PDA, Cadence!" Lyla growled.

Austin chuckled against my lips.

"They're so cute!" Tara exclaimed.

Austin broke away. "I guess that means you're fine."

I smiled. "Yeah, sorry. You really don't want to know why I left."

"Period pain," Lyla said.

I glared at her as Aaron and Gareth stared at their plates, turning red.

Austin kissed my cheek. "Lucky you have chocolate. That's supposed to help, right?"

I laughed softly, looking into his eyes again and forgetting my troubles.

At home, I climbed into bed with my scrapbook. The first time, we hadn't done a group date, but I had spent that evening with Austin and Aaron. My heart warmed with the memories. Although things were slightly different, they were mostly the same.

Someone sat by my feet. I gasped, pulling back. "Angel?"

He smiled sadly at me. "You might want to turn that back on."

I followed his gaze to my phone. "Oh."

I snatched it up.

"Why are you doing this to him?"

My heart felt like it tore itself in two. I clutched at my chest from the pain. "I can't break up with him over the phone."

"Are you sure that's what you want?"

I pursed my lips, my chin quivering as I stared down at the picture of Austin. "Yes. I did this for Austin and Melody."

"I told you, Melody will always be yours."

I shook my head, confused. "What does that mean?"

"Mortality isn't the beginning or the end." He stood, offering me his hand.

With a sigh, I took his hand and stood. He wouldn't give me any more on Melody, so I decided to go along with what he wanted to show me.

We stepped through my bedroom door into James's room. I drew a sharp breath as he paced the room, ruffling his hair.

Dusty sat on his bed, his brows furrowed and wearing a deep scowl. "That *is* really weird."

"I can't help thinking she must still be upset about how I reacted to Mel bringing home a guy. I mean, I was being way too overprotective. Maybe she's thinking I'm like that with her. I hate this distance. It makes things a million times worse than they should be. If she were here, we'd have had it out that night and that would be it. But this? This is driving me mad."

"Is this tonight?" I asked.

The angel nodded, gazing ahead.

"She hasn't said anything about it to any of us," Dusty responded to James.

"It's just so frustrating." James rubbed his temples. "I don't mean to be overprotective, but Mel doesn't exactly have a great track record. Can you blame me?"

"Mmm." Dusty stared at his lap.

"Can you maybe get Geri to talk to her?" James swung to face Dusty, hands on his hips.

Dusty's head snapped up. "Who? Mel?"

"No." James ran his hands through his hair.

"Oh, Cadence. Of course." Dusty cleared his throat. "What makes you think Geri would listen to me?"

James raised an eyebrow. "Really? I'm not oblivious to your sneaking around."

"Don't tell Dad," Dusty muttered, staring at his hands.

"I'm not stupid. Of course I won't." James sat beside him, resting his head on his hand. "I just want her back."

"You can't have Geri." Dusty smirked.

James punched his shoulder. "Moron."

Dusty chuckled, rubbing his arm. "Seriously though, I really don't get Cadence lately. She's all weird and elusive."

"Do you think . . . ?" James swallowed, looking to Dusty. "Do you think she might be cheating on me?"

Dusty scoffed. "Cadence? No way."

"It's just . . . she seems to be *busy* a lot lately. I wouldn't blame her. She's gorgeous and amazing, and I'm not exactly—"

"I really don't think she's cheating. That's not her. Yeah, there's definitely something weird going on, but I doubt that's it."

James's face fell into his hands. "I just love her so much. I have to get out there to be with her. When we're together, everything is always okay again. I don't know how much more of this I can take."

I swung to the angel. "Stop. I can't watch this."

He raised his hand and the scene froze. He stared me dead in the eyes. "What do you see?"

"I see that I'm destroying him." I walked over, squatting in front of James. "I can't keep on like this. He deserves so much better."

"All he wants is you."

I sighed, letting a tear fall. "It can't be him. It's supposed to be Austin. I did all of this for Austin."

"James already loves you. Austin's on his way, but he's not quite there yet. Which heart do you think will break the most?"

I leapt to my feet. Fists clenched, I yelled, "It's *always* been Austin. How can you say that?"

His dark eyes turned cold and everything went black. As light faded back in, my bedroom formed around us. The man stood in the corner with his back to me. "Choose wisely, Cadence. It's not just about their hearts; yours is at stake too."

In a flash, he vanished.

I swung to my bed. Usually, the angel left me feeling better, but this time I felt worse. It was like he wanted me to choose James, but he *knew* I did all this for Austin and Melody. He knew I loved Austin long before James stepped into the picture.

The scrapbook on my bed made me stare. It sat open where I'd left it, on the page about Austin and Aaron. I flicked it over to Austin's journal entry.

Aaron really likes Cadence, which is impressive for him because he usually doesn't like my girlfriends. He wouldn't talk to me for a week after I slept with Lena, and he avoided Kira at all costs. But not Cadence. He said, for once, I picked a girl with a brain and a personality to go with her pretty face, and I completely agree with him. Cadence is unlike any girl I've ever met.

I hugged the scrapbook, thinking about the way Austin had looked at me earlier. Everything was falling back into place. How could anyone doubt Austin and I were meant to be together?

Chapter Fourteen

Over the next few weeks, I spent every spare moment with Austin, and when we were in classes or working, we texted constantly.

The night Geri called, I desperately wanted to tell her, but I couldn't. How could I tell her that I planned to break up with James, and that I was already dating someone else?

"James and Dusty are harassing me," Geri told me as I lay on my bed. "They want to know why you're acting so weird."

"Weird?" My stomach tied in knots.

"Yeah." Hesitance made her voice catch. "Honestly, I think you're acting a bit strange too. Why are you avoiding James?"

My cheeks burned as I rolled to face the wall. "I, ah, I need to give him some space."

"What?" she said sharply.

"All of this . . . it just isn't fair to him. Next time I see him, I think I'll—"

"No, no, no, no!" Her voice grew higher in pitch. "You better not be thinking what I think you're thinking. You can't . . . you guys are soul mates. The distance is just getting to you."

"Geri—"

"Dusty said you were thinking this at the wedding. You *can't,* Cadence. You love him, I know you do, and I know you think you're doing this for him, but if you break up with him, you *will* crush him."

A tear ran down my cheek. "I can't keep doing this to him."

"Cadence." She let out a long sigh. "I love you, no matter what. You know that, right?"

"Yes," I replied weakly.

"Just be patient, okay? You'll see him soon, and—"

"I can't get back for the winter break. I can't get the time off work."

She hesitated, then sighed again. "Okay. But you'll see James again soon, and I know when you do that everything will be fine again. He's planning on moving out there to be with you. That's how much he loves you."

My lip trembled. She, like everyone else, wanted me to be with James, but that was because she didn't know Austin. If I could just show them, they'd know Austin was perfect for me.

"It'll be okay, Cay-Cay," Geri said gently.

"Enough about me," I said hurriedly, to hide the pain in my voice. "You need to tell me the deal with you and Dusty."

"Dusty?" She laughed uncomfortably. "What makes you think there's a deal with me and Dusty?"

"Really?" I smirked, twisting my hair off my neck. "Hmm, it might have something to do with the fact that you talk about him *all the time*."

"He's your brother, so, you know, substitute."

"Uh-huh."

She groaned. "Fine. We're sort of seeing each other. Sort of. Not technically. He's still in high school, so it's totally weird."

"But you really like him." I rested my head against the wall to keep my hair up.

She squeaked. "Yeah. I shouldn't, but I do. I can't help it. He's so . . . irritatingly adorable."

I grinned, chuckling. "That's a pretty accurate description."

"What's wrong with me?" she growled.

"Nothing. He's way into you, has been for ages now."

"But he's *Dusty*. He's your brother. I've known him forever."

"So?"

She let out a heavy sigh. "So I really like a high school guy who I've known since he was a snot-nosed fifth grader. But I can't stop. He calls me and I get light-headed. He asks me to hang out with him and I can't say no. He kisses me and I get giddy—"

"Kissing?" I grinned, folding my legs as I sat forward. Although I'd caught them in the act before, this was the first time she'd admitted it.

"Yes, we kiss . . . a lot more than I'd like to admit." She groaned again. "He just looks at me like I've always wanted a guy to look at me, and knows me so freaking well." She paused, then whispered, "He's tried to sleep with me."

"What?" My voice rose in pitch.

"But I won't. He's too young, and I'm so not there yet. Now I know why you freaked out so badly when you and James slept together the first time. It's absolutely terrifying! Even though he tells me he loves me, I can't—"

"He *what?*" I just about jumped off my bed.

"He . . ." She coughed. "He tells me he loves me."

"Geri! That's *huge*."

"I just . . . I don't know. How did you know?"

I paused, contemplating how best to answer. With James and Austin, I'd known in different ways and at different times of our relationships. "I don't know. I think it's unique for everyone. But I knew I cared about him more than anyone else, and I wanted him to be happy. I knew he was safe, and he cared about me. I don't know. It's like being best friends on steroids."

She giggled.

"It just feels . . . good. It's like when the butterflies and romantic daydreams wear off, he's still there, and everything is okay, like it should be."

"Wow," she said breathlessly. "And you want to break up with James when you feel like that?"

My voice caught. *No . . . yes . . .* "Oh, Geri."

"I love you, Cay. Don't do it if you don't know for sure. You know it will break your heart too. Don't think you have to do this for him, to save him from pain. I know you love each other."

"I thought we were talking about Dusty," I said as a tear ran down my cheek.

She giggled. "Sorry, we were. But you helped me answer my question."

"And?" I wiped my eyes.

"I think I might love him too."

I grinned. "Geri."

"I know!" She let out a sigh. "Why him?"

I chuckled. I couldn't be happier for her, even if she didn't think he could work for her yet. They would be wonderful together. Nothing would mean more to me than seeing her happy, my brother or not.

Despite our conversation, I continued to avoid answering James's calls, texts, and emails. My guilt became stifling. The worst thing was that I still loved him so much. But he knew me so well—*too* well. After several weeks of only a few short texts and emails, I received a call from Dusty's phone.

"Hey, Dusty," I said.

"Not Dusty," James responded in a firm voice. "We need to talk."

I glanced around the library and rushed into a study room for some privacy. "James . . ."

"You've been avoiding me." There was no mistaking the pain in his voice. "What's going on, Cadence?"

"I, ah . . . I've been busy."

"Don't lie to me. I'm so tired of you telling me you're busy. Come on, we've always been able to talk."

I locked the door. "I know. I'm just overwhelmed right now. There's a lot going on, and I'm not sure how to handle it all."

He sighed. "Cadence, you know I can help you, even if it's just to talk things through."

I took a deep breath and sank onto the floor. "James . . ."

"Are you coming back for winter break?"

I rubbed my forehead. "I can't get off work."

"*What?*"

"I tried!" I said honestly. "After four weeks off last winter, and the two over the summer for Harper's wedding, I had to choose winter or Christmas, and I want to go home for Christmas this year."

"Is that why you've been avoiding me?" he said in a tense voice. "Because you didn't want to tell me you weren't coming back as planned?"

I sighed. "Yeah."

"Oh, Cadence." The line fell quiet. I could almost hear him ruffle his hair. "Then I'll come to you."

"No, James!" The very thought that he and Austin might cross paths terrified me. What would that cause? I could lose them both rather than just one . . . I needed time. "You need to focus on graduating and securing that job at the lab."

"No, I need to see you. You're more important than all that. I can tell you're struggling right now."

"Please, James. If you're here, I'll be worried about your job and your studies as well as my own classes and work, and—"

He huffed, his frustration with me growing by the moment. "Fine, I won't. You won't see me until Christmas, is that what you want?"

"No," I said in a small voice.

"Then what *do* you want, Cadence?"

I rubbed my eyes with the heel of my hand. "I just don't know."

He swore loudly in frustration. "Cadence, this is nuts. I have *no* idea what's going on, but it's messing around with you and you need to do something about it. Why won't you talk to me? Is it my fault?"

I covered my mouth to stifle my sob. "No, it's not your fault. I just . . . I'm just . . ." The line fell silent while he waited for me to continue. "I . . ." I grabbed my hair. "I just don't know."

"Don't know what?" he asked, raising his voice.

"Don't yell at me!"

"Seriously? You're driving me crazy! If you're done, then just say it! I'm tired of these . . . this . . . whatever's going on! I'm *done*, Cadence!"

The line fell silent. He'd hung up on me. James *never* hung up on me. Did that mean we were over? That was what I wanted . . . right?

But then, why had it left me with such a deep, hollow pain inside?

James stopped all communication with me. I tried not to let it get to me. It meant we were over and he'd made the decision for me, but it still hurt so much. Austin noticed

I'd become quieter than usual, but instead of asking about it, he took me out to distract me and cheer me up.

Austin hummed softly beside me. We'd been dating for two months, and every moment I spent with him made me blissfully happy. Being with Austin made the pain of losing James vanish. Being with Austin seemed to heal everything.

"Ah!" He yanked out a women's wet suit. "I knew it was in here somewhere. You're a little taller than Mum, but it should fit."

I took the black and purple wet suit. "You know the water will be freezing."

He scoffed. "We're going to an inlet that stays warmish."

"Warmish?" I chuckled, pulling off my shirt to reveal my one-piece swimsuit.

As I slipped the shirt over my head, I caught him glance away from my boobs. I tried not to smirk as he swiveled in search of diving gear for me. Austin had always been respectful, even when he wanted to jump me.

We rode out in George's boat to the island, chatting and laughing the whole way. We pulled into the inlet, and I smiled, remembering. The water, despite being "warmish," would be too cold for me, and I'd stay in only to let him finish his lesson with me.

He lowered the anchor, and ran through all the instructions of what I needed to do. Like riding a bike, I hadn't forgotten a thing. I checked all the safeties, the oxygen tank levels, and strapped it on my back without a problem.

He stared at me, blinking. "I'm impressed. You *are* a fast learner."

I chuckled nervously, thumbing to the water. "So, how do I do this?"

He helped me slip into the chest-deep water, and slowly started introducing me to breathing. Conscious of looking too obvious, I took my time. Plus, it had been so long since I'd last gone diving with him, it really did feel odd breathing through the mouthpiece.

Finally, we started our swim around the inlet. With only small fish, crustaceans, and mollusks, there wasn't much to see, but this wasn't a sightseeing dive. Austin led me along, pointing to clams or fish excitedly. Even underwater, his passion showed.

As he pointed to an uncomfortably large crab that I refused to get anywhere near, I remembered the most important detail of this trip. This was when I first realized I loved him. After our dive, while I shivered and ate lunch on his boat, I'd watched him talk so passionately about the ocean that I just *knew*. If he could be that passionate about the ocean, maybe he could feel the same about me.

But this time . . . as he led me back toward the boat, I watched him, amazed at my incredible opportunity to fall in love all over again. Although I already knew I loved him, I didn't know how he felt yet. *When had he fallen in love with me?* Whenever I'd asked, he always answered with "the moment I saw you," but I didn't believe that.

Back on the boat, he handed me a salad sandwich and juice. The boy was healthy, I had to give him that, but the sandwiches were the only thing he knew how to make. He'd always been terrible at cooking, and so took pride in his sandwich-making skills.

As he talked about the creatures we'd seen, I felt as if he had wrapped me in a warm blanket, even though I was shivering. Everything about the trip was so *Austin*. No pretenses, no flashy attempts to impress me, he was just *him*, like I'd always remembered him.

"So, I hope you don't mind me always bringing sand-wiches," he said as he tossed a crust to a sea bird.

"It's totally fine," I said, grinning. "You've seen the inside of our fridge at the flat. Lyla and I eat terribly. You're actually doing me a favor."

He chuckled and dug into his bag. "I need to take a photo of this. Cadence's first diving trip."

"More like paddling with fancy equipment."

I grinned right before he snapped the shot. "Perfect."

I touched my ratty, wet, windswept hair. "If you say so."

"You're always beautiful." He leaned in and kissed me.

I clasped his face, leaning against him.

He broke away. "You're freezing cold."

"I'm sorry to tell you, but your *warmish* gauge is broken."

He grinned and kissed me again. Wrapping his arm around my waist, he pulled me onto his lap and wrapped me up in his arms. His body radiated heat somehow. No wonder he could swim in such cold water all year round.

He broke from the kiss and wove his fingers into my hair. "You know, you're the only girl who has let me take her diving."

"Paddling," I corrected.

He smirked. "Paddling. It's seriously hot."

"It's actually freezing."

He tickled my ribs. I squirmed, giggling.

"It's hot that you'd do this with me." He met my gaze, and I saw it. Right there. Gazing out at me was the love I used to see. But the memories of it, being so faded, didn't do it justice. I never wanted him to stop looking at me like that. Seeing my own feelings reciprocated after so long . . .

I sighed, stroking his cheek. Without looking away, he caught my hand and kissed my palm. It dawned on me that this moment, for both of us, was when we first fell in love.

Chapter Fifteen

The weekend before our end of semester exams, Austin came to pick me up. He told me to wear a nice dress or skirt, so I wore a black pencil skirt with a burgundy wrap. I felt so nervous. I knew this was the night he would take me out to dinner with his parents, and afterward, since Lyla would be out clubbing, we'd return to the flat together . . .

The knock on the door startled me out of my memories. I rushed to answer it. Austin blew me away. He looked so incredible in his fitted, black pinstriped pants and white dress shirt.

Austin grabbed me by the waist as he handed me a bunch of flowers. "Are you okay?"

"Holy cow, you're hot."

He laughed. "Oh! You're swooning." He tossed the flowers onto the couch. "I've never done that to a girl before. I must say, it's a pretty awesome feeling."

I ran my hand down his arm. "I still can't believe all of this is just from diving."

His arms tightened, pulling me up against him. "There's no one else I'd rather impress."

My knees wobbled as he nibbled on my ear.

He chuckled softly. "You know, it's a good thing we'll be sitting tonight because you're a bit shaky on your legs."

"Shut up." I forced myself to calm down, then picked up the flowers. "These are beautiful. Thank you. Let me just put them in water and we'll head out."

He followed me into the kitchen, and while I searched for a tall glass, his hand rested on my behind. I froze, my nerves rising in anticipation of what would happen later.

"Wow, this skirt makes your butt look incredible." His hand ran over it, taking in the curves, and gave it a firm squeeze.

I gasped and swung around to face him. "Don't do that, or we'll never get out of here."

His eyes twinkled at my implication. "I'm okay with that."

He rushed at me, grabbing my breasts and kissing my neck. He was already raring to go, and as my hands rested on his hips, I realized I was too.

"Austin?" I said breathlessly.

"Yeah?"

"We can't stand up your parents."

He pried himself off me. "Yeah." He reached around me and plugged the sink. "This will do for now."

He turned on the faucet. Our eyes locked as the water filled the sink, the tension rising between us. There was no doubt where the night was headed.

When he turned off the water and severed our eye contact, I took a sharp breath, stunned by the power he had over me. He rested the stems in the water and grasped my hand. "Let's go."

He took me to a stunning restaurant on the riverfront. I found myself breathless all over again. The first time we'd gone there to meet his parents, I'd stood completely in awe of the view, and he had to pull me away from the window to eat. This time, I mustered up my self-control and simply gazed out in awe as we followed the hostess to our table.

His parents already sat waiting for us, and greeted me warmly. Linda sat directly across from me, and took my hand and held it tightly while she talked. The way she looked at me reminded me of the way Karen had always looked at me, but I forced that thought aside. James and I were over, and it was for the best. I had Austin back. The life I'd had torn away from me was on its way to being restored.

The meal tasted divine, and the company was delightful. I loved his parents as much as I always had. When the dessert came out, Austin's hand rested on my thigh. I glanced at him and our eyes met. My cheeks warmed and I dropped my gaze. His lips pressed against my forehead as he stroked the hair over my shoulder.

Sighing with contentment, I glanced up to see Linda smiling at us with a tear in her eye. I hadn't seen it the first time around, but this was the moment she saw we were in love. She'd always seemed to know, but right then, reflected in her eyes, was the turning point where she saw her son in love, and it made her happy. I loved being able to see so many things I'd missed the first time.

We finished and headed to the cars to say goodbye. Linda held me tightly and kissed my cheek. "Cadence, it's been lovely getting to know you. Don't be a stranger. You're always welcome in our home."

"Thank you, and thank you for such a wonderful evening."

She smiled at me before kissing Austin's cheek. "Drive safe, son. We'll see you at home."

"Okay, Mum. Bye."

He rested his hand on the small of my back and guided me to his car. We drove in a comfortable, content silence back to the flat. But when we arrived, and he walked me to the door, I grew nervous. Could I go through with what we'd done the first time? James had broken up with me, so

I wasn't cheating, but what would Austin think of me not being a virgin? For the first time in a long time, I regretted sleeping with James.

As I went to unlock the door, Austin's hand rested over mine, steadying it as I slid the key in the lock. His other hand pressed on my waist, pulling at the tie on my wrap. "Let me come in for a little while."

I nodded as he turned my hand to unlock the door. He grasped the handle and opened it. He pushed me through and used his foot to shut it behind him. "Cadence?"

"Yes?"

"You have no idea how beautiful you are."

I was putty in his hands. He reached back and locked the door, then pulled the tie on my wrap undone. I faced him as he slid the burgundy fabric away to expose my cami. Wrapping my arms around his neck, I kissed him, pulling him back toward my room through the darkness.

As we stepped through the door, he rushed to unbutton his shirt. I pulled away from him and backed toward the bed. I flicked on my bedside light and pulled the cami up over my head.

He shut the door and locked it, then tossed his shirt on the floor, exposing his magnificent chest and torso. My legs turned to jelly and I sank onto the bed. He stood over me as he undid his pants and I fumbled to remove my skirt. His thumbs slid under his boxers, drawing my gaze to his crotch.

"Cadence?"

My gaze lifted to his face just before he kissed me. He lowered me under him on the bed. My body pulsed with excitement. "Oh my . . . Austin."

He opened my legs and wrapped them around him. He wrapped his arms around me, pulled me up onto his lap, and kissed my neck. I moaned as he made love to me, my whole body aching at how familiar, yet new, he felt. His hands stroked down my back, making me quiver.

"Austin, I love you."

Wait, did I just say that? My eyes shot open as he pulled back from me.

"What did you say?" he asked.

"I, ah . . ." I covered my face as my cheeks burned. *He* was supposed to say it before I did.

I'd screwed up.

"Did you say you love me?"

He peeled my hands back from my face so he could look into my eyes. What I saw gazing back at me surprised me, I knew that look well. He loved me too, and his adoration poured out of him.

"Yes."

His arms wrapped tightly around me again, and he kissed me. I stroked his face, my heart pounding in my chest. His lips broke away, but he held me close as he gazed into my eyes. "I'm so glad you said it first. I wasn't sure if you were as committed to this relationship as I am.

I thought maybe you were just having a good time, and I didn't wanna screw it up. I love you too, Cadence. I can't stop thinking about you. You drive me wild with just a glance. I swear, if I could, I would never let you go and keep you in my arms forever."

We gazed into each other's eyes, our feelings intensifying and spilling over. I stroked his cheek with my thumb. "Austin."

He lunged at me, kissing me with such passion I thought my heart would explode. He lowered me back down underneath him.

Afterward, I lay curled up beside him as he fell asleep, wondering why he hadn't admitted his fear to me the last time. Then again, he hadn't needed to. I'd been a virgin. When we first started to make love, he'd paused and looked down. "You want me to be your first?"

I nodded, knowing I'd turned red.

He leaned down and wrapped my legs around him. "Oh, Cadence, I love you."

Giving him my virginity had told him how I felt, that I was serious about him. But not being a virgin this time, I'd needed to express my feelings to him vocally before he felt safe to say it. I nuzzled into his chest and sighed. His arm tightened around me and he kissed my head. At least this was the same, the safety I felt in his arms.

"Say it again, Cadence," he said softly.

I smiled in the darkness. "I love you, Austin."

He let out a long, contented sigh. "And I love you."

I hated it when James snored. I rolled over and thumped him. "Shut up."

Austin jumped. "What?"

I yelped, startled. "Oh! I thought you . . ." I shook off my confusion. *Austin* was with me. "You were snoring."

He chuckled and nuzzled into my breasts. "I do that sometimes."

I realized there was sunlight outside. I sat up and looked at my phone. 7:23 a.m. "Shoot! Austin! You stayed all night."

"So?"

"So? Weren't your parents expecting you home?"

He encouraged me to lie back. "They won't care. Come on, you've probably spent the night with someone before, right?"

"Yeah, and my dad practically broke the door down at five in the morning and banned him from seeing me."

Austin's head lifted, and his eyes sparkled. "Seriously? Wow, your dad is freaky. I'm kinda nervous about meeting him."

"Ha . . . me too." I wondered how that conversation would go. *Oh, by the way, James and I broke up and I'm already dating this other guy. Sorry about the inconvenience.*

I was such a prat.

Austin shifted over me. "How many guys have you been with, anyway?"

I held up my index finger. I didn't want to talk about it—I felt dirty for not waiting for Austin like I had the first time.

"Just one, huh?" He grinned and stroked my hair. "That makes me feel pretty special." He softly kissed me. "To be honest, you're my third. My twelfth grade girl-friend, then a girl I dated for a while last year."

"I saw you with her once."

He raised his eyebrows. "When?"

"That day I dropped all my books when my phone rang and I was running late."

He laughed. "Oh, yeah, we were still together then. I felt a little guilty that I was so attracted to you while I was still with her, but we broke up about a month later, which seemed to fit nicely with our little exchanges."

I giggled. "That was pretty awkward."

He shifted and pushed my legs open. "I thought it was pretty cute. You were so shy, and always blushed like crazy."

"I wasn't sure what to do," I said softly as he kissed my neck. "I had my boyfriend back in Sydney, and then all of a sudden, there you were."

His lips lifted from my neck. His nose brushed against mine as our eyes met. "It doesn't matter anymore. We're together, and I've never been happier. I love you, Cadence."

Caressing his face, I whispered, "Oh Austin, I love you too."

He made love to me again, slowly, gently, lovingly. When we finished, he sat up and looked at the time. "It's almost nine. When are you working today?"

I rolled over and grabbed his pants for him. "One. You should shower."

He grinned. "Care to join me?"

"Oh no," I laughed, "that shower barely fits one person. You go first."

He pulled on his pants, bending over and running his hand over my shoulder and down my back. I shuddered when his lips pressed against my skin. He pulled the blankets up around me before he opened the door.

Lyla swore loudly. "Austin! What the . . . you stayed the night?" Her head appeared around the door and she grinned at me. "Nice, Cadence."

Heat crept up my neck.

She turned back to Austin. "Wow, you should just walk around like this. I'm sure no one would complain."

He laughed. "Sorry, Lyla. I'm taken."

She smirked. "Obviously."

I groaned and buried my face into my pillow. Austin laughed again as he moved off into the bathroom, and once the door shut, she rushed to me.

"Cadence! Wow! This is . . . wow!" She sat on the bed beside me, and I clutched nervously at the blankets. "So you guys are pretty serious."

"Yeah." I smiled. "He told me he loves me."

She shrieked. "Are you serious?"

I nodded.

"Oh wow!" She rested her hand on my shoulder for a second before she pulled away. "You're totally naked, huh?"

"Yeah."

She giggled and jumped to her feet. "Tara is about to get a call!"

"Lyla!" I reached for her, but being naked, I couldn't stop her as she rushed out of my room, slamming the door behind her.

I lay back, resting my hand on my forehead. I felt happy. Austin filled my heart and made me feel so beautiful. Things would be back to how they were soon, and my redo would be worth it. I would save him, and we would be happy just being together with our little family.

My phone rang. My hand flopped around in search for it as I remained lying on my back with my face covered. I found it and hit answer. "Hello?"

"Cadence, I have to see you."

I sat bolt upright. "James!"

"It's killing me," he said in a gravelly, distressed voice. "I'm sorry I yelled and hung up on you, but you're acting so strange lately that I'm afraid I'm losing you. I have to see you. I have to know everything's okay."

"But . . . what? James, I thought you dumped me."

"No!" he exclaimed. "Oh Cadence, no! I'd never! How could you think that?"

"You . . . I . . ." *Crap*! When he'd said he was done, I could have sworn . . .

"I have to see you. We have to work this out."

"But how? I can't get back there—"

"I'm coming to you. I'm searching for flights right now."

"James . . ." I had to keep my voice calm. If I sounded alarmed, I'd never talk him out of it. He'd show up and find me with Austin and everything would fall apart. "Don't. You need to save your money to pay your tuition fees and your rent—"

"Don't try to talk me out of this. My mind is made up."

"James . . ." I rubbed my forehead. If he discovered me with someone else, it would hurt him more than anything. I needed to cut him off. I'd just slept with Austin because I'd believed James and I were over! I couldn't hurt him by dragging things out. "Try to be rational."

"Rational?" His voice rose. "Cadence, I can feel you slipping away. I'm losing my mind with worry. If I could just see you, you'll remember how in love we are, and you'll remember your promise to me. You're just running again, and I'm not going to let you get away."

I let out a long breath. I didn't know how to respond to that. His voice alone stirred up my feelings for him, and his passion made me want to kiss him and tell him everything would be all right. But I couldn't, not after the step I'd just taken with Austin.

"Cadence?" he said quietly. "Tell me that you still love me."

I couldn't lie to him. "I do still love you."

He let out a long sigh. "I hate fighting with you."

"I know. Me too."

"I have to see you."

"Coming out here isn't the answer," I said, rubbing my eyes. "I'll try to work something out so I can see you, okay? Maybe I can trade some shifts and arrange a long weekend or something."

He let out a long breath, releasing all his tension. "That would be great."

"I'll let you know."

"Okay. I love you."

"I love you too," I responded softly as the shower shut off. I hung up, and hurried to gather my clothes together.

Yes, as much as I would hurt from it, I had to end it with James. Prolonging things would only make matters worse.

Chapter Sixteen

I wished the plane had more people in it. I waited for everyone else to get off before me, and moved slowly through the terminal. When I saw the bathrooms, I hurried in and threw up. James would be devastated, and the thought of the pain I'd inflict on him tore me apart.

But I couldn't see him anywhere. *Great, he's late.* I struggled to keep my stomach down on my way to collect my suitcase. It didn't take long to come through, and as I yanked it off the carousel, I heard my name. I couldn't turn toward the voice. It meant facing the one thing I dreaded.

A hand joined mine on the handle of my suitcase.

"I've got it," James said gently. My gaze followed his arm up to his face. His smile grew wide from ear to ear before he clasped my face and kissed me.

His familiar smell, kiss, and touch sent a rush through my body. I grabbed him, pulling him up against me, but he broke away, his incredible gray-blue eyes gazing into mine. "Why do you taste like vomit?"

"I . . . threw up."

"Gross." He dug into his pocket and handed me some gum. "Are you sick?"

"My stomach was unsettled the whole trip."

"That's not like you." He wrapped his arm around my shoulders as he tugged my small suitcase behind him. "You never get airsick."

"I know." I rested my head on his shoulder, finding comfort in his arm.

"Well, since you've only got two days, do you want to go to your parents' first?"

I sighed, forcing myself to remember why I came. "No, let's go somewhere private, just me and you."

"My room is always—"

"No," I said sharply. "Somewhere we've never been before and won't ever go again."

He gave me a quizzical look. "Okay."

He drove us to Bicentennial Park in silence. I couldn't even look at him. He found a quiet corner, and we walked hand in hand along the edge of the tree line.

Finally, I looked up at him. "James . . ."

His head turned to me, and I saw that he sensed something coming. "Let me say something first."

"Okay."

He took a deep breath. "From the day you told me you were going clear across the country to go to school, I was afraid I'd lose you. But I knew if I really loved you, I needed to let you spread your wings, so I did. I've missed you every day. You left me with such a wonderful promise, it made the distance seem not so far."

He pulled us to a halt and turned to me. "I know these past few months have been rough, and I understand that you don't want to talk to me about it, but we can't just give up because of that. We've been together for four and a half wonderful years, and I've been crazy about you for every single moment. We've given each other so much and loved each other so completely that I know we can get through this. Don't give up on us, Cadence."

My resolve faltered. I couldn't look up at him. "You knew I came to break up with you."

He clasped my face and forced me to look at him. His eyes filled with tears, but none had fallen.

"I thought, maybe . . ." He blinked, and his tears fell. "No, Cadence. Don't do it. *Please* don't do it."

I couldn't look away from his eyes. They gazed so steadily into mine as his emotions flooded out of him. Pain, grief, sorrow.

"But I . . . James . . ." My voice caught. I couldn't say the words.

How could I end it when I loved him so much?

"I'm not going to let you go without a fight," he said in a hushed voice.

My heart fluttered as his eyes grew bluer, reflecting his determination. Without thinking, I grabbed the back of his neck and kissed him. His arms wrapped around me and he clung to me, kissing me with a deep passion. I didn't think of Austin once as James took me back to his home and we made love.

When I awoke and saw James still asleep beside me, I knew I was in trouble. I loved both him and Austin, and neither more than the other. My heart was torn in two— the love of my youth, the one I'd given my everything to, or the one I loved first, the love I'd sacrificed everything for.

James stirred and noticed me looking at him. He smiled and wrapped his arm around me. "Hello, beautiful."

I nuzzled closer to him without looking away from his face.

"What should we do today?"

"Stay right here," I whispered.

He kissed my forehead. "Okay."

I dozed off again in his arms. When a soft tap came on the door, he shuffled out of bed, careful not to disturb me as he hurried over.

"What's up?" he asked in a whisper.

"It's me, bro, open up."

"Dusty?" I gasped, suddenly wide awake.

"Hey!" Dusty spoke loudly. "Dude, are you cheating on my *sister*?"

"No, Dusty, I'm not!" James replied.

"There's a girl in there! I heard her!" Dusty kicked at the door. I pulled the blankets around me just in time as it burst open. "Cadence?"

"Dusty, get out!" I hollered.

"I didn't think you could get back!"

"I couldn't. I'm leaving tomorrow."

"But . . ." He scratched his head, and then his eyes widened. "Oh gross! You're totally naked!"

Feet rushed down the hallway, and Sam and Tom's heads popped in.

"Perverts!" I yelled.

James shoved them all out and slammed the door shut. "Cadence . . ."

"I'm on it." I jumped out of bed and dressed.

We hurried down the stairs. Dusty stood in the living room with his hands on his hips, waiting for us. I couldn't get a read on him. He wasn't quite irritated or frustrated, but there was a hint of excitement. He pointed at me as

I walked toward him. "You could have told us. Harper's dying to talk to you."

"It was last minute," James said. "I made her come out here."

"Oh." He looked between us. "For just a day?"

"Yeah. We needed to talk." James wrapped his arm around me. "She was going to dump me."

I dropped my gaze at how upfront he was about it.

Dusty turned on me. "What? Are you insane?"

"Hey, Dusty, calm down." James rested his hand on Dusty's shoulder. "As you can see, everything's fine. She's still my girl." He stroked my hair and kissed my forehead. I hoped my guilt wasn't showing on my face.

"Ooh, Cadence," Dusty scolded. "We talked about this. I think you need to transfer back here. Being so far away is messing with your head."

"I'm halfway through my course," I protested. "I can't up and change now!"

"Dusty, enough," James said calmly.

Dusty backed down immediately. I was impressed— no one had ever made Dusty back down like that before, in either timeline.

"So why does Harper need to talk to me?" I asked, wishing to change the subject.

Dusty gave me a wicked grin and patted his abdomen. "You'll just have to wait to find out."

"Oh, she's pregnant, of course. This is about the right time."

Dusty and James stared at me, their jaws hanging. James shook his head. "There you go again with your weird psychic thing. Next you'll be telling us its gender."

"I'd feel safe betting it's a boy." I grinned. "I bet she'll breed boys like a freaking rabbit."

Dusty burst out laughing. "Don't tell her that! She's convinced it's a girl, because she doesn't want another unruly, spoiled boy like her nephews." He dug his phone out of his pocket and slipped into the kitchen to call her.

James leaned down to whisper, "If you say it's a boy, I'm going to take your dad up on his hundred dollar bet. You're always right with things like this."

He pulled out his phone and called my dad. I grabbed his arm to try to stop him, but he held me back while smirking. "Dave! So I was thinking about your offer, and I think I'll take it. One hundred on it being a boy."

Dave? Did he seriously just call my dad *Dave*?

"Excellent. I'll need that hundred." He paused, then grinned at me and winked. "Nah, I've got this in the bag." He laughed. "We'll see in a few weeks, I guess . . . all right, mate. See ya later."

He shoved the phone back in his pocket. I gazed at him in shock, knowing he'd basically just taken a hundred dollars from my dad.

"Don't worry. I'll spend every cent on you." He kissed me softly.

Harper came around within the hour and told me her news excitedly. We bounced around and shrieked together before she grabbed my hands and held them against her belly.

"I can barely believe it," she said. "In here is my child. Daniel is ecstatic. He's hoping for boys to pass on the family name, but I want a little girl. I refuse to name her something musical, though. Daniel's agreed on Susan."

I giggled. "Susan sounds perfectly ordinary."

She smirked. "Good."

While I waited at the airport for my flight, I clung to James and listened to his heartbeat. I had no clue what to do. Both he and Austin were wonderful, and I wished someone could spell it out for me, or even better, make the choice for me.

James stroked my hair. I looked up at him, and he smiled. "I'm glad you came, and I'm glad you didn't end our relationship. I'll do all I can to make the distance easier on you, I promise."

I pressed my cheek back against his chest. "You're so wonderful, James."

He chuckled. "I try, but you can stroke my ego as much as you want."

I giggled, but cut myself short when the speakers blared with the announcement for my flight to board. "I guess I have to go now."

He squeezed me tightly and gave me a long kiss goodbye.

As we parted, he watched me until I disappeared through security.

On the flight, I thought about James. He made my whole body tingle with delight, and I thought maybe I was wrong about him. Maybe I needed to end it with Austin instead. James had done so much to be with me, and made me happy for so long. He was a part of me. My family loved him, even my dad. But then again, what about Melody? My beautiful Melody . . .

Five hours later, as I made my way through the terminal at Perth, I heard Austin's voice calling my name. Like I had with James, I felt sick. He came up beside me and casually wrapped his arm around my shoulders. "How was your brief trip, sweet Cadence? Family all fine? What was so urgent?"

I went to grab my suitcase, but he plucked it up before I had the chance. He grinned and tilted his head for me to follow. We walked toward the parking lot.

"Harper's pregnant, and she wanted to tell me in person."

"Hey! That's awesome!" He grinned. "More family for me to meet."

I was so screwed.

Chapter Seventeen

The last week of the break, Lyla took a trip with her family, so Austin practically lived at the flat with me. He claimed I needed someone to watch over me so I didn't get lonely, but I knew he just wanted to take advantage of the privacy. However, with my relationship with James still alive, I refused to sleep with him again. It just complicated things more than I wanted to deal with. He didn't ask why and just understood, like he always did.

On Wednesday, we were curled up on the couch, enjoying a quiet night in, when someone knocked on the door. I grunted at the disruption and rushed over to answer it. There came a shriek, and a body flew at me. The floor rushed to meet us, and I was pinned between it and her.

Curls fell into my face as she laughed. "Ha, ha! I've never knocked you down before. I win! For once, I *win*!"

She sat up while I rolled over, winded.

"Geez, Geri! What are you doing here?"

"Dusty and I decided to visit and surprise you."

Dusty! I sat up. He stood by the door, staring at Austin on the couch, his expression one of complete horror. Austin leapt up and offered his hand. "You must be Dusty. Cadence wasn't exaggerating when she said you looked just like her."

Dusty's gaze fell to his hand. "Do you live here?"

"No—"

"Are you Lyla's boyfriend then?"

"No, I'm Cadence's boyfriend."

Dusty turned red with rage. I'd never seen him look like Dad until that moment.

Geri slapped me across the face. "What the *hell*, Cadence?"

"Hey!" Austin hurried toward me. "Don't treat her like that!"

Geri pointed at him. "You shut up! How dare you presume to be her boyfriend?"

"Austin, get out!" I climbed to my feet.

He grabbed me around the waist. "No. I'm going to stand by you."

"Austin, please, let me deal with this."

He caressed my face. "They're your family—"

"Stop *touching* her!" Dusty's bellow made me cringe. He marched over and pulled Austin's hand off me. "Get away from her."

I grabbed Austin's hand and pulled him to the door. "Please go."

He met my gaze, and I saw his pain. "What's going on?"

"I'll explain later, but I need you to go now."

He chewed on his tongue, then nodded. "Okay. I love you."

Knowing Geri and Dusty were listening, I hesitated to respond. "I love you, too," I replied softly. "Please go."

He nodded. I watched him walk to his car before I shut the door. I didn't dare turn to face Dusty and Geri. I knew exactly how they would be looking at me.

"You *love* him?" Dusty hissed in a low voice. "What about James, Cadence? Is *this* what all that break-up talk was about?"

My face fell into my hands. "Yes."

He grabbed my arm, pulling me around roughly. "No. Just *no*. I don't know who he is, but he *has* to go."

"I can't believe you would do this," Geri said, tears in her eyes. "It's not like you. I thought you . . ."

Shoving Dusty out of the way, I rushed to her. I couldn't lose her again, not like this. Not after I'd done everything I could to avoid losing her friendship. She folded her arms and stepped back, avoiding eye contact.

"Geri, please. There's just some things you don't understand. This is way more complicated than you know."

"No, it's not!" she yelled. Her gaze lifted and burned into me as tears streaked down her cheeks. "You're with James. You've always been with James, and you'll always be with James. He . . . you can't love *him*!"

I shook my head and grabbed my hair. Then I remembered something I'd told her years earlier. I looked into her eyes. "Do you remember when we were in ninth grade, and I told you I liked a guy named Austin?"

She stared at me, confused, but slowly nodded. "Yeah, I thought he was a lame excuse to not date anyone."

I pointed toward the door. "*That* is Austin. One and the same. He's real."

"B . . . mmm . . . ah . . ." She seemed unable to form any words. The possibility that someone she thought to be pure fantasy could suddenly be very real had to be a hard concept to wrap her head around. "But . . . how? He lived clear across the country. How did you even meet him back then?"

I shook my head. "I can't explain it. But, in a way, this whole time I've been cheating on him with James."

Geri's eyes widened, her confusion growing. "But . . . what . . . ?"

"She's lying, Ger." Dusty marched forward and grabbed my wrist. "This crazy talk ends right now. James might think it's cute, but it just bugs me. This guy goes. Stop being such a slut."

His words felt like knives in my heart.

"We came to see you because James is concerned there's a problem here you're not talking about, and now we know what it is."

"Austin isn't the problem! I'm the problem. I thought James dumped me, so I let Austin in. But when I found out it was a misunderstanding . . ." I huffed. "I don't know what to do anymore."

"It's very simple!" Dusty threw his hand in the air. "Dump him and stay with James!"

I shook my head. "I can't."

"Why not?" he said with a growl.

"Austin's . . . he's . . . I can't tell you why! If I do, all of this will go away and everything I've worked so hard for will be gone."

Dusty shoved me against the wall. "You're making no sense. You're talking to James right now."

"Dusty, don't be so rough," Geri said timidly.

Dusty ignored her and pinned me against the wall by pressing his forearm against my chest and leaning into it. He pulled out his phone and called James.

"Hey," I heard James say.

Dusty hit the speaker. "James. We're with Cadence."

"Cadence?" His voice rose with excitement. "Can she hear me?"

"Yeah, you're on speaker."

"Good. How are you, beautiful?"

"I'm fine . . ." Dusty shoved me hard and I winced.

"Hey, what's going on?" James asked. "Cadence, you sound like you're in pain."

"Yeah, she's in pain," Dusty responded with a snarl. "I'm inflicting it on her. Do you wanna know what's been going on?"

Geri snatched the phone, hitting mute. "Dusty, you idiot! Don't tell him. He'll be crushed. Let's just work this out without him knowing. It'll be better that way. Think about James's feelings. He loves her so much that this will tear him apart."

Silence. Dusty stared into her eyes as she gazed steadily back, her jaw clenched.

"Hey, are you still there?" James's voice rang out from the phone.

Dusty hit the mute button again so James could hear. "Yeah."

"Is everything okay?"

"Yeah. It turns out she has rats. Big, dirty, greedy ones." He glared at me. "She can't afford a decent exterminator, so she's been dealing with rat traps. But they haven't been working, and she's been waking up with them in her bed."

I looked down in shame at his hidden meaning.

"Geez! That is pretty bad. I knew she had mice once, but not rats. I could send some money—"

"No need," Dusty said. "I'm going to take care of it."

He pushed harder into me, causing Geri to grab his arm and whisper, "Dusty, you're hurting her."

"Thanks, Dusty," James said. "And Cadence?"

"Yes?" I forced out.

"You don't need to be afraid to tell me things like that. I shouldn't have teased you about the mouse. That probably didn't help. I know you're trying to be independent and find your own feet, but everyone needs help sometimes."

"Thanks, James."

"I love you, beautiful."

"I love you, too."

Dusty hung up the phone, shoved it in his pocket, and turned on me. He grabbed my arms and slammed me against the wall again. "You selfish, lying slut! You told two guys you love them in the same half-hour!"

"That's because I do!" I yelled back.

"No, you don't!" He grabbed my hair and slammed my head against the wall.

"Dusty, stop it!" Geri grasped his elbow.

He ignored her. "Now, Cadence, you listen to me. You only love James. This other guy is just a rebellious streak or something. Tomorrow morning, he goes."

I stared Dusty firmly in the eyes. "I know I'm not being fair. I just need some time, and I won't be bullied into making my choice either."

"James is your soul mate."

I laughed shrilly. "You have no idea! You don't even know Austin. You don't have a clue how complex this is. They both could be, if I let them. I need to do this on my terms, *not* yours."

"Dusty, let her go," Geri said.

Dusty tilted his head to look at her. "She's been lying to us all, especially James."

"I don't think she's lying. I know her, and I believe her when she says there's more to this than she can explain. I remember her talking about Austin in ninth grade, so this is somehow all connected. There's always been something weird about the things she seems to just *know*, and I think this is part of it. Let her go, and let her make the decision on her own."

Geri was easily the best friend in the world.

Dusty let me go and stepped back, folding his arms. "If he comes around while we're here, I'll kill him."

I sighed. "I'll let him know."

A soft tapping on my window woke me. I lifted my phone to check the time, but I saw I had a text. I opened it and read the message from Austin.

I'M COMING OVER.

The tapping came again. Shuffling up in my bed, I pulled the curtains back to see him looking in at me. He popped off the screen while I unlocked and opened the window.

"What are you doing?"

"I had to make sure you were okay," he whispered. "Your brother seemed really upset, and when you sent me that text telling me to stay away for a few days, I was concerned."

Without any effort, he lifted himself up and through the window. I felt glad Geri took Lyla's bed instead of my floor, while Dusty slept on the couch.

Austin closed my window, then sat cross-legged on my bed. "I'll get the screen later."

"Austin, Dusty will kill you if he finds you here. He's seriously pissed at me. He'll have no problem with—"

He cut me off by kissing me, lowering me underneath him before breaking away to whisper, "So, what's going on?"

I sighed. "It's complicated."

He kissed the tip of my nose. "I'm listening."

I groaned. "It's just . . . you know about my high school boyfriend, right?"

"Right."

"Well, they want me to be with him, which is completely understandable because they both love him, especially Dusty, who sees him as a brother. It's just, it tears me apart, you know? I love you so much, but they don't see it because all they see is . . ." I paused, knowing I had to be careful with what I said. "He's a good person, Austin, and he's always treated me well, so they see me with him, and that's it."

He buried his face into my shoulder. "What can I do?"

"I don't know." I ran my fingers through his hair. I shut my eyes and remembered the years of marriage we'd shared and how happy I'd felt. "You mean everything to me—you've always meant everything to me. I wish I could explain that without hurting them."

He rolled onto his side, pulling me up against him as our legs entwined. "Why don't we all do something tomorrow? We could go out to Rottnest and do one of the biking trails?"

Dusty wouldn't be eager to agree, and I felt hesitant because of James. But if I wanted to get a clear gauge on if—under the new circumstances—my family could accept Austin, this would be the time.

"It would have to be handled carefully," I said. "And don't do any boyfriend things. We'll just be friends, okay?"

"Okay."

We fell asleep in each other's arms.

Thwack!

"You filthy pervert!" Dusty hollered. "Sneaking in through the window during the night!"

He hit Austin with my textbook again, but Austin grabbed it and jumped to his feet. Dusty backed away, sensing Austin's superior strength, but he kept his glare firmly locked on Austin. "She's *not* yours!"

"You need to get off her case and let her make her own decisions!" Austin said with a snarl. "How old are you, anyway? Seventeen, right? What makes you think you have any right to control your older sister?"

"What makes you think you have a right to jump in bed with her?"

I rushed over and forced my way between them. "Stop it!"

Dusty's arms wrapped around my waist, and he swung me around, blocking off Austin. "You stay away from her!"

Austin tore him off me and pinned him against the wall. "I don't want to fight you. Cadence explained to me what's going on, and I'm going to respect your feelings on this, but *you* need to respect hers. I'm in love with her. I'm not going to give up without a fight, no matter what you say."

Geri's hand wrapped around mine. I squeezed it, knowing she understood that I felt torn. Austin was just as bold and in love with me as James.

"Cadence," she whispered in my ear, "I'm so glad I'm not in your shoes. I wish I could help you."

Austin released Dusty and walked into the living room. "Now, let's make this a pleasant day, shall we? I was planning to take us all biking out at Rottnest Island, so, Dusty, go get some comfortable shoes on, because I'm going to kick your trash out there."

Dusty's gaze flew up, and his nostrils flared. He had the same competitive streak as me, and Austin just slapped it in the face. Austin, sensing he had pushed Dusty's buttons the same way he pushed mine, smirked and pulled off his shirt. With Austin's chest exposed, Dusty stood taller and stuck out his chest. Being nowhere near as big, he held his shirt down as Austin walked by us and into my room to grab his clothes.

"Oh my gosh," Geri said, wheezing. "He's so built."

Dusty threw her a filthy look before grabbing his clothes and rushing into the bathroom.

Geri followed me as I returned to my bedroom, and stared at Austin's chest. "Wow! How can I make Dusty get one of those?"

"Diving," Austin and I said in unison.

Geri cleared her throat, and offered her hand. "I'm Geraldine Turner."

He took her hand and gave her a crooked smile. "Austin Jones. It's a pleasure to finally meet you."

"Oh my gosh," she squeaked. "I think I'm falling in love, too."

He laughed, and just for effect, he kissed her hand. "You are quite lovely yourself, but alas, my heart is already taken. I have a thing for blondes, after all."

I scoffed. "You do not. You dated a brunette and a redhead before me."

He lifted me off my feet. "Yes, and they never quite made the cut, did they? But you, oh, you dazzled me from the moment I laid eyes on you."

My heart skipped a beat as he moved closer to kiss me.

"You did that to James, too," Geri whispered.

My heart fell, and I turned away from the kiss.

Austin kissed my cheek instead and said, "Well, she's incredible."

I blushed as our eyes met and he smiled.

The boat ride out to the island was silent. Dusty sat back, smoldering, his glare burning into Austin's back. Geri sat between Dusty and me. She kept shuffling while refusing to make eye contact with anyone.

Austin pulled into a dock. We alighted and followed him toward the bike rentals. Once we had our bikes and a map, Dusty shot off, determined to beat Austin to our picnic place. Austin sighed and mounted slowly. "He's really determined to hate me, huh?"

"It's not you," I answered.

He shrugged. "I guess I'll have to take some shortcuts to keep him in his place." He gave me a quick peck on the lips before hurrying away.

Geri and I moved much slower. She wanted me to hang back with her so she could talk to me, and I was more than willing to oblige. Once we'd mounted our bikes and made our way across the island, she spoke. "I don't really know what to think about you right now."

I sighed. "I know. I really believed James had broken up with me. Then, when he called me apologizing, I tried to break up with him, but when I went to do it, he just . . ."

"I understand," she said after a pause. "I didn't want to like Austin when I saw him with you last night. In fact, I hated him. But he's nice, and just as good for you as James. But I love James, and you've always loved James. So . . . what are you going to do?"

For a moment, I considered calling for my angel, but I remembered him telling me it wasn't his place to tell me which choices to make. "What do you think, Geri?"

She groaned. "I'll always say James, but it's not my choice. When I saw you and Austin together earlier, and the way he looked at you, and you him, I knew your love was real. So maybe you should choose him? But then again, you and James have exchanged that same look hundreds of times."

"You're not helping me at all."

She chuckled. "I could offer myself up as a sacrifice, but I don't think Dusty would be too happy with that."

I laughed and hurried to change the topic to her relationship with Dusty. Her whole face lit up as she went on and on about it, and we laughed at how my dad had no idea how to react to it. He'd always been protective of Geri, since she was in our home so much, but seeing her with his only son sent him into a fierce internal conflict. He didn't know which one he needed to protect the most, and usually just yelled at them both and walked away.

When we arrived at the beach, Dusty sat in the sand sulking with his knees under his chin while Austin set up the picnic.

"What's up with him?" Geri asked.

Austin smirked. "I beat him by almost five minutes."

"He really is just as bad as you, Cay-Cay." She walked over and sat beside him.

Austin's index finger ran down my arm. "Everything good between you and Geri?"

I nodded, smiling. "She's the best friend in the world."

He wrapped his arm around my waist and pulled me against him. "You only deserve the best."

He nibbled on my earlobe, making me giggle.

Dusty shoved him, knocking us apart. "I'm hungry, woman-stealer."

Austin pursed his lips, but didn't respond.

When the day was finally over, and Austin dropped us off at the flat and went home, Geri wrapped her arm through mine as we walked inside. "Cay, I love you no matter what."

My chin quivered as tears welled in my eyes. "Thank you, Geri."

"I don't," Dusty said, folding his arms as he flopped onto the couch. "I pretty much hate you right now."

His words stung. I pulled away, slamming the door to my bedroom behind me.

Chapter Eighteen

Geri made sure James wasn't told about Austin. She was by far the most understanding person when the news came out to my family. When Dad called me, furious, I could hardly speak.

"Cadence, you better explain yourself to me."

Being home on my own, I curled up on the couch to whisper, "It's complicated. Please, it's not—"

"You're cheating!" he yelled. "It's not complicated. Being lonely is no excuse, since you're the one who left."

A lump formed in my throat.

"How long has this been going on?"

"Dad—"

"No, I don't want to know. But it ends right now. How could you do this to James? How could you lie to all of us?"

I covered my face as I cried. "I'm not doing this to anyone. I've tried—"

"You most certainly are! You will end this affair tonight, do you hear me? Before that boy finds out what you've done. He's been nothing but loyal to you, and this is how you repay him?"

I sobbed. "I didn't mean to."

The line fell silent as I cried onto the throw pillow.

"Cadence?" he said gently. "Don't be *that girl*. If this is about you finding yourself, about knowing if James is right for you or not, then you're doing it all wrong. When things get hard between me and your mother, we resolve it between us. We never step out on one another. That's not an appropriate way to solve things."

"I know," I whispered.

"Then end this. Promise me."

I squeezed my eyes shut. I could've easily agreed and kept going, but that would've been lying. I had to figure out on my own—in my own way—what I needed to do. Who I needed to choose. "Dad . . ."

"Yes?"

"I'm so confused."

"There's no need to be."

"But there is. There's so much . . ." My voice cracked. "You don't understand. *I* don't even understand everything. I won't break up with Austin. I have to sort out my feelings on my own."

His rage exploded. He yelled all kinds of foul things at me, demanding I end it with Austin. Mum was sorely disappointed in me, and later would only reply to my emails in short, single sentences. I never heard from Harper, so I wondered if they even told her.

Austin was incredibly understanding. One night, after another huge fight with Dad, he took my hand while I cried and drove me to his family home. When we arrived, he parked in the driveway and waited as I gained control of myself. "Cadence?"

"Yeah?" I rubbed my eyes.

"Do you . . . I mean . . ." He sighed. "I'm here for you no matter what, so if you feel like you need some time to help your family adjust, then I'll step back."

I gasped as my gaze shot up to him. "You wanna break up with me?"

Alarm flashed through his eyes. "No! That's not what I meant. I just . . ." He sighed again. "I love you so much, and I feel like I'm causing you grief."

I clasped his hand. "You're not causing me grief. You make me happy."

He smiled and squeezed my hand. "That's all that matters to me. I hate seeing you so sad all the time."

I took a sharp breath. "I've been a real downer, haven't I?"

He leaned forward and caressed my face. "No. Just, when your family gets on your case, you hurt for several hours afterward. I wish I could take it away and just see you smiling all the time."

I smiled, which made him smile.

"Come on. Mum's making stroganoff. I'm sure that will cheer you up."

Oh! Linda's stroganoff! I shot out of the car.

Austin rushed up behind me, chuckling. "Wow, you're eager."

"I love stroganoff!" *Especially Linda's.*

We entered his home, and I smiled at the warm, cozy, familiar feel of it. They lived in a lovely home in South Fremantle with three bedrooms, a living room at the entrance, and a kitchen that opened up to a family room with a huge flat screen and a pool table. A large, brown leather couch sat against the wall facing the TV, where George worked on his laptop.

Linda noticed us enter first as she pulled the stroganoff out of the oven. "Oh, Austin! You've brought us a lovely guest."

I smiled and rushed over to her. She set down the dish and hugged me. "Hello, sweetie."

"How are you, Linda?"

"Wonderful. Austin tells me you've been having some troubles with your family."

I slumped. "Yeah."

"Not to worry. When they meet him, they'll see what a good boy he is and everything will be fine."

She smiled up at me, making my heart fill with hope. Yes, I'd always loved Linda.

"Austin, have you set the table?" George asked, not looking up.

"Dad," Austin huffed, but hurried to do his chore. "You know, I'm not a kid anymore."

Linda chuckled and kissed his cheek. "You'll always be my boy."

I smiled warmly at their interaction.

We sat together at the table and fell into an easy conversation about school. Austin was doing very well, which wasn't surprising. He was far brighter than me, and the only reason I earned better marks in my own course was because I already knew it. I felt so proud of him as he explained things way beyond my comprehension. Linda's pride in him sparkled in her eyes.

Once I finished my first plate, I dug in for seconds. "Linda, this is divine!"

She laughed. "Thank you, Cadence."

"No, seriously, you should sell it."

She beamed. "I'm very flattered."

"You need to show me how you make it, because wow!"

Austin laughed. "I'd sure like to have you . . ." He stopped and shook his head.

George glanced at him and changed the subject. "So, Cadence, what do you hope to do with your degree?"

I swallowed my mouthful so I could answer. "A lot of people become PE teachers or coaches, but I wanna get on staff with an AFL team."

He nodded thoughtfully. "You should try to get in with my team, the Dockers."

I grinned. After I graduated before, I was put on staff with the Fremantle Dockers. "I can certainly try."

"Dad is obsessed with them," Austin said. "A few weekends ago, when they played Sydney and lost, he told me I had to break up with you because he didn't want a Sydney girl around!" Austin laughed merrily. "Mum slapped him and made him apologize before she reminded him it's just a game."

George grunted. "Stupid Swans. Buncha cheaters."

I smirked. "At least they don't have the refs on their side like the Melbourne teams do."

George raised his eyebrows and laughed. "True! Oh, those Melbourne teams—"

"Look what you've started," Austin grumbled. "This is one of his favorite soapboxes: unfair refs. He goes on and on about it every time one of the Melbourne teams plays the Dockers."

"Well, it's appalling." George folded his arms.

"We know, dear," Linda said, patting his arm.

George met my gaze and nodded. "I'll take you to a game sometime. Would you like that?"

I grinned. "I sure would."

George's eyes gleamed, and I knew he was sold on me.

Austin wrapped his arm around me. "Are you trying to steal my girl?"

George waved his fork at him. "No, I'm trading in kids. At least she's interested in football. All you ever did was complain, when I took you."

"But I never complained when you took me diving."

George smirked. "Ah, you have me there. Okay, I guess I'll keep ya."

I smiled as they continued their friendly banter, and after a short while, Linda returned to the kitchen. I decided to follow her, and found her preparing a bowl of custard while heating a sticky date pudding.

"Oh!" She smiled as I entered. "What are you doing in here?"

"I thought maybe you'd like some help."

She shook her head. "No, this is very easy. Go back in with Austin."

I leaned over the counter instead. "How much has Austin told you about what's going on with my family?"

She met my gaze and sighed. "All of it, dear."

My gaze fell. "Oh."

"But"—she touched my cheek so I'd look at her—"I know you love him, and he loves you. Once they see what you have, they'll be as happy as George and I are for you."

"You think so?"

"I know so." Her gaze lifted over my shoulder. "She's still here, Austin, don't worry."

I looked back as he wrapped his arms around my waist. He smiled as our eyes met, and my heart melted.

Later, we went into his room. The decor, with everything ocean-based, was very different from James's: his books were all about coral and marine life, his bedding was dark blue, and the one picture hung on the wall was of a yacht. On his bedside table rested a small picture frame.

While he talked about the time he and George found themselves diving with a great white shark, I turned the picture around to look at it. "Oh!"

He turned to me. "What?"

I lifted the picture of me grinning in a wet suit after my first diving lesson with him. "You framed this?"

He plucked it from my hands and blushed. "Yeah, it was a good day, and you look gorgeous in it."

I hadn't known that in the first timeline. I stepped toward him and slid the picture from his hand. "You think I'm gorgeous in a wet suit with ratty, wet hair?"

He smiled down at me as his breath grew shallow. "You're always gorgeous, especially when you smile like that."

I leaned closer to him and wrapped my arm around his waist. "Like what?"

His hands shot to my face and he planted his lips firmly against mine. I moaned as I pressed against him, my feelings for him pulsing through me. I broke away and asked softly, "Austin, why do you love me?"

He met my gaze. "How could you even ask me that? Cadence, you're everything I've ever dreamed of and more."

He tried to kiss me again, but I pulled back. "But why? I've never understood how someone as amazing as you could love me."

He stroked my cheek. "Because you're smart, and sweet, and charming, and have this crazy side to you that completely throws me off guard."

I leaned forward to kiss him, but he continued. "Sometimes, I wonder that about you too. How could someone like you love someone like me? Then I just feel grateful that you somehow do."

I ran my fingers through his hair as he shut his eyes and sighed. "Austin?"

"Mmm?"

"I love you so much."

A wide smile spread across his face as his eyes opened to meet mine. "Cadence, I don't think I'll ever stop loving you."

He leaned down and kissed me.

Chapter Nineteen

Spring flew by, and the end of the semester rapidly approached. I dreaded going home for Christmas, and Austin knew it. Being privy to all the drama and fights with my family, he'd done everything he could to ease my mind.

Meanwhile, despite my best efforts, James kept persevering. I hated the idea of breaking up with him in any other way than in person, and knew he deserved that, but he made it so hard. I'd start our conversations closed off, trying to push him away, but he always ended up making me laugh and pulling me back in.

"Did you know Geri and Dusty are taking a trip next year?" he told me, as I tried my hardest to get off the phone to study. "Geri's pushing for Europe, but Dusty's dead set on the United States."

"I know. Geri told me," I said, distracted.

"We should go with them."

I hesitated. "I have uni, but you can go. You'll have graduated."

"And be a third wheel? No thanks. You know they'll be all over each other."

I couldn't help grinning. I loved that they were together.

"They can be so full on, but then they'll flip and be really distant. I think that's Geri, though. Dusty's all go in that relationship."

I chuckled. "Yeah, Geri's still wary. She's into him, but she's still worried about his age. I think when he finishes his HSC she'll be more open to moving forward."

"I'm glad his exams are all at the beginning then, because he's driving me crazy."

I smirked, giggling as I leaned back in my chair.

"Oh, hey, I saw Michael today."

"No way." I sat up straight. "How's he doing?"

"Great. He's doing some super brainy four-year engineering course at Sydney Uni. You really did hang out with a bunch of nerds. I had no idea. I thought I was dating a popular chick."

"Shut up!" I laughed.

"Seems I was wrong. He told me that other group that sat by the football field was the popular group. How did the most beautiful girl in school not end up in the popular group?"

"Because I dated a loser." I shook my head, slipping onto my bed.

"Ouch. Poor Tyler."

"Tyler?"

"You dated him before me. I didn't know you until after you'd joined the nerds."

"Oh my gosh." I flopped back on the pillow. "But you joined your grade's nerds."

"Because I thought *they* were the cool kids." He sighed. "I trusted you too much."

My heart sank. "Yeah, you probably did."

"But it all worked out. I'm about to graduate university! How insane is that?"

"I'm proud of you," I said honestly. Despite everything, I truly meant it. I wanted James to be happy and successful with his life, even if it meant living without me.

"Thanks, beautiful. That means everything to me."

Tears rolled down my cheeks. Hearing him talk like that weakened my resolve. With James filling my heart, I considered breaking up with Austin after our conversation.

But then, I saw Austin again. He grinned as he approached me in the campus corridor. "There's my gorgeous woman."

I stopped, dodging his gaze as I bit my lip.

He kissed my cheek as we ignored the people passing by. "You had another confrontation, didn't you?"

How could I answer that? How could I say I was struggling with my feelings between him and someone else, when he, like James, treated me so wonderfully? I grew frustrated and confused, not wanting to be unfair to them.

"Everything will work out." He slid his arm around my waist as he tucked my hair behind my ear. "I love you, no matter what, so I'll be here for you."

I wrapped my arms around his neck, burying my face into his shoulder. "You're so wonderful."

I had to resolve my feelings, and I needed to do it soon. Why did they both have to be so perfect for me?

Why did I have to love them both?

On our weekly Friday night date, Austin pointed suddenly at my handbag during dinner. "Is that your phone?"

"Hmm?" I glanced down in my bag and saw James across the phone's screen. "Oh!"

I snatched it up, hoping Austin hadn't seen it.

He chuckled. "Are you going to answer it?"

"Yes." I smiled, but felt nervous at the same time. I pressed the answer button. "Hey."

"Hello, beautiful," came James's chipper voice.

"Hey, I can't talk right now. Can I call you back?"

"Ah . . . okay. Is everything all right? You sound kinda edgy."

"Sorry, I'm just distracted."

"Okay. Call me when you can. I miss you, and I love you."

"You too. Bye." I hung up rather abruptly, and hoped James hadn't noticed.

"Who was that?" Austin asked casually as he took a bite of his salmon.

"One of my friends from high school."

"Geri?"

"No."

"Michael?"

"No."

"Ah . . ." He gazed at me and tilted his head. "I don't think you've mentioned any others."

"It was James." I watched his face to see how he'd react.

"Oh." He grinned at me. "Nothing I should be worried about, right?"

My stomach tied in a tight knot. He apparently didn't remember the one time James was mentioned as being my boyfriend. "Ah . . ."

He chuckled. "So, anyway, I wanted to discuss something with you."

"And what's that?"

"I'm planning on going with you for Christmas."

If it could have, my jaw would have hit the floor with a thud. I couldn't believe that, despite my family's contempt for him, he still planned on coming with me, just like in the first timeline, to . . .

Oh my gosh . . .

"Do you think that's such a good idea?" I asked, knowing I needed to break up with James first.

He nodded. "I do. I think if they see how much I love you, then they won't be so concerned anymore. Plus, I . . ." He cleared his throat and dropped his gaze.

Oh no . . . *oh no!*

"Cadence, let's go for a walk after dinner, okay?"

"S-sure."

We made our way to the beach and watched the sun set over the ocean. He held me against him as we walked, until we found a quiet place and sat together. He stroked my hair as I leaned against his shoulder. I sighed, contented until he spoke. "Cadence, you're the best thing that's ever happened to me."

I held my breath, knowing what was about to happen.

"I'm so in love with you that nothing else seems to matter in comparison to being at your side. You're beautiful, and smart, and sweet, and I just can't get enough of you." He paused as his hand slid into his pocket, and he hesitated. "You love me too, don't you?"

"Yes," I answered breathlessly.

His eyes flashed with hope, and his hand slipped out of his pocket. "I've been meaning to ask you this for a while, but I've been a bit nervous that you might reject me." He took my left hand. "Cadence Anderson, will you marry me?"

I thought my heart would leap out of my chest as he slid on my engagement ring. All thoughts of James rushed out of my mind, and my memories and feelings from the first timeline consumed me. Those three diamonds on a yellow-gold band with an intricate design holding them together were so familiar and so beloved . . . . I lifted my hand to examine it. "Austin!"

"I know we haven't talked about it or anything, but I love you, and I want to take care of you for the rest of my life. That's why I want to go with you for Christmas—so I can ask your dad's permission."

He had done everything *exactly* the same. I couldn't believe it. It suddenly felt like everything that happened since the first time I'd experienced this moment just vanished. I clasped his face and answered the same way I did before. "Oh, Austin! Yes, yes, yes!"

A fleeting smile swept across his face before he kissed me. He laid me back on the cool sand as he kissed me passionately, his fingers weaving through those of my left hand. My stomach filled with butterflies. My Austin, my husband.

He took me back to the flat, but with Lyla there, he didn't stay. He gave me a long kiss goodnight by the door before we tore ourselves apart. He watched me as I stepped inside and said, "I love you, Cadence."

I shut the door behind me and sighed, clutching my heart.

"Hey, Barbie," Lyla said from the couch. "How'd it go?"

"Perfect," I sighed.

She swung around, and her gaze fell on my hands over my heart. "Oh my gosh!" She jumped up and grabbed my left hand. "No way!"

I bit my lip and grinned like a school girl.

"You have to tell Tara right now or she'll *kill* you!"

I giggled. "I better get on it." I rushed into my bedroom and called Tara.

She shrieked with delight. "You and Austin! I can't believe it! I never would have picked him to be one of the first to marry from our grade. But this is seriously amazing."

I giggled.

"You know, I get all the credit for this. I made this happen."

I laughed. "Yes, thank you."

She squealed. "Dibs on bridesmaid."

We talked for about half an hour. After hanging up, I lay on my bed and raised my hand to stare at the ring. It looked just as beautiful as I remembered. I daydreamed of what was to come and all the happy times we had ahead.

My phone rang. I fumbled through my handbag, pulled it out, and looked at the caller ID. *James.* I almost vomited. My finger trembled as I hit answer.

"Hello, beautiful. Are you still busy?"

"No," I answered softly.

"Good, because I really want to discuss something with you."

"Oh."

He chuckled. "Are you sure you're not busy, because you sound distracted."

"No . . . no, I'm getting ready for bed." I really needed to stop lying to him. He didn't deserve this.

"I have some great news."

"What's that?"

"It looks like I'm going to be graduating with honors!"

I sat up, feeling a rush of excitement for him. "James, that's wonderful!"

"I know, right? And it's all thanks to you. You inspired me, Cadence, you always have. And I want you to know that things are lining up for me to move out there in March, once I've received my diploma. I'll be bachelorified."

I giggled at his made-up word.

"Ah, Cadence, life is looking up. I'm so excited. Finally, we'll be together again."

I rubbed at my eyes as tears started to form. "James?"

"Yeah?"

"You shouldn't be with me."

There was a long pause. "Cadence, don't you dare start that again."

"Really, I mean it. I . . . I cheated on you."

There was another long pause before he said, in a low voice, "What?"

"That's why I was acting so strange. I thought you broke up with me, and then when you called me and it turned out we hadn't . . . it was why I tried to break up with you. That was the rat in my bed Dusty was talking about."

He swore loudly over and over. "Cadence! No!"

"I'm sorry, James!" Tears streamed down my cheeks. But I felt relieved to come clean. He deserved better than to be treated the way I was treating him. I loved him too much. He kept swearing, over and over, while I silently wept. "The guilt has been eating at me. You deserve better than me."

"No!" he said fiercely. "Just . . . no! You just won't do it again. It's because we've been apart for so long, that's all. You'll be here soon for Christmas and you'll see, you'll remember how we are. I'm not going to let you go. We're going to get married, and have beautiful babies, and live happily ever after. This is just a roadblock. I mean, we've been together for so long, it kinda makes sense you'd wanna try something else. But we're in love—we'll make it work."

I cried softly into my hands. He wasn't going to let me go. I yanked off my ring and tossed it across the room. What had I done? How could I choose Austin over James?

"You still have your ring, don't you?" he asked.

"Yes."

"Then wear it. Make it clear you're taken so guys don't try anything on you again."

"James, I'm a terrible person. You can do better."

"No, you're not!" he said firmly. "There's no one better than you. Stop trying to protect me and push me away."

I sniffed, struggling to compose myself. "Why do I have to love you so much?"

He let out a long sigh and his tone softened. "Cadence, I love you too. When you get here, everything will go back to normal, I promise."

"Okay, James."

"Cadence?"

"Yes?"

"I forgive you."

Loud sobs burst from me, and I buried my face in my pillow to smother them.

"Everything will be okay. I love you so much. I'll let you go now, okay? I know that you'll need some time."

"Okay," I whispered through my sobs. He really deserved better than me. I couldn't believe he forgave me so easily.

The connection cut off as I continued sobbing into my pillow. What was I going to *do*? I had been so certain I had chosen Austin until James called. But I had to choose one of them, and soon. Both of them just laid their hearts on the line for me.

I jumped up, plucked Austin's ring from the floor, and whipped James's ring out of my jewelry box. They both looked so beautiful and represented perfectly my relationship with each of them—with James, beauty, passion, and endurance, while with Austin, a simple, classic elegance. I slipped on one ring, then the other. I pulled them on and off until I became mad with conflict. I tossed them both onto the desk and rushed out of the flat.

"Cadence? What's wrong?" Lyla called after me, but I didn't stop.

I rushed to my car and sped to the nearest beach. I needed to clear my head. I needed to escape and sort out exactly how I felt.

I stumbled down the sand, my mind spinning. James still wanted marriage, and Austin planned on coming with me to visit my parents, to ask Dad for permission to marry me. My parents hadn't even accepted Austin yet. They still thought I should be with James.

I found a quiet place among the rocks and pulled out my phone. I had to talk to someone.

"Hey, Cay." Harper yawned. "You realize we're two hours ahead, right?"

"Harper, I really need to talk to you."

"Are you okay?" Her voice reflected a more alert tone.

I started to cry.

"Oh my . . . Daniel!" I heard her husband in the background. "I need to talk to Cadence. I'll just go in the next room."

I heard some shuffling, and the sound of a door closing, then: "What's going on?"

"I'm . . . I'm . . ."

"Cadence, I need words."

"*I'm in love with two guys!*"

Pause. "What?"

"I'm in love with James still, so much, but . . ." I bit my lip and rubbed my eyes. "I'm in love with Austin, too."

"Who's Austin?"

"I'm surprised no one told you. I met him here. He's amazing, and he wants to come back with me over the holidays, to ask Dad to marry me."

"Cadence, how did this happen?"

"It just did."

"But why were you looking around in the first place? Were you bored with James or something?"

"No! James is so wonderful, I just . . ." I rubbed my eyes.

"Just what, Cadence?" She wasn't angry at all, but patient, wanting to understand.

"There's just some things I can't explain. I loved Austin before I even met him, so when he came along, all I could see was him, and when I'm with him, there's only him. But then, when I'm with James, it's the same."

"Oh, Cadence."

"I know!" I sobbed.

She sighed. "Try to think about it differently. Who can't you live without?"

I paused and carefully considered her question. They both fulfilled me so completely. I pulled my hair with frustration. "Both of them."

"You can't *be* with both of them."

"I know!" I growled. "It's just . . . I know what life with Austin will bring. We'll have a family together and be so happy, but James—I don't know."

"You've been with James for years. How can you not know? How would he be any different to what he is now? Why couldn't he give you those same things?"

She was rooting for James; that was obvious, and not surprising.

"Tell me what to do," I said.

"Oh, Cay, I can't do that," she said in a gentle voice. "It's your life, so you have to decide on this one."

"You're no help."

She huffed. "I know. I'm the big, bad sister."

"No . . . I'm sorry."

"It's okay. I get that you're torn up right now. You just have to be really honest with yourself. Who will make you the happiest?"

I didn't answer.

"Well, it's late here, and I'm not sleeping well as it is. So, call me if you need to talk some more."

"Thanks, Harper."

"No worries, baby girl."

I hung up and hit my phone against my forehead over and over. How could I choose one over the other? They both meant so much to me. James intoxicated me. He captivated me with just a gleam in his eye. He had been my best friend through thick and thin, had endured my dad's wrath just to be with me.

But Austin was the reason I had done *everything*. I had a deep love for him that grabbed my heart and clutched it tightly. Those years of blissful marriage tugged at me, and the memories of him playing and laughing with Melody filled my heart. I couldn't forget that. I couldn't forget our baby and how much joy we'd shared.

I jumped to my feet and yelled, "Angel!"

A bright flash made me shield my eyes, and the sea foam and waves crashing toward the rocks froze in midair.

The man in white stood in front of me, his pure white clothing blinding me with its glow.

"Yes, sweet Cadence?"

"What do I do?"

"I've told you before, I can't advise you on this."

"How do I choose?" I screamed at him. "This is insane! I love them both the same amount, but in different ways. I can't . . . It's just . . . I can save Austin if I stay with him, and we can live out the life we had taken away from us."

The man frowned. "Cadence, your contract states that you cannot change fixed moments in time."

My jaw wagged soundlessly. I stepped closer to him. "What does that mean?"

"You cannot save Austin."

I jumped back, alarmed. "But all of this, I did all of this to save him. You said—"

"I never said you could save Austin. I agreed that he would be alive again, and yes, you can save Melody, but no matter what happens, Austin will die that day. Whether you choose him or not."

I stumbled back onto a rock in shock. "But . . ."

"That's why you were given James." He moved closer and gazed steadily into my eyes. "So you had an alternative from the sorrow and grief. James isn't meant to die for many years, but Austin's fate is sealed."

"But why?"

His gaze fell, and he turned away from me. "Not all fixed events are major disasters. There are many small events that are necessary for the world to continue on its planned course."

"Then my choice is obvious," I said softly. "I choose Austin."

He swung around and gazed at me, wide-eyed. His voice rose as he said, "Even though you know he *will* die? Even though James won't leave you a widow at twenty-five? Even if you risk losing James entirely and being alone?"

"Yes."

The man rested his hands on his hips, his expression stone cold. "Why?"

"Because I love Austin, and I want him to be happy. He gave so much for me, and even sacrificed his life trying to save our daughter's. I can't let him live out these last few years with a broken heart, and never give him the two things that made him happier than anything else: Melody and me. If he's going to die, then I want him to die happy."

"So you choose him out of *pity*?"

"No! I choose him because *I love him,* and he deserves to be loved by someone he loves. I will gladly stand over his grave and grieve, if I can just have another five years of marriage with him."

The angel glared right into my face, his dark eyes burning. "You were given James to save you from this grief! Do you mock this gift by turning your nose up at it?"

I gazed steadily into his eyes. "If that's how you see it, then so be it. But I choose my husband all over again. Austin deserves nothing less than the happiest last few years I can give him."

The man in white stepped back, his teeth bared. "Then you will suffer from watching him die again and, more significantly, *you will lose James.*"

"I understand completely what I stand to lose, but no matter what, I'm staying with Austin."

He vanished, leaving an outline of his bright light in my retinas. Blinking, I tried to regain my night vision as the waves fell crashing over the rocks.

Chapter Twenty

We celebrated our engagement at Austin's home. George sat watching the TV, yelling at the screen every so often, while Linda chuckled and shook her head.

"Hey, Dad," Austin said, stepping in front of the TV.

"Move it, kid," George responded with a growl.

"Cricket's boring."

"I can still discipline you, if I want."

Austin laughed. "Come on, Dad! Cadence is here because we're celebrating our engagement. The game isn't going to go down the crapper if you look away for half an hour."

"It just might. You know—"

Linda cleared her throat. "Dinner's ready."

We shuffled in around the table and laughed together. Linda kept tapping my hand and squeezing it, while Austin's hand, when he wasn't eating, stroked my leg.

The phone rang. Austin shot up and rushed over. "Mal?"

George and Linda fell silent.

"What do you . . ." Austin huffed. "Just once, Mal, this is . . . . No, I'm not throwing my life away on some . . ." His brows furrowed as he glanced at me. "Ah . . ." He turned his back to us. "Fine, just fine! I try to reach out to you, and this is what I get? . . . Dad's gone. He doesn't want anything to do with us . . . . Whatever, bye."

Austin returned and flopped into his chair. The room fell dead silent. Austin glanced at me and sighed. "At least your family wants to be involved, even if they don't approve."

I rubbed his shoulder. "I'm sorry, Austin."

He shrugged. "No big deal. I never see him, anyway. He's on another hunt for Dad and refuses to meet you unless we go join him. It's so pointless." He glanced at Linda. "Sorry, Mum."

She smiled. "It's okay. I have George now."

After the meal, Austin rushed to the bathroom. Linda wrapped her arm around my shoulders as she guided me back into the family room. "I'm sorry about Mal. He was once a nice boy like Austin, but when his father left, he changed, and when his wife divorced him, he only got worse."

"That must break your heart," I said.

She nodded. "But he's a grown man now, so what can I do? I'm just grateful Austin isn't that way, and that he found you."

I smiled. "I'm grateful I found him, too."

The toilet flushed, and then Austin's door slammed. Staring down the hallway, I wondered if I should go see him.

"So, Cadence," Linda said with a sigh, gently guiding me toward the couch. "When will we get to meet your parents?"

Half an hour later, Austin returned. When he came back, he was red-faced and irritable as he sat beside me and folded his arms. I rested my hand on his thigh and gently squeezed it. His gaze fell to my hand before he wrapped his arm around me protectively and kissed my head. "I'm sorry about my brother. He can be so . . ."

"I'm sorry, Austin."

He sighed. "Well, what can you do?"

Austin fell asleep on the plane to Sydney. I felt so nervous and afraid, and I'd made it a point not to let James know when I would be landing. I'd arranged for Harper to pick us up, as she was eager to meet the man who "stole my heart from James."

When I saw her, her belly—she'd always been so slender—popped right out in the front. Her face lit up when she saw me, and I ran into her arms. "Harper!"

"Cay! It's so good to see you again."

"Look at you!" I beamed, running my hand over her belly.

"I know. My body is completely destroyed now, so I might as well have a soccer team."

I laughed. "Still a bit sore about it being a boy?"

"You have no . . ." Her gaze lifted over my shoulder and her jaw fell. "*Wow*."

Austin's hand appeared beside me. "Austin Jones. You must be the infamous Harper."

She blushed. "Holy cow!" She grabbed his hand. "It's nice to meet you."

He laughed and rested his hand on the small of my back. "Cadence has told me a lot about you."

Her blush deepened. "Ah, well, I'm sure she's exaggerating."

He grinned. "I doubt it."

Harper nearly melted. She didn't react like this to him the first time. In fact, I couldn't recall her reacting to him at all. As he turned away from us to head toward the bag collection, I slapped her shoulder. "Stop it."

"Oh my gosh!" she said under her breath. "Okay, James was always a hottie, but he's, like, *wow*! Nice trade-in."

I scowled. "It wasn't a trade-in. It just happened."

"Cadence, hon, he's smoking hot! I *really* approve, but you and James were tight. Are you sure you want to do this?"

I nodded. "Austin is the best choice for me. I love him so much . . . and not just because he's hot." I grinned, seeing her eyebrows rise. "James is very attractive too, it's just . . . I want to be Austin's happiness. I can't explain it."

She sighed. "Dad's prepped to rip him apart."

"I'm not surprised."

We paused and our jaws dropped as he lifted both our suitcases over his shoulders. *Show off.* He approached us, smirking, and I rolled my eyes. "You ladies ready?"

"Mmmhmm." Harper gazed at him dreamily.

"Harper, think Daniel. *Daniel.*" I said slowly.

She blushed and shook it off. "Let's go."

Austin behaved like his usual charming self the whole way to my parents', while Harper remained beside herself as he won her over.

When we pulled into the street, I took a deep breath. Austin squeezed my shoulder and grinned. He looked far less nervous than I felt. He nodded to my ring, and I slipped it off and handed it to him. He needed to talk to Dad before we made our engagement public.

We pulled up and climbed from the car. Austin went around and pulled our bags out as he gazed up at the house.

"So this is the place you grew up." He rolled the bags behind him as he stepped up beside me. "Are you ready, sweet Cadence?"

"Why do you seem to pick guys who give you stupid pet names?" Harper asked under her breath.

We approached the front door, and Dusty stepped out. He leaned against the doorframe, glaring down at Austin.

Austin climbed the stairs to meet him. "Hello again, Dusty."

Dusty scoffed. "You're staying in Harper's room, where I have every intention of hog-tying you in your sleep before dragging your body down—"

"Stop it, Dusty," I said sharply.

"He disgusts me." Dusty marched back into the house.

I groaned. I understood how he felt, and that his loyalty remained with James, but that didn't mean I liked it.

Austin's fingers ran through my hair, catching my attention. Our eyes met and he smiled, kissing my forehead. "It'll be fine. He's only that way because he loves you."

I wrapped my arm around his waist, grateful for his understanding.

"Oh!"

I turned at the sound of Mum's voice. Her hand rested over her heart as she looked Austin over. "You must be—"

"Austin," he responded, with his friendliest smile. "And you are obviously Cadence's mother, Harmony. I can see where she gets her beauty."

Mum flushed. "Ah, I've heard that before, yes."

Crap, James always said that to her.

"Come in, please." She stepped back, holding the door open for us.

She watched Austin with narrow eyes as he passed, then glared at me. This wasn't a good start.

I took him to Harper's room, where he stared at the portrait on the ceiling.

"Hey, that's pretty amazing." He dumped his suitcase on the bed and tilted his head to look at it. "Did Harper paint this?"

"She sure did." I smiled as Harper stood back blushing.

"It's great. You can really feel the love in it. It must have been great growing up here."

"Most of the time," Harper responded, elbowing me in the ribs with a smirk.

"So, I'm feeling a bit gross from the flight," he said. "Where can I take a shower?"

We both pointed to the door down the hall. He whipped off his shirt, making Harper whimper softly, then grabbed the towel Mum left on the bed for him. Harper and I both stared at his exposed torso as he walked toward us.

"Thanks." He kissed me quickly, but then decided he wanted more and gave me a long, deep kiss.

Harper sighed wistfully as he pulled away. "Okay, Cadence. I'm sold."

While Austin took a shower and I unpacked, Dad arrived home. He came straight to my room and shut the door. "Cadence, we need to talk."

I sank onto the bed, waiting for him to rip into me, but he sighed and sat beside me instead.

"I know I've always been hard on you and James, but I believed you'd end up marrying him. This has shocked me beyond words. I can't believe *my* Cadence would cheat, and then have the gall to bring him here and flaunt him around."

My cheeks burned with shame as my gaze fell. "Dad, it's more complicated than that."

"No, it isn't. James has wanted to marry you for years. He asked me when you were still in high school! I'll admit, I'm glad you refused him that young, but I thought after some time you'd be ready and would accept. But this, you going off with some stranger, and for what? Because you were lonely, maybe?"

"No, Dad. Please, Austin—"

"I pursued her, sir."

I jumped at Austin's voice by the door. Dad shot to his feet and stood tall as he stuck out his chest. Austin rested his hands on his hips, linking his thumbs through the belt loops on his jeans and putting his shoulders back to show his size under his white t-shirt. He met Dad's gaze, refusing to be intimidated.

"When I first saw Cadence, I thought she was the most beautiful girl I'd ever seen, and I had to get to know her. To be honest, it took me a while to even get her to look at me, and when we had the opportunity to meet at a Christmas party last year, she was definitely hard to pin down."

He glanced over at me and smiled affectionately at the memory. "I don't know all the details about this guy everyone is set on her being with, and although she did resist me, I was persistent. I couldn't get her out of my head, and even after I'd been told she'd been in a very long relationship and would likely have a lot of baggage, it didn't matter. I *had* to know her.

"With the help of some mutual friends, we started talking, and she let me in. What I found was better than I could have ever hoped for, and I fell in love instantly. Cadence is amazing. She's bright, and warmhearted, and has this insane need to win at everything." He chuckled and gazed at me. "And more than anything, I want to marry her."

Dad took a sharp breath and stood taller. "You what?"

"I want to marry her." Austin met his gaze and stared firmly into it. "I know you don't know me, but she does, and she loves me. I'll do everything I can to make her my wife and look after her as long as I live.

"Now, I'm asking you, sir, to allow me to marry your daughter."

Dad's eyes narrowed on him. "No."

I jumped up beside him and grabbed his arm. "Dad!"

"I said no!" He shook me off.

"But, Dad, I love him!"

He prodded my chest. "You've already told me that once. It's starting to sound a bit fickle and hard to believe."

His words were a huge slap across my face. I fell back onto the bed, crying.

"Cadence." Austin stepped toward me, but Dad blocked him off.

"I want you out."

"Dad! Stop it!" I said pleadingly.

"*Shut up, Cadence!*" he yelled. I jumped, having never had him take that tone with me. "Apparently, I still need to protect you from yourself. This boy has swept you off your feet and made you lose your senses. He even admitted it!"

"That's *not* what he said!"

He ignored me and turned back to Austin, advancing on him, but Austin stood his ground. "I said, get out of my house."

"I won't leave without Cadence."

Dad grabbed him by the shirt to throw him against the wall, like he'd done to James many times, but Austin held his ground and shoved Dad back.

"I won't be bullied," Austin said in a calm voice. "Cadence warned me you would be ruthless, but I won't give up without a fight. She's already consented to marry me, so asking you is simply out of respect."

Dad's glare shot to me. "You *what*?"

"Yes, Dad, we're engaged," I responded.

He looked back at Austin and grabbed his hands to pull them off him. "Well then." Austin stepped back from him as he straightened his shirt. "Cadence, you must leave too."

I gasped. "Dad, you can't be serious!"

"I didn't raise you to be like *this*! The Cadence I raised is honest, and loyal, and doesn't go sneaking around and getting engaged in secret."

"Dad, I—"

"No! I don't want to even look at you!"

We fell silent as I stared at him, gaping, tears streaming down my cheeks. "Dad, please . . ."

He walked down the hallway. "You have twenty minutes to repack and be out of here."

Austin rushed to me and caught my shoulders as I sank onto the bed in despair. "We'll fix this."

I shook my head. "No, I've screwed up worse than ever."

"No, you haven't. We'll go find a hotel and try again tomorrow once things have cooled off a bit. I won't let you lose your family over this. They love you, I know they do, so we just need to give them some time to adjust."

He packed up my suitcase again. "It'll be fine. You'll—"

"I'm not going to let you leave," Dusty said from behind Austin. Austin turned to look up at him as he continued. "I heard what you said, and I think, maybe, if you love her that much, I could talk Dad into letting you stay."

I gasped. "Dusty—"

His gaze lifted to me, and I saw sorrow in his eyes. "I love you, Cay, and although James is like my brother, you come first. And knowing you tried to resist makes me feel like I do still know you, and you weren't just looking around."

He grabbed my hand and pulled me to my feet. "Come on, let's have it out with Dad together."

As he wrapped his arm around my shoulders, I smiled at him. I had my brother back, and as he looked back at Austin and cocked his head for him to follow, I knew he would accept him too.

We walked out to the living room, united as we stood in front of Mum and Dad for the showdown.

Chapter Twenty-One

Screaming and yelling filled the house. Finger-pointing and accusations flew as the fight turned into loud, jumbled noise. Mum and Dad yelled, Dusty and I yelled louder, and Harper even joined in. The only person not making a sound was Austin. He remained silent, but kept a supportive arm around my waist.

"This is disgraceful!" Dad yelled.

"Dad, you're being ridiculous!" Harper hollered.

"I can't even look at you right now!" Mum sobbed, waving her hand at me.

"Cadence is still my sister!" Dusty said fiercely. "She's staying right here, *and with* Austin, too!"

"Ooh, boy . . ." Dad glared at Dusty.

It went on for more than an hour. Finally, things seemed to burn out, and the yelling faded. The final verdict: Austin and I stayed, but Dad did not like it one bit.

That night, I lay in bed unable to sleep, my mind consumed by my feelings and thoughts of James. I had to see him. I had to end it and not let him overwhelm me.

I arose and left early, knowing it would be his day off. I slipped a note for Austin under the door, telling him I'd gone to visit an old school friend before I hurried out of the house.

When I pulled up in front of the townhouse, James stood outside, shirtless, washing his car. I tried to push aside my feelings of attraction to him at the sight of his lean, muscular shoulders and chest. He waved carelessly, apparently assuming I was Dusty, but when I stepped out, he did a double take. "Cadence!"

My stomach churned as my fears and nerves consumed me. "Hello, James."

He grabbed a towel and rushed toward me. "I can't believe . . . . You never gave me any details."

I couldn't look him in the eyes. "I know, I . . ."

He grabbed me in a tight embrace. "I've missed you! Let's go inside. I'm pretty hungry because I haven't had breakfast yet, so if you want—"

"Let's just talk," I said, my shoulders slumping.

He swore. "No, you're going on a guilt trip again." He caught my hand and led me inside to the couch.

Those few steps brought me to tears. He would kick up a hard fight and make it impossible for me to let him down gently.

"Cadence," he said softly as he knelt before me. "I told you not to worry about this. I've forgiven you, so you should forgive yourself."

I shook my head. "It's not that simple."

He clasped my face. "Yes, it is. I've finished my course, and after graduation, I'm coming to be with you. Don't let this get in the way of us."

Sobs wrenched from deep inside me. How could I hurt him?

I had to—I'd made my choice.

"James, it's over."

He hesitated. "Well, I'd guessed as much when—"

"No, you and me. *We're* over."

He shook his head. "No."

"James . . ."

"No!" He jumped up and sat on the couch beside me. "You promised me we'd get married."

I nodded. "I know, but—"

"I'm not going to let you go. I know this is because you think you're hurting me with this other guy, but—"

"James, please stop. We're done." I moved to stand, but he caught my arm and held me down.

"Then tell me you don't love me."

I took a sharp breath. "James, I—"

"Look me in the eyes and tell me you don't love me, Cadence, and I'll let you go!"

I looked into his eyes, those eyes that I'd always loved and found myself lost in, and couldn't do it. My gaze fell as I turned away and tried to stand again.

"You do still love me," he said in a tight voice. "Then, why are you pushing me away?"

He couldn't know about Austin—that would be a devastating blow—and the images of James as a vegetable rushed through my mind. "I can't hurt you anymore."

"*This* hurts me."

My face fell into my hands and I sobbed. He clasped my face and pulled me in for a kiss. His familiar lips sent a shudder through me. He pulled me into his arms as our kiss deepened, and he wiped away my tears.

He lifted me, and without me realizing it, he'd carried me into his room and laid me on his bed.

"I love you, Cadence," he whispered as he slid down my jeans. His hands caressed my body as he slowly peeled off my clothes.

"James," I said breathlessly.

He bent over me and kissed under my eyes. "Yes?"

"We can't . . ."

"Can't what?" His fingers stroked me between my legs, making me groan. Before I knew it, we were making love with such fiery passion. I was lost in him, in his eyes, his touch, his voice whispering in my ear how beautiful I was and how much he loved me.

My fingers found their way into his chestnut hair as he kissed my body and loved me like he never had before.

"Oh, James," I whispered in his ear. "How do you just know how to get to me?"

"Because I love you," he answered. "And there's no one I know better than you."

As we finished, he wrapped his arms around me and we softly kissed. We gazed into each other's eyes, communicating feelings between us that words couldn't express.

He softly stroked my back, the one trigger that always made me fall asleep. When I awoke, several hours had passed, and James lay asleep beside me. Covering my mouth as I pulled away, a pit formed in my stomach for betraying Austin. I had to leave, and never come back. I just couldn't face James again.

I dressed quickly and silently, then rushed to his desk to write him a note.

James,

I'm so sorry. You deserve better than this. Please don't fight for me anymore. All I will give you is pain. I wish I could leave you more than just a note after everything we've been through together, but I know talking to you will only prevent me from leaving and hurt you more.

I'm so sorry, and I wish you the best in the future.

Cadence.

As I rested the note on his pillow, I stared at his face one last time, taking in every detail to remember him exactly how he was when we loved each other. Then I dug into my handbag and pulled out his ring, placing it carefully on top of the note. I turned and froze as I heard movement behind me.

"Cadence?"

I couldn't look at him, so I rushed to the door.

He leapt out of bed and held it shut. "No."

"James . . ."

"You're not running away." He locked it and reached for my note. I gasped and reached for the door, but he grabbed my arm. "A note?"

Tears burst out of me. "I keep trying, but you keep stopping me."

"Because you love me!"

"There's someone else!" I yelled, avoiding his gaze.

"He's confused you! I felt it when we made love. I see it in the way you look at me. You love me, Cadence."

My face fell into my hands as I cried. I did love him, so much, but I needed to be with Austin. I loved him, too, and I needed to make sure he was happy before he died. I needed to give him myself and Melody, and I needed that too. I grieved so much for him and Melody that I needed to have them back. Everything I had done was for them.

James rested his hand on my shoulder. "Don't go back there, or wait for me to come with you. Defer for a semester so we can work this out."

"It's . . . I . . ." I shook my head, forcing my tears aside. "We're over."

I grabbed the handle and unlocked it, but he pulled me back.

"No." He grasped my face and kissed me again.

I moaned, aching for him as my heart broke. I pulled back as a sob wrenched free, and yanked the door open. "Goodbye, James."

"No!" He went to rush after me, but still being naked, he paused to grab some pants.

I hurried down the stairs and out of the house. As I opened the car door, he pushed it shut.

"James, please!"

"I'm not going to let some guy get between us. You made a mistake. Everyone makes mistakes."

"He's not a mistake," I responded softly.

"Then I'm a mistake?" he yelled.

"No." Tears streamed down my face again.

"Then why are you cutting *me* off? What has he done to you?"

I bit my lip. "I can't explain without you . . . without you . . ." *Turning into a vegetable.*

"Without me what?"

I finally looked up at him. He had tears running down his face, and it tore me apart. I couldn't help brushing his cheek with my thumb to wipe them away, but then I stopped myself. "Please, let me go."

"No." He wrapped his arm around my waist and pulled me in for a kiss. I moaned and caressed his face as my heart pulsed inside me. Was I making the right choice? James made me feel so incredible, but I needed to think of Austin and Melody.

I broke away, deliberately avoiding looking into his eyes. I tried to push him off, but he held me tight and kissed me again. My heart melted as I kissed him back, my love for him filling me up.

My phone vibrated in my handbag. Breaking from the kiss, I looked into my bag to see Austin calling. I swore and pushed James off.

"Did you just swear?" He raised his eyebrow.

"Shut up."

"Who is it?"

I turned away from him, my guilt for him, Austin, and everything consuming me. "I need to go."

"It's that guy!" He grabbed for my bag.

I held it closed as I pulled the car door open and tossed it inside. "James . . ."

"Let me talk to him, and I'll fix all of this."

I gasped. "No! James, I can't . . . you don't know how complicated this is! He's . . . he was . . ." I couldn't tell him Austin had been my husband before, as much as I wanted to, as much as I almost did.

"Give it to me!" He grabbed for the door and pried it open.

"No!" I grabbed his arm, forcing him back.

He shook me off and dove back in, grasping my bag.

"Stop it!" I grabbed his arm, and he shoved me off. I stumbled back and into Tom. I winced as my head impacted Tom's shoulder. Tom grabbed my arms as James swung back, his eyes wide with alarm as he realized what he'd done.

"What's going on?" Tom asked.

James swore. "Cadence, I didn't mean to . . . are you okay?"

I nodded. He hadn't meant to shove me, but I rubbed the back of my head as pain throbbed through it. "I have to go."

"We're not done," James said firmly. I pushed by him to get into the car, but he caught my arm. "We're *not* done."

"Yes, we are, James." I pulled free.

"Cadence . . ."

My phone started ringing again. We stared into the car. "I have to go."

His lips pressed into my hair where I had hit Tom. "No, you don't."

I took a sharp breath as his hand brushed my neck. "No, no, no. I can't do this. Not again. You need to stop."

I pushed him back, and before he could react, I shut the door and locked it behind me.

He tugged at the handle. "Cadence!"

I turned the keys to start the ignition.

"Cadence! Don't do this."

I put the car in reverse.

"I love you, my beautiful girl. Please."

I looked up at him as the words danced on the tip of my tongue. *I love you, too.* But to say them would be unfair, so I bit them back and reversed out of the driveway, tears streaming down my face.

Austin sat quietly beside me on the sectional. He knew something was wrong from the moment I arrived home. But he didn't ask, and just let me cry on his shoulder. I'd settled down, and curled up beside him so his warmth encompassed me. Even in the early summer heat, it felt comforting.

He flicked through the channels on the TV, and, finding nothing of interest, said, "Why don't we go do something?"

"Okay. Like what?"

He chuckled. "You're the local, you tell me."

I looked into his eyes and sighed at the love I saw in them. Guilt made my heart twinge as a flash of James only a few hours earlier, gazing down at me while we made love, shot through my mind. I needed a diversion. "How about we go up the mountains? It will be slightly cooler, and I know a great candy shop where we can go crazy and give ourselves a sugar high."

"I think that sounds like a great idea."

I hurried to change into denim knee-length shorts and a loose, pale blue t-shirt before we left. The trip came as a welcome distraction as I took him to see tourist hotspots and looked out over the stunning views of the bushland.

We stopped at the candy store last, and he bought me several bags of my favorite treats, which were mostly different types of chocolate.

"I love spoiling you." He grinned as he paid for them.

"You know you don't have to," I said, offering him some money again.

"What's mine is yours." He handed me my bag full of treats.

When we arrived home, Dad paced the living room, and Dusty sat on the couch with his elbows on his knees, holding his head. That wasn't a good sign.

As soon as the door opened, Dad swung around and pointed at me. "You, my room, right now."

My hand tightened nervously around Austin's.

"Without him," Dad said firmly. "Dusty, you come too."

Dusty kept his head low as he scurried away.

Austin squeezed my hand. "I'll be right here, so don't worry."

He released my hand and nodded for me to follow Dad.

In Dad's bedroom, Dusty sat staring at his hands on the bed. I touched his shoulder, but he flinched away. Dad shut the door behind him and spoke in a low voice. "I believe you recognize this."

He tossed James's ring on the bed.

I gasped. "He came here?"

"He just left," Dusty said quietly. "He's never going to speak to me again."

"Oh no! Dusty, I'm so—"

"You're not sorry, Cadence." Dad scowled. "So don't even say it. He came here and told me you tried to end it with him, but you couldn't deny that you still love him. So he's going to fight for you."

"I told him not to," I said softly, but firmly. "I told him he deserves better than this."

"I told him the same thing," Dad said harshly, making me wince. "But he said despite your weakness, he wants to forgive you and move on, and he left the ring for you for when you're ready."

I shook my head. "I can't keep doing this. I don't know what else to do. I've tried ending it over and over, but . . ." I trailed off. He refused to let go because he knew he still had a hold on my heart. The only thing I could do was stay away from him so he didn't sweep me up again. "I love Austin, Dad. Being with him makes me happy, and I know it's the right thing for my life. James, he's . . ." My voice caught. "He . . . I'm . . ."

"Despite everything, you still love him," Dad said gently.

I nodded.

He took a deep breath and slowly released it to calm himself. "But you love Austin more?"

I hesitated, but slowly nodded. "Austin would sacrifice everything for me, even his life, and in some ways, I feel like I've already done the same for him. Just so you know, I didn't come to this decision easily. There were many factors that pulled me in both directions, but when it came to it, the one I wanted to do everything I could to make happy for the rest of his life was Austin."

Dad rested his hands on his hips as he slowly looked me over. But Dusty spoke first. "Why not James?"

I sighed. "James will always be my first love, and the best friend I've ever had, but Austin is my match. I can't explain it, but I just know I'm meant to be with him."

Dusty reached over and plucked up the ring. "I guess I should give this back to him."

I gently placed a kiss on his cheek. "I'm sorry this hurts you so much. I hope it doesn't end your friendship with him."

He scoffed. "It probably will. I think he only tolerated me to keep you happy."

"Dusty!"

He shook his head. "I guess I'm about to find out."

He shuffled off the bed and headed out to the car.

Dad surprised me by grasping my shoulder. "I think maybe I've misunderstood your feelings and that young man's intentions. Why don't you send him in here to speak with me?"

Gasping with surprise, I jumped to my feet and threw my arms around him. "Thank you, Dad. You'll love him too, you'll see. He's what you've always wanted for me."

I rushed out to send in Austin.

Dusty returned in a mellow mood, but not devastated, telling me his friendship with James remained intact. That was a relief.

Dad's conversation with Austin resulted in him giving permission to marry me. So, on Christmas, with the whole family around, we announced our engagement. Although it still startled my family, they accepted my choice and did all they could to get to know Austin.

Toward the end of our visit, we set a date and booked our wedding.

On New Year's Eve, my annual visit from the man in white came. When time froze, I broke away from Austin's kiss. I stared at him, sorrow for all those years with James making my heart heavy.

"Cadence."

I turned, keeping my hand on Austin's knee. "I've made my choice."

He bowed his head. "I know. But are you sure?"

"Yes." I looked to Austin, touching his hair. "More than ever."

"Let me show you something."

His hand rested on my shoulder. The room shifted. I gasped as I found myself on the end of James's bed, him sitting on his pillows cross-legged, staring at my ring. With bloodshot eyes, his lip trembled as he fought back his emotions.

James shook his head, squeezing his eyes tightly shut. He clutched the ring and launched to his feet. Grasping my note, he tore it in two before he marched downstairs.

"Wow, James." Tom stopped him by the living room. "Don't do this."

He pushed Tom aside. "I can't let her go. She's everything to me."

"Maybe you should give her some space."

"*Space* has been the problem." He ground his teeth, squeezing the ring. "Five years. How can one person mess with her head enough to wipe out five incredible years?"

I swung around. "Don't make me see this. I told you I'd made my choice."

The man in white ignored me, watching James.

Tom sighed, shaking his head. "I don't know. Cadence hasn't been herself lately."

"Exactly." James stared at the ring. "Her dad's on my side. If we talk to her together, maybe she'll see sense."

Tom's brows furrowed. "Mate, don't—"

James marched out the door.

The scene changed, and we appeared at the house. James waved the ring in Dad's face as Dusty stood in the corner. "She promised. Help me talk to her."

Dad shook his head. "I don't know what to do, son. She won't listen to me either."

"Damn it." James marched through the house to my room. Dad and Dusty rushed after him, trying to block him off. Outside my door, he paused, looking across the hallway into Harper's room.

Dusty rushed over and shut the door.

"He's here." James ran his hand through his hair. His chin trembled as he looked at the ring again. Then, he rushed into my room.

I followed him, wishing I could take his pain away. More than anything, I wished I could explain everything to him, to explain about Austin, and Melody, and him. If anyone deserved an explanation, it was him. But too much was at stake, and an explanation like that would turn him into the one thing I dreaded for him.

"Cadence." He set the ring on my dresser and sank onto the desk chair. "I don't understand. She loves me, I know she does. She couldn't deny it when she came to me, and the way she looked at me . . ." He grasped his hair. "It hurt her to break up with me. I know it. I know her so well I could see it all over her."

Dad rested his hand on James's shoulder. "I wish I could explain, but I don't understand either. I don't doubt that she still loves you too. But I can tell you that this Austin will kick up a fight for her as well."

"His name is Austin." James's eyes darkened. "That's such a stupid name."

"I don't think you should be here when she gets back," Dad said firmly.

"When *they* get back." James stood, taking a deep breath. "Make sure she knows I'm not giving up on her. We'll get married once we get past this."

"James," Dusty said weakly. "Can you get past this?"

James nodded, meeting his gaze. "It hurts like crazy, but we've shared too much for me to forget her. I've always had to fight for her, and I won't ever stop."

James stormed from the house, leaving Dad and Dusty in my room, staring at the ring.

The man rested his hand on my shoulder. "Cadence—"

"Don't." I pulled away, covering my face. "I hate that you showed me that."

Darkness encompassed me, and then slowly faded back to New Year's. I stared at Austin, refusing to acknowledge the man's lingering presence.

"Is there anything else you'd like to review?" he asked.

"Like more of James's heart being ripped out?" I responded bitterly. "I told you I'd made my choice."

"James will save you from grief."

I sobbed, covering my face. "Stop."

"Very well, sweet Cadence. But don't blame me for not warning you."

He disappeared, but thankfully, time didn't start again until I'd pulled myself together enough to smile as Austin broke away from our kiss.

Chapter Twenty-Two

*B*ack at the flat with Austin, we called Tara and Aaron over. I told Lyla and Tara they would be bridesmaids with Geri and Harper.

Lyla grinned. "I hope you don't expect to live here afterward."

"No." Austin chuckled. "We'll be looking for a place to rent elsewhere."

"Good." Lyla winked at me playfully. "By the way, don't pick green. Green doesn't look good on anyone."

"That's good, because we're going for yellow," I said. "It's going to be a beach wedding, so—"

"But you said it was in July!" Tara exclaimed.

"Yes, we're having a beach wedding in July on Rottnest, where we had our first real date."

She pulled a disgusted face. "It'll be freezing cold!" She pointed at Austin. "She's perfect for you. She's just as insane as you are with all your 'diving in the middle of winter' madness."

Austin laughed.

Soon, we returned to school for our final year, and I spent my days balancing study, work, and wedding plans.

I had almost finished writing my paper. Glancing over at my clock, I saw I had five minutes before Austin would arrive to go look at a townhouse together. A sudden pounding on the door made me jump.

Lyla grumbled the whole way to the door. "What?"

"Where's Cadence?"

I jumped at the sound of Melanie's voice. I rushed over to lock my door, but came face-to-face with her as she grabbed it to stop me. We stared into each other's eyes. Hers burned with a rage that terrified me, but at the same time, I saw the same pain I'd inflicted on James. I stood, my stomach knotting as I waited for her to speak.

"We need to talk."

I shook my head and stepped back. "No . . ."

"Yes! We've been friends for a while now, and I know all of this is just not you!"

"Mel, please, I can't explain—"

"Why not? James is devastated. You just walked out on him! You've been with him for five years, and that's all you can do? Tell him that you can't be with him, that there's some other guy who's convinced you to be with him instead, and he just needs to understand?"

"Cadence, what's she talking about?" Lyla asked.

My face burned. "Mel, let's go for a walk."

Melanie glanced back at Lyla. "Fine."

We hurried out to a nearby park, where we stopped by a bench. I stood with my eyes down, while Melanie glared at me, her arms folded. "Well, Cadence? Explain."

I took a deep breath. "There are some things that I can't tell you—"

"You can't be serious—"

"—but I *can* tell you this!" My gaze shot up to meet hers and she clamped her mouth shut. "I still love James—"

"Then why—?"

"But there's something else I need to do before I can be with him. I have things in my life that are so important that I needed to cut him off, or I'd only hurt him more than I already have. I know it's hard for him, and it's hard for me, too, but . . ." I bit my lip and shook my head.

"This is the right path for me. It always was, and I don't want to change it."

She stared at me, completely baffled. "You've always been kinda weird, but that just doesn't make sense. Whatever you need to do, James will gladly do it with you."

I sighed and rubbed my eyes. "Not this."

She shocked me by grabbing my wrist and pulling it away from my face. As she stared at my hand, I realized the mistake I'd made.

"You're engaged?" She threw my hand aside. "*I can't believe this!*"

"Melanie . . ."

"You've been putting James off for years, and now you're marrying someone else? Is that why you were putting him off? Because this other guy has you brainwashed into thinking he's the one, and not James?"

"No. It's not like that—"

"Geez, Cadence! I never thought you'd stoop this low!"

"Melanie, please—"

"No! This is easily the worst thing you've ever done!"

My face fell into my hands as I cried. "I know."

"Don't cry! You don't deserve to cry. You did this."

"Hey!" I flinched at the sound of Austin's voice. He ran up beside me and stood between us. "Don't talk to her like that!"

Melanie's eyes widened as it dawned on her who he was. Her gaze shot to me, narrowing as she snarled, "This is him, isn't it?"

"Melanie—"

"Shut up!" She pulled her phone out and took a photo. "You know where this is going."

"Melanie!" I lunged at her.

She pulled away and slapped me hard across the face. Austin grabbed me and pulled me behind him. "Get away from here! No one treats my fiancée like that. If I ever see you again, I'll press charges for harassment!"

Melanie folded her arms and scowled at me. "Nice, Cadence. Have a nice life."

She marched away, and as I watched, she typed a text and hit send.

My heart tore in two. With that simple action, James and I were completely through. No more chances, no more possibilities. He'd never be willing to come back to me. I burst into tears and collapsed onto the bench.

Austin's arms wrapped around me in an instant, pulling me into his chest. "What was that about?"

"That's James's sister," I said through sobs. "My boyfriend from high school. He's going to hate me forever now."

"Wow, you guys must have been a pretty serious item."

I nodded. "I'm a terrible person. He'll hate me, knowing I chose you over him."

There was a moment's pause before he said, softly, "Cadence? Were you still seeing him when we got together?"

I nodded slowly, and covered my face with my hands. "I'm sorry, Austin. That's why I resisted you in the beginning. But that night when we got together, you were so wonderful that you just stole my heart. I'll understand if you leave me for this. I've done a terrible thing to you."

He stroked my hair as I sobbed. After a few minutes, he said, "But you chose me. Why would I let you go when you love me so much that you risked estranging everyone you love for me?"

He lifted my chin so I had to look into his eyes. "Thank you for coming clean. I kind of suspected there was something going on that you were conflicted about, and when I saw another engagement ring in your suitcase when we left for Christmas, I didn't know what to think. But this makes sense. I don't blame him for fighting for you and wanting to be with you, but I'm grateful you chose me, despite how hard it would have been for you. I love you more than anything."

I buried my face into his chest and sobbed from relief. No more secrets, no more guilt, and he still wanted to be with me. My Austin, just like it had been before . . . except, somehow better.

I looked up into his face. The intensity of his love for me poured out of him, and I knew our love was stronger than it had ever been before. I was stronger; I was wiser. I had grown enough to match him in every way, whereas before, I realized, he really had been looking after me all the time. He'd protected me from my ignorance, but now, I knew my ignorance. I'd faced it in what I'd redone. Geri, James, Harper, Dusty, Mum, Dad, and even Melanie, my relationships had been altered by my change in perspective. My eyes were wide open now, and our love was stronger because of it. I could carry myself at his side instead of leaning on him for protection.

"Austin?"

"Yes, my sweet Cadence?"

"Don't ever let me go."

He smiled and pressed his forehead against mine. "I'll be with you forever."

Chapter Twenty-Three

July arrived, and so did my family. Dusty and Geri came over first. They flew in from the United States a few days before the rest of the family arrived. They had jetted off together on a backpacking trip at the beginning of the year—Geri deferred the last year of her degree and would return to finish in the New Year.

Dusty and Geri camped out in the living room of the flat. A few days later, the rest of my family arrived. Tara's family generously offered a room in their home for Harper's little family, while Mum and Dad stayed with George and Linda, and just like before, they all got on like a house on fire. They stayed out late like teenagers, and during the day, George and Linda took them around Perth and its surroundings. Mum and Dad finally seemed to accept Austin, and Mum whispered to me the night before the wedding, "Cadence, I couldn't have made a better match for you if I tried. I'm sorry I was so hard on him."

That made my heart sing.

The day arrived. Lyla, Tara, and Geri helped me dress, tied up my gown under a long trench coat, and covered my hair with a heavy veil. Harper met us down at the harbor and helped me onto the boat driven by George.

"That's a good look," he said teasingly to me.

I pulled the coat tighter around my dress. "Yeah, I thought I'd try classy for once."

He laughed.

We sped to the island while my four bridesmaids chatted excitedly together. I simply sat and listened, basking in the fact that I had Geri and Harper alongside Lyla and Tara this time around.

Mum and Dad met us at the jetty. Mum rushed forward and helped me out of the boat, then wrapped her arms around me. Dad hung back and watched us be escorted to the small venue to finish preparing.

Once I was ready, I stepped in front of the mirror. My long-sleeved wedding dress looked perfect. The lace bodice with the plunging V neckline had been the seller for me the first time, and so I'd gone straight to it this second time. To my delight, it fit like a glove. I remembered no longer squeezing into it once my middle expanded after childbirth.

As I gazed in the mirror at the final result, Dad stepped up behind me and rested his hand on my waist. "Where did my little girl go?"

I giggled. "You've been saying that for years."

His knuckle brushed my cheek. "But now she's completely gone, and all I see before me is a beautiful young woman. You look so much like your mother did."

I turned to face him. "Please don't make me cry. You'll ruin my makeup."

He chuckled. "I'm sorry. It's no secret that I always favored you. But you are so much like your mother in every way . . . except that mad aggression you get when playing sports. I have no idea where that came from."

I laughed. "Oh, Dad. That's all you."

He grinned, and then glanced around. "They're all gone. I guess that means we should head out too." He clasped my face and kissed my forehead. "He's a good choice, sweetheart. I know he'll make you happy."

Tears welled in my eyes, and I struggled to hold them back. "Thank you. I love you so much. That means everything to me."

"I love you, too." He looped my arm through his.

He led me down to the beach, where the gentle, cool sea breeze made me tremble. But my trembling turned to shivers of anticipation as a rush of excitement filled me. How many people had the chance to relive their wedding day, to feel the joy of that moment a second time over?

We stepped into view of the group gathered in the wedding marquee, decorated with white and yellow. Austin turned to the entrance, and our eyes met. He wanted to run to me and throw his arms around me as I walked toward him—I could see it in his eyes. His love was written all over him, and my heart fluttered with excitement. My Austin, mine again.

We stepped in front of him, and he barely noticed Dad offering him my hand. His gaze fixed on my face, making me blush, which in turn, made his smile widen. Dad cleared his throat, and Austin snapped back to reality. He grasped my hand and nodded his thanks, before Dad kissed my cheek and went to sit with Mum.

Without looking away from my face, Austin wrapped my arm through his and we stepped up to the white, wooden altar. As we proceeded, he struggled to take his eyes away from me. I bit my lip, trying to suppress my flattered smile. When we turned to each other to exchange rings and vows, he smiled with relief that he had a good reason to just look at me. My cheeks warmed again.

The marriage celebrant finally said, "I now pronounce you Mr. and Mrs. Austin and Cadence Jones. You may kiss your bride."

Austin's hands shot to my face, and he pulled me against him as he kissed me passionately. I grabbed his shirt under his jacket and clung to him, reveling in the moment and grateful it was just as wonderful as I'd always remembered.

When our lips parted, he held me close, our eyes locked. "I love you so much, Mrs. Jones. You are the most beautiful woman I've ever met."

I caressed his face, wishing the moment could last forever. "I love you too, Mr. Jones."

We walked along the beach and around the township for photos before returning to the venue for the reception. What a crazy, laugh-until-your-sides-hurt party, with beautifully touching moments dispersed throughout. Austin rarely broke contact with me. Whether he held my hand, or his fingers were on my back as he rested his arm on the back of my chair, he always touched me.

In our first dance, he pressed against me and softly sang in my ear. The moment was so beautiful and romantic that a tear ran down my cheek.

During the daddy-daughter dance, Dad held me close and said, "I'm so proud of you, Cadence. He's truly worthy of you."

I wrapped my arms around him and squeezed him tightly.

As the dancing moved into more of a party feel, I needed to use the restroom. Harper and Geri rushed in with me, as Lyla and Tara were well on their way to being blind drunk. Harper and Geri held up my dress as I sat to relieve myself.

"Well, this is awkward," I said.

Geri giggled. "Oh, we've been through worse. Do you remember that time I puked on you?"

"I remember dodging it." I grinned.

"You stuck your fingers in it and picked up the drugs I had forced down my throat."

"Oh, yeah. That was gross."

"Sick," Harper grunted. "You guys are weird."

"Harper, I held your dress at your wedding."

She smirked. "Just hurry up."

"So, why aren't you taking advantage of the booze fest?" I asked, while reaching for the toilet paper.

"I'm knocked up again," Harper replied under her breath.

"Seriously?" I laughed, having forgotten how close together her first two were.

"Yeah, and this bugger better be a girl," she groaned.

"I'm betting on another boy."

She slapped my shoulder. "Shut up! Damn it! Now you've jinxed it! You're always right with these things."

"Sorry, Harper."

"I don't wanna spill to your dad that Dusty and I got married in Vegas," Geri responded softly.

Harper and I both did a double take and yelled, "What?"

Geri blushed. "Yeah."

"Geri!" I clutched her arm. "Why didn't you tell me?"

"We didn't want to say anything until after your wedding. We didn't want to steal your thunder."

I signaled for them to look away so I could stand and fix my clothing. "Geri, this is a big deal! Come on! I wanted to be at your wedding."

"We're going to have a small ring exchange in a few months with a reception, but we just wanted to be married right then."

I did a little dance on the spot and hugged her. "This means you're really my sister now! I'm so, *so* happy for you!"

She giggled. "Thanks, Cay-Cay."

When I let go, Harper wrapped her arms around her. "I always saw you as Cadence's irritating twin, so having you as an official member of the family won't make much difference."

Geri laughed. "Thanks, you guys. I know having you both on my side will make a big difference when we finally break it to your dad."

"Cadence!" Dusty's voice echoed around us.

"Speak of the devil." I winked at Geri. "Hang on. I'm just going to wash my hands."

"Hurry up! You need to get out here."

The urgency in his voice startled me. I looked to Geri and Harper, who both seemed as confused as me. I hurried to wash my hands and rushed out. At the door, Dusty grabbed my arm, glanced around, and tugged me out into the small courtyard.

"Dusty, what's going on?"

A tall, lean man stepped into the courtyard. I gasped. "James!"

He walked toward me, tears streaming down his face. "So it's true. You got married to someone else."

"I'll let you talk," Dusty said as he backed away.

"No, Dusty!" I panicked, knowing how easily I gave in to James. "Stay . . ."

But he had gone.

"You look more beautiful than I could have ever imagined," James said in a hushed voice.

I turned to face him. "James, please . . ."

"I waited so long for you, and then this other guy comes along and steals you away. It was supposed to be us."

He advanced on me, and I backed into a tree. He caressed my cheek tenderly, making my heart race. "Tell me you don't love me. Tell me that you feel nothing for me."

My breath caught. I couldn't tell him that. "James, I love Austin—"

"So what? Do you still love me?"

"Please, don't . . ."

He moved closer to me, moving in for a kiss. I whimpered and turned away. "Don't do this."

"You still love me," he said firmly. "Why are you doing this?" His hand fell from my cheek and wandered down my neck and exposed collarbone. "Look into my eyes."

I shook my head. "No."

"Why not?"

"Because, when I look in your eyes, I can't resist you. I have to resist you now. I'm committed to Austin. I *married* Austin."

He moved closer, and I pressed my hands against his chest, trying to hold him back. "Please, James. I can't do this."

"Hey!" Austin's voice boomed across the courtyard.

James pulled back. Using his distraction to my advantage, I ducked away and rushed to Austin. Austin wrapped his arm around me and touched my face. "Are you okay?"

I nodded.

He turned his attention to James. "This is my wife. I don't know who you are, but don't ever touch her like that again."

"Oh, is that so?" James sneered.

I grabbed Austin's hand, sensing things were about to turn ugly. "Let's go back inside."

"You dirty thief," James said with a snarl. "You did something to her to steal her away and make her think she loves you. But she loves me. She loved me long before you came along."

Austin turned to face him. "You're the high school boyfriend. James, isn't it?"

"Austin, don't provoke him," I said softly. "He's very strong, and a good fighter."

"Yeah, Austin, don't provoke me . . . oh, you already have." He advanced on us, and Austin pushed me behind him. James stood over him. He was a full head taller, but Austin didn't back down.

"Move on, buddy. She chose me."

James grabbed Austin's shirt. "I'm gonna . . ."

Austin grabbed him right back. "You're gonna what? There's no point in fighting, because she's still gonna leave with me."

"Austin, don't . . ." But I couldn't say more as James roared and tried to shove Austin to the ground. But Austin, being stronger than James expected, held his stance.

He shoved James off him. "You're making an idiot of yourself."

"Austin!" I gasped. "You don't need to be cruel! Let's just go back inside."

Austin turned to me and wrapped his arm around my waist. "I'm sorry. You're right. We're supposed to be enjoying ourselves. This is our night." He leaned in and kissed me.

The kiss tipped James over. He tore Austin away from me and hit him across the face.

"You bastard!" He swung and hit him in the face again. "Do you have any idea what I've done for her?"

Austin caught his fist as he swung again and shoved him back, swinging at him. He contacted hard across James's jaw, but James kicked out and knocked him over. James jumped on top of him and raised his fist.

"No!" I rushed over and grabbed his arm. "James, stop it! Please, stop!"

James's head shot up and our eyes met. Fury and agony poured out of him. But as he stared into my eyes, his arm relaxed and his rage faded away, leaving only the pain.

"Stop fighting for me," I whispered.

He took a sharp breath.

"I've made my choice."

His face twisted with pain. He pulled his arm free of my grasp and climbed to his feet. "Well, Cadence, I hope you never regret it, because I will never take you back after becoming your second choice."

He dug into his pocket and grabbed my hand. He slammed the ring into my palm, and without looking at me again, marched out of the garden.

Squeezing the ring tight, I watched him go, my heart aching for him. Tears streamed down my face. Even after choosing Austin, I still hadn't wanted my relationship with James to end. He'd been part of me for so long that it felt like someone had removed a limb.

Austin rested his hand on the small of my back. "Cadence, I'm so sorry."

I threw my arms around him and buried my face into his chest as I cried. He held me, softly kissing my ear and head.

We stood there for several minutes before Dad rushed out. "What happened?"

I felt Austin look up to him, and when he didn't say anything, I assumed he mouthed it. Dad rested his hand on my back. "Sweetheart, let me get Geri and Harper to clean you up. This is your night—you need to enjoy it, not hide out in the garden crying. Let's try to get your mind off it. Your mother and I have put a down payment on a house that's being built. By the time it's done, your lease will be up, and you'll be able to move right in. But when you open the card, you need to pretend to be surprised. Your mother will kill me if she finds out I told you without her."

I giggled, then took a deep breath and turned my head to look at him. "Thanks, Dad."

He touched my cheek, gently brushing my tears away. "Anything for you, baby girl." He looked to Austin. "I'll be just one moment."

Austin nodded as Dad hurried away.

Geri and Harper dragged me into the bridal room and fixed my hair and makeup in a matter of minutes. By the time they finished, I couldn't tell at all that I'd been crying.

"I'll kill Dusty," Geri said. "That was a dirty trick. I knew he told James all the details, but I didn't realize they'd planned on having him try to steal you away."

"Geri," Harper said firmly as she watched my face. "Let's not talk about it."

I noticed my chin quivering and stopped it. Forcing my thoughts of James aside, I took several deep breaths and turned toward the door. "All right. Let's do this."

As I reentered the hall, Austin met me with a smile. He took my arm, and soon after, the call for the bouquet toss came. I made my way to the front and watched where Geri went. It would land in her hands whether she wanted it or not. She stood to the side with Dusty to watch. *Ha!* I had a good arm, so it could easily make it over the crowd gathered to catch it.

I took careful aim and threw it hard. I spun just in time to see it hit Geri in the face and land in her arms. The surprise on her face made me laugh, and she glared at me. "I'm gonna get you, Cay-Cay!"

"What are you talking about? I'm a sports nut, right? I throw hard."

She opened her mouth to retaliate, but Dusty covered it. "Thanks, Cadence."

Austin stepped up beside me and set down a chair.

"So, I hear it might be a family tradition to use the teeth." He took my hand to help me sit, and then knelt in front of me. "I like family traditions."

His head disappeared under my skirt. I squealed. Everyone laughed, except Dad, who slapped his forehead. "Harper!"

She grinned at him and shrugged.

Austin's hair tickled my thighs as he took complete advantage of having his head under my dress, kissing my leg several times before he grabbed onto the garter. As he pulled it off, his hands wandered into places that made me blush, and I glanced around, hoping no one noticed.

He reappeared to cheers and laughter. He grinned and flung the garter, causing a tussle to break out, and Aaron won it. He glanced to Tara, who scoffed and walked away. He laughed.

The time came for us to leave. Austin took my hand as the love tunnel formed, and Geri rushed to get my bag from the bridal room, while Harper snatched my clutch.

"Congrats, little sister," she said in my ear. "Be happy, and try not to get pregnant as quickly as I did."

I laughed. "Thanks, Harper."

I gave her a quick kiss on the cheek.

Austin kissed my hand and met my gaze. "Are you ready?"

I nodded, and he gave my hand a tug. We dashed through all the guests, and at the end, we found ourselves by the door, facing our car for the ride to the hotel. Dad caught my shoulder and kissed my cheek with tears in his eyes. He took Austin's hand and embraced him. My heart swelled as I remembered this same moment from the first time, and I loved that it hadn't changed.

Mum wrapped her arm around my waist and kissed my cheek, before she did the same to Austin. Linda stepped forward and kissed my other cheek, then squeezed Austin affectionately.

Austin helped me into the car, and we waved goodbye.

Chapter Twenty-Four

Austin hummed as he lay on the bed gazing out at the ocean. My head rested on his chest as I dozed. As the last day of our honeymoon on Hamilton Island, we'd decided to spend it in bed. We'd spent most of our two weeks diving and snorkeling around the Great Barrier Reef. The weather was terribly cold, but Austin didn't seem to notice, and enjoyed warming me up in our hotel room afterward.

For our last day, all I wanted was to be curled up under thick blankets in Austin's arms. His warm body comforted me, and the vibrations in his chest as he hummed lulled me to sleep.

"Cadence?"

I jumped at the sound of voice. "Yes?"

"Why did you pick me?"

I squeezed his waist. "Because I love you."

"But you love him, too."

My head shot up. "Are you doubting me?"

He smiled and caressed my cheek. "No. I'm just wondering."

Shuffling up closer to him, I said, "I'd choose you a hundred times over. You make me so happy."

He wrapped his arms around me and lowered me underneath him. He kissed me deeply, lovingly, as his hands wandered over my naked body. When his lips broke away from mine, he whispered, "I'd give anything to protect you and be with you. I'll never let you go. You're my everything, and I'd do anything to make sure you're always happy."

I pulled him down to kiss me, and we made love.

After the honeymoon, we returned to finish our degrees and moved into our tiny townhouse. We struggled along, like most newlyweds, but after graduation, Austin got his dream job—conservation of the ocean around Rottnest Island and Perth.

I signed as one of the trainers with the Fremantle Dockers, which impressed George to no end. It required some travel around the country throughout the football season, which meant free trips to Sydney for the away games there.

At the beginning of the next year, I returned to university and earned a graduate diploma in sports management.

I discovered I was pregnant a year after that. Once the morning sickness passed, I found myself gazing in the mirror after my shower, examining my belly. My little Melody grew inside of me, and I felt excited to see her again.

Austin walked in and ruffled his hair. "I feel disgusting. Do I smell disgusting?" He lifted his arm.

"Oh, geez!" I shoved him away. "Seriously, everything stinks to me right now. Get in the shower."

He laughed and turned on the water. "You know, if it's a girl, Harper's going to be furious."

I giggled. "Oh yes, she will be."

He turned to face me. "You think it's a girl, don't you?"

I rubbed my belly. "I sure do."

"Hmm, then we better start thinking up musical names, because, from my experience, you're never wrong about these things." He turned off the water and looked at me. "You know what? I'm working on collecting samples today, so I don't need a shower."

He grabbed his deodorant and rolled it on, then yanked his wet suit up to his waist.

I rolled my eyes.

"What was that for?" he laughed.

"You're such a man."

He grabbed me around the waist from behind, and nibbled on my neck, making me shriek and giggle.

"Yes, but I'm *your* man." He held me tightly as his hands drifted down and caressed my abdomen. "She'll be beautiful. My girls. I must be the luckiest man alive."

Several months later, I went into labor. Mum and Geri were with us as I went through it. As a nurse, Geri was a huge relief to have in the room with me. She stayed calm, and when the hospital's nurse wasn't around, she kept a close eye on my progress.

But Austin was all I wanted. I clung to his hand as contractions hit me, and he kissed my head, telling me I was so brave.

"Austin?" I said between contractions.

"Yes, my sweet?"

"Don't let go of my hand."

He chuckled. "I won't, even if you break every bone in it."

I gave him a sarcastic smirk. "You're so . . . . *Argh!*"

I threw my head back as another contraction hit.

Finally, Melody crowned, and I pushed hard. Austin clung to my hand as he watched his little girl arrive into the world. When she opened her mouth and screamed, his whole face lit up, and he gave me a wide, proud smile.

The midwife lifted Melody onto my chest while she wiped her clean. Austin kissed my head as he held us both in his arms. Nothing could have been more perfect than that moment.

Once I was cleaned up and covered, Dusty and Dad entered to see Melody. Dad held her with a proud smile, before walking over and kissing me on the head. "I'm so proud of you, sweetheart."

Austin stepped up beside Dad and lifted Melody from his arms as my family gathered around me to talk. I watched Austin while he sat with Melody and talked to her softly, stroking her cheek with his finger. It was a beautiful moment, and I felt so glad she had such a loving father. But then it dawned on me. Austin only had eighteen months left. The thought made tears burst from my eyes, and my family stopped their conversation abruptly.

"Cadence, honey," Mum said. "What's the matter?"

Austin's head lifted, and he looked over at me. "Cadence, what is it?"

But I couldn't speak. My heart ached too much.

Austin stood and asked for everyone to step out. He came up beside me and stroked my hair. "Why are you crying?"

"I just . . ." I took a deep breath to compose myself. "I just love you so much, and Melody is so lucky to have you as her daddy."

Tears formed in his eyes. "Oh, my sweet Cadence. We really are so lucky, aren't we?" He placed Melody in my arms. "You're going to be a wonderful mother."

That night, for the first time in years, I called for the angel. I'd only seen him briefly on New Year's for my yearly recap and goal setting. He seemed content to just let me live my life.

"Angel?" I said softly, as I watched Austin sleep on the couch that had been converted into a makeshift bed.

The beeps and humming of the air conditioning fell silent, and the man appeared at the door, wearing white scrubs. "What is it? You haven't called on me for a while."

I looked back at Austin. "It's almost over, but I'm not ready to lose him again." Tears streamed from my eyes, and I sobbed. "Are you sure there's no way to save him?"

He walked up beside me and folded his arms. "Absolutely none. Whatever you do to prevent it will just lead him to a different death. He must die at his allotted time."

My face fell into my hands. "I'm not ready. Why can't he stay to watch Melody grow? Why can't he stay to be her daddy and protect her and love her?"

"I'm sorry, sweet Cadence. But remember, death is not the end. He will be able to watch over you from the next life, and he will continue to love you. I promise you that. Don't despair."

My head shot up to respond, but he had gone.

I did everything I could over the next few months to make them beautiful and happy for Austin. We went on family outings every weekend, we visited with his family regularly, and with mine too.

When Melody was nine months old, we visited Dusty and Geri in Sydney. Geri was five months pregnant with their first child and, despite her medical training, wanted my and Harper's guidance through the pregnancy.

"There's just things you don't comprehend as a nurse," she said to us. "Like how the smell of raw meat makes you feel sick, so cooking dinner is just out the window." She sat on the couch in their flat's living room and sighed. "And all the peeing, and swelling, and aches and pains."

"Stop whining, Ger," Dusty said teasingly as he walked into the room. "You need to toughen up."

"I'm going to smack you," she said with a grumble.

We laughed. Dusty hurried over and plucked Melody off the floor. "Austin, Daniel, let's take these monkeys to the park and let these hens cluck for a while."

"Great idea," Daniel responded as he jumped to his feet.

Austin grabbed one of Harper's three boys and winked at me. "Have fun, ladies."

He and Daniel stepped out. Dusty went to follow, but I said to him, "Hey, how's school coming along?"

He paused and turned back to me with a grin. "Great. I'm probably the smartest person in my course."

Geri groaned and shook her head.

"You finish at the end of the year, right? Do you think you'll earn honors?" I asked.

He scoffed. "Without even trying." He moved to turn, but paused. He glanced around, then turned back to me. "So, now that Austin's not here, James asked about you the other day."

I gasped, and Geri slapped his thigh. "Shut up, you moron!"

"What? It's not like he wants her back. He's dating that hot Emily chick."

My cheeks burned.

Harper jumped up to intervene. "Dusty, just go, would you?"

Dusty shoved her aside. "He asked how you were doing, and I told him you work for the Dockers during training and stuff, but since you have a kid, you don't travel with them anymore. I also told him you're going to start earning your master's next year."

"Why did you tell him all that?" I asked softly.

"Because he hasn't asked about you since your wedding. I thought it was a good sign that he's moved on, and I wanted you to know."

"Oh." My heart sank. I didn't know why I had expected him to still want me after what I did.

"He's doing well, too. His team has made some awesome discoveries, and he traveled to Europe recently to develop some theories over there. He's just raking in the cash."

"Seriously, Dusty, get out," Geri said sharply.

"Cay, you should get in contact with him. I'm sure he'd be happy to be friends again, and I know he's forgiven you."

"Leave, you oversized brat!" Harper yelled. "Don't you see she still carries a torch for him? Yeah, she loves Austin, but James still sits quietly in a small corner of her heart."

"Wow, great imagery," Geri said.

"Thanks." She turned back to Dusty and poked his chest. "Now go and play with your brothers-in-law and your niece and nephews, and *stop causing trouble*."

Dusty looked at me and raised an eyebrow. "You still have feelings for James?"

"Get out!" Geri and Harper yelled.

"Okay, okay. Geez." He rushed out the door with Melody clinging to his hair.

Geri and Harper continued talking about Geri's pregnancy, but I fell quiet. I knew they were watching me, but I didn't care. I tried not to think about James, because it only hurt, but Dusty had stirred things up again. James had asked about me. Was Dusty right about that meaning he was ready to move on? I felt sharp pang in my heart as my old wound reopened.

Geri and Harper didn't dare ask me about it. They knew what I was thinking and feeling, and didn't want to make it worse. We just wanted to brush it under the rug and forget about it.

The whole family came out to visit us for Melody's first birthday. She was all smiles and giggles as she chased her cousins around and basked in the overload of attention. Geri had given birth a month earlier to a preemie boy, but he was strong and doing well as she rocked him in his car seat.

Everyone laughed, having a great time as I pulled out the cupcakes to sing "Happy Birthday." I sat beside Melody as Austin squatted in front of her, while she tried to squash a whole cake into her mouth. He laughed at her and took a photo before setting the camera aside and wiping icing all over her face. She burst into giggles and grinned at him. He laughed again as he stood and wrapped his arm around my shoulders.

I grabbed his hand and sighed, enjoying the moment with my little family. Then, I had an idea.

Later that night, once we were in bed, I said to him, "Let's have another baby."

He looked up from his laptop and raised an eyebrow. "What? Now?"

I nodded. "By the time I fall pregnant and go through the pregnancy, Melody will probably be two. That's a perfect age gap."

"Ah . . ." He looked at me and closed the laptop. "I don't think we're ready for another one. You're about to start school again to earn your master's, and that's going to cost us a lot of money."

"I don't have to do it," I said quickly. "Our family is more important."

He shook his head. "I don't think *I'm* ready for another one just yet. Maybe in a year, but—"

"Please, Austin." I didn't mean to beg, but a year wasn't an option. He only had six months left. "I'm really ready for another. Melody is so beautiful, and seeing Geri with our new nephew made me want another."

He sighed. "Not right now, my sweet. Let's give it a few months, okay? This year has been hard, with you being so caught up with work and taking care of Melody. I feel like we need some you and me time now that she's more independent."

"But I've been trying to do everything I can to make you happy," I said, concerned that I wasn't making his last stretch of life enjoyable for him.

"I know you have." He reached out and touched my face. "And I appreciate it, I do, but to be honest, I think you're getting a bit burned out. I've noticed your energy has been low, and you're a bit short-tempered. I want you to be happy more than I want another child, and right now, I don't think you could handle another child, emotionally."

I leaned back against my pillow. "I'm getting burned out?"

He sighed. "Come here."

He wrapped his arms around me, and I rested my head against his chest. "Cadence, you've always been remarkable. You're hardworking, smart, determined, but you've been carrying a lot on your plate recently. Why don't you just relax and let me take care of you for a while? Focus on your schooling, and have the team cut back your hours. We don't need the money—I'm doing just fine with work—so the less you have to do, the better. It would make me happy to see you smile and laugh again like you used to."

I looked up into his eyes. "I've really been that different?"

He shrugged. "You're tired, mostly. Being tired all the time has been dragging you down."

Resting my head on his shoulder, I nuzzled into his neck and clung to him. "Maybe I should cut back on my commitments. If nothing else, at least I'll see you and Melody more."

He smiled. "I definitely won't complain about that."

I fell asleep in his arms, and the next day, as promised, I cut back on my hours. When I went back to school, I only went part time. I loved it, too. Austin was right about me being tired, because as soon as I was doing less, I felt more energized and happier while I was with our family.

We went to the park together whenever we could. About month later, I took the photo that Dad gave me that day in the hospital, the one I'd stared at for years.

Austin kissed Melody's cheek as he set her down, her legs already running before she touched the ground.

"You know, I need to teach her to swim. She'll want to start snorkeling before we know it."

I chuckled, elbowing him. "It's almost summer, so swimming lessons would be in order."

"Essential." He kissed my hand.

I opened the picture on the phone, a deep melancholy washing over me. Things had come almost full circle, and here was my picture I'd cherished for so long, fresh and new again.

"You know what would make that picture better?" Austin slipped my phone from my hands. He caught Melody again, and took a picture of us together.

He was right. I'd cherish that photo so much more. I had it printed off instead.

As we came down to the final few months, I grew more desperate. If I couldn't save Austin, then I needed to have one more child with him. Every day, I would drop hints, but he continued to refuse.

A week before he was due to die, I broke down in tears in the shower. It was coming up too quickly, and I was terrified. He burst into the bathroom and pulled me out of the shower to hold me. "Cadence, what's wrong?"

"You . . . and I'm . . . Austin, you . . ."

He sighed. "Is this about the baby thing?"

I couldn't even respond. I just clung to him, reveling in how alive he was and not wanting to let go.

"Oh my sweet, I didn't realize it meant that much to you. If it's what you really want, let's do it."

I looked up into his eyes, wishing I could tell him everything, but knowing I couldn't without losing more than ten years of hard work and Melody. "I just love you so much."

He held me tightly in his arms as he kissed my head. Tears streamed down my face as I wished his arms would never let me go and his kisses would never end.

Chapter Twenty-Five

The day Austin was to die, I struggled to function. I dropped off Melody with Linda like I usually did when I went to school, but instead, I skipped my classes and sat on the beach where he proposed. The whole day I sobbed and sobbed. I didn't even know I could cry that much.

Finally, I looked at the time and saw that he would be home. I rushed to return, wanting to spend every second possible with him.

As I entered, he popped his head out of the bathroom door and grinned. "Hey, hon. I didn't expect you home this early. I was going to surprise you by having Melody and dinner ready, but I guess not."

"My last class was canceled," I lied, "so I came home to spend time with you both."

"Well, come in here then."

I walked into the bathroom where Melody splashed around in the bathtub.

"Dinner's in the oven," he said. "Nothing hard, just a frozen lasagna, but hey, I'm not a chef."

I smiled and sat on his lap. "It will do."

He wrapped his arms around my waist and kissed my cheek. "Did you know that you're beautiful?"

I giggled. "I'm glad you still think so after I destroyed my body through childbearing."

He lifted my shirt. I squirmed and tried to hold it down. He laughed. "Stop fighting me." He rested his hand on my abdomen. "Are you talking about this?"

I nodded and gazed down at my stretched and scarred skin.

"This," he said gently, "is the most beautiful part of you. It's evidence of how much you love me and Melody."

His words almost made me burst into tears again, but I forced them back, wanting him to see me nothing less than happy for his last few hours.

We chatted and laughed together over dinner, and when we put Melody to bed, I took him into our room and made love to him slowly and with all the passion for him I held inside me.

"Oh, Cadence," he said softly as he held me afterward. "I should have agreed to get you pregnant again months ago."

I forced a smile. "It's not just about that. I wanted to make sure you know how much I love you."

He ran his fingers through my hair. "Sweet Cadence, I already know how much you love me, and I hope you know I love you just as much, maybe even more."

I traced his features, trying to burn them into my memory. "Promise me you won't ever let me go."

He smiled warmly. "I'll never let you go."

He soon fell asleep, but I refused to. Once he drifted into a deep sleep, I crept into Melody's room and carefully lifted her out of the crib so I wouldn't wake her. I carried her back to our room and set her on the bed.

I pulled on some pajamas, and with great care not to wake him, I slipped pants onto Austin. Then I curled up beside him, holding Melody in my arms, and stared into his face while he slept.

When the first small quake hit, it came with a crack and a rumble. I bit my lip to stifle a sob. Austin sat up and looked around. "What was that?"

"I think I felt something too."

He looked down at me and saw Melody in my arms. "Why is . . . ?"

The second, more violent quake hit.

"Get on the floor!" He pushed me off the bed. I hit the floor with a thud, and a sharp pain shot through my shoulder. I held Melody in my arms, and the force of me hitting the floor underneath her woke her.

"Mamma?"

"Shh, sweetheart." I kissed her head, as Austin climbed on top of us.

Then the real quake hit. The whole house shook and groaned.

"It's going to collapse!" My voice trembled with fear.

"It'll be all right. Don't panic, or you'll scare Melody." Austin stroked my hair.

"Austin . . ."

A chunk of ceiling fell on top of him. He grunted in pain, but wrapped himself around us, covering my head.

"Austin!" I whimpered. He met my eyes. "Austin, I love you."

"Sweetheart, don't be scared. We'll be okay."

"Have I made you happy?" I asked desperately.

"Oh baby, you're the best thing in my world. But don't be scared. We'll be okay."

A loud crack and rumbling shook the house as Melody's room collapsed. I screamed and clung to her. She'd died in that room before, and I had to keep her safe now.

Melody screamed and cried. "Mamma! Dada!"

Austin touched her golden hair. "It's okay, baby girl . . ."

Something fell on his legs. I felt them crack over me, and he wailed.

"Austin! Austin, please look at me!"

He met my gaze, and he saw what I knew. His face fell. "No, don't be right."

"I love you."

A beam cracked him across the head. He fell limp over me, and I sobbed. Melody's crying frightened me, so I shifted her between my body and the bed, with Austin over her. I ran my hand through his hair as I whispered to him. "Austin, oh please, Austin. I don't want this to be real."

I rested my fingers on his neck. He still had a pulse. I gasped, hoping maybe the angel was wrong, but as more blood poured out of the back of his head, his pulse slowed.

The quake stopped. Everything fell silent. With our home now a pile of rubble, it felt eerie.

"Austin," I said breathlessly as Melody cried. "Austin, wake up. Fight, please fight. I'm not going to let go of you, so don't you dare leave me again."

But as I lay there, trapped under the rubble, his pulse weakened, until it finally stopped. "No!" I felt for his chest and tried to do CPR the best I could. "No, Austin, please!"

Sirens rang out in the streets, and I panicked. He couldn't die! I wasn't going to let him die. "Austin!" I screamed. "Somebody help me!"

A few moments later, several sets of feet ran toward us. "Where are you? Keep calling out."

"I'm here, in the back of the house! Please, I think my husband's dying!"

The aftershock came. I watched the remnants of the wall shake, then tumble. I screamed and wrapped my arm around Austin's head, while holding down Mclody. She screamed too, and when something hit my head, her screaming rang in my ears as I fell unconscious.

Chapter Twenty-Six

They told me that the earthquake lasted only thirty seconds. To me, it had been the longest thirty seconds I could ever remember.

A rescue team dragged me from the rubble, with Melody still screaming beside me. They found us quickly because she hadn't stopped crying. The world blurred, and I struggled to focus on what was going on.

"Melody . . ." I managed to mutter as a paramedic examined me on a board.

"Your child is just fine," he said in a soothing voice, but I panicked.

"Austin!" I tried to sit up, but he pushed me down.

"You've got head trauma, ma'am. Don't move."

"Where's my husband?" I sounded hysterical, but I didn't care.

He grabbed my shoulders as a second paramedic rushed over. "Ma'am, I need you to relax."

I don't know why he said it. The second paramedic injected me with a sedative.

"No . . ."

They held me down while it took hold. It didn't knock me out, but my whole body relaxed.

"Tell me your name," he said as he flashed a light in my eyes.

"Cadence."

"Cadence what?"

"Cadence Jones."

"How old are you, Cadence?"

"Twenty . . . twenty-five."

He continued talking to me, asking me easy questions to keep me conscious and calm. Finally, the paramedics lifted me and wheeled me toward the ambulance. But as we passed into the front yard, I saw, obscured from view, a body bag.

"Austin!" I moaned, the drugs stronger than my body.

As we reached the ambulance, Linda rushed to me.

"Cadence! Oh Cadence, sweetheart!" Tears streamed down her face.

"Where's Austin?" I asked breathlessly.

A loud sob wrenched from her. "He'll be right along, honey. You just relax and heal, okay?"

"I want Austin." I looked back toward the body bag; standing over it was the man in white. Startled, I lifted my head to look at him. Time hadn't frozen, and people rushed by him, completely unaware that he stood there staring at me.

"You!" I screamed, forcing my body to overcome the drugs. "You give him back to me!"

Linda and the paramedic looked at me like I'd gone crazy, but I didn't care. I tried to sit upright, but the paramedic held me down and tied me to the bed. Wailing in frustration at being bound, I screamed, "Give me Austin!"

The man in white glanced down at the body bag before moving toward me as I slipped into the ambulance. He stood at the doors, and his dark eyes locked with mine. "I warned you."

"No!"

The doors shut, closing him off from my view. I sobbed loudly as the paramedic saw to my injuries. Beside me, Linda lay on the second bed and wrapped her arms around a small body. I turned my head and saw her soothing Melody. Melody looked shaken and pale, and kept letting out soft whimpers as tears streamed down her face.

"Melody!" I gasped. My little girl was alive, and she even appeared uninjured. She'd been saved.

Linda looked up at me and smiled gently. "She's fine, Cadence. Frightened, yes, but nothing serious. You and Austin saved her."

I rested my head back and closed my eyes, letting my tears fall.

A steady beep brought me out of unconsciousness. My eyes felt heavy. I struggled to open them. The distinct aroma of cleaning products hung in the air. My brain switched on as I realized where I was and forced my eyes open. The beeping sped up. White walls encircled me in the hospital room; directly across from me was a closed bathroom door.

I shot upright in panic. *No! No, it couldn't be.* But then, I noticed Melody beside me in a small children's bed, fast asleep. She was safe. I'd saved her. But Austin . . . I needed to see Austin. Reaching behind me, I found the button to call the nurse. A moment later, she entered. "Hello, Mrs. Jones. It's nice to see you awake."

"Where's my husband?"

She avoided eye contact. "You sustained some head trauma, so just relax."

"I want to see my husband!"

"Cadence." Geri's voice came from the door. "Don't bully the nurse. Trust me, it sucks."

Her voice was flat, and she kept her eyes low as she approached me. "Your family will be here in a moment. They just went to get a bite, since we've been up all night to get here. We came straight in, but didn't want to disturb you and Melody. I said I'd stay, so they could go."

She stood at the foot of the bed, her arms folded. "You're lucky to be alive. Your neighbors died. Apparently, there was an old mine shaft that had been forgotten about under your neighborhood. They're saying the construction put pressure on it, and after the rains wore it down, it just collapsed."

She stepped beside me. Her hand wrapped around mine, but she couldn't look me in the eyes. "How are you feeling?"

"I know he's dead," I said in a hushed voice. I glanced over to check the day. My time had passed. The contract was no longer valid. "I knew this day would come."

Her eyes lifted and met mine with confusion. "What?"

"There's so much I want to tell you now, but I need to see Austin."

She tilted her head, her curls bouncing over her shoulder. "Cadence—"

"Cadence!" Mum rushed at me and grabbed my hand. "Oh, Cadence! I'm so sorry!"

I bit my lip as I forced back my tears. "Let me see Austin."

Dad stepped forward to grab her shoulders. "Cadence, why don't we—"

"I want to see Austin," I said forcefully.

He nodded and asked the nurse to bring me a wheelchair. As Geri and the nurse helped me into it, Melody awoke and called for me. Dad grabbed her and hugged her tightly, then set her on my lap.

As Dad wheeled me out, Dusty and Harper rushed over and paused in front of me. Dusty's face had turned red and blotchy from crying, while Harper just looked pale and in shock. Dusty rushed in behind me. "Let me push her."

They all came with me to the morgue as I fought to suppress my fear. I swallowed the large ball in my throat as the morgue doors opened and I was pushed through. But I couldn't do it. I grabbed the wheels, bringing us to an abrupt halt.

"I just need a moment." Taking several deep breaths, I forced my emotions down. I had to see Austin. "Okay."

Dusty pushed me forward, and Austin's body was brought out for me.

"Harper?" I grabbed at Melody. Harper understood and lifted her off my lap.

Forcing myself to stand, I leaned over and looked into Austin's face.

"Austin?" I touched his hand. It felt ice cold. I couldn't contain my emotions any longer, and I burst out in loud sobs. "No, *no*! Not again! Why couldn't I save you? Why did this have to happen again?"

Grasping his face, I pulled his head against my chest and cried. My face stung from the tears, my throat ached from the emotion, but still I cried. "I did everything I could. Why couldn't I change this? Why did you have to go?"

"Cadence, honey," Mum said gently, as she rested her hand on my shoulder. "It was an accident. There was nothing you could have done. He protected you and Melody. Knowing you are both alive and well would make him happy."

My fingers ran through his thick, dark hair. "Why couldn't I change this?"

No one answered. They all must have thought I snapped.

They took turns staying with me over the next few hours as I whispered to Austin, begging him to come back. Finally, Dad rested his hand on my shoulder and said, "Sweetheart, it's time to go."

I shook my head.

"Yes, honey. You need to eat something and rest. You need to recover to take care of Melody. She still needs you."

"Melody's alive," I muttered as I released Austin's head.

"Yes, sweetheart. Melody's alive."

I straightened, and gently clasped Austin's hand in mine before looking up into Dad's eyes. "She didn't die this time."

Concern furrowed his brows. "No, she didn't die."

I grasped his hand. "Daddy, take me away."

Tears tumbled down his cheeks as his chin quivered. "Okay, my little girl."

part three:

life

Chapter Twenty-Seven

All I could feel was numbness. If I felt anything else, I'd lose it. I sat in the back of the car with Melody in the car seat beside me. She didn't understand what was going on, but she knew everyone was sad, and for some reason, Daddy wasn't around anymore.

Ahead of us, the hearse turned into the graveyard. I watched Dad's hands on the steering wheel as he turned the car. My mind had to focus on alternatives to the funeral. The service had been held in a small Anglican chapel, which had been filled to the brim with friends and family from all over. Even Malcolm came. I'd never seen him cry so much. I didn't think he'd cared about his little brother at all.

The car pulled up in a parking space not far from the gravesite. Mum and Dad climbed out, but I couldn't move. I stared toward the open hole in the ground, dreading the moment when it would be filled.

Harper opened my door and reached over to unbuckle my seat belt. "Come on, baby sister," she said gently. "You've been doing great. You're so brave."

Melody's door opened, and Geri reached in for her. Harper grabbed my hand and gently tugged it to coax me out of the car. I stood beside Harper and tried to focus on how pretty she looked with her hair back in a braid and her black, figure-hugging dress and coat. But as she led me out to the open grave, my emotions pushed up and caught in my throat. I held them there while my eyes burned. I didn't want to cry.

Harper took me to the side of the grave, and Geri set Melody beside me. I grabbed her little hand and held it tightly, while Mum came up next to me and wrapped her arm around my waist. I felt so glad no one talked to me. Condolences were the last things I wanted, especially pity.

The casket was brought out, and Linda sobbed. My own feelings swelled, and I gulped hard to hold them in, but I was losing the battle. The graveside service began, and the gathered family all cried. My whole body started to shake.

"You're allowed to cry," Mum said in my ear.

I shook my head as my chin quivered.

She took a shaky breath through her tears. "Cadence, you don't have to be brave. He was your husband. Let it out."

"Mum, please." A tear ran down my face.

Dad looked across at me from her other side. "Sweetheart, don't be afraid to feel it."

"Dad, I . . ." But I covered my mouth as a sob forced itself out. My gaze locked on the casket as my family rested flowers on it. Then, my turn came. All eyes turned to me as I stood with my hand over my mouth, quivering and unable to move.

Linda stepped over and took Melody's hand so she could rest a daisy down for her daddy. I fell apart. Dusty and Dad rushed over and caught me as my legs gave out from my uncontrollable sobbing. I knew everyone was watching me, and the sound of tears being shed filled the air.

Then, silence.

Gasping, I forced myself to stand and gazed around. "Angel?"

"I am here." His hand rested on my elbow. I turned to see him staring at the casket. "You were warned this would happen."

"I know." My voice shook with grief. "But I had to be with him again. I just love him so much."

"And he loved you." He helped me stabilize myself while I gained some control.

"Why are you here?" I finally asked.

"To inform you your contract has expired. You no longer need to comply with its terms, and you can live your life as you wish."

"What little life I have left to live."

"Oh, sweet Cadence," he said with a sigh. "Follow me."

He took my arm and turned me around. "Look at everyone here, and tell me what you see."

The first person I laid eyes on was Geri. Her gaze focused on where I had collapsed in Dusty and Dad's arms. Tears streamed down her face as lines of distress covered her brow.

"Have you forgotten all the good you have done with the better choices you made?" he asked. "Look at Geri— your best friend through thick and thin. You lost her the first time around, but this time, she has become *family*. In the first timeline, she never knew your husband died, and she spent her days at the hospital working extra shifts to fill the void in her life. She craved for someone to love, while Dusty was no longer in her life.

"Dusty, meanwhile, though he had the appearance of a happy life as he graduated with honors and began his career as an architect, was addicted to porn and spent his weekends at strip joints, having sex with any girl willing. He felt the void in his life, too, but in this timeline, they found each other and are happy with their little boy."

He walked me down the line, and we stopped in front of Harper with her three sons around her and Daniel's arm around her waist. "When Harper heard Austin died in the first timeline, she didn't want to come. She never felt close to her family, and her little sister was always the favorite, so why would she need her to pack up all the kids and fly across the country when Mum and Dad would do? But this time, her family means everything to her. You are her best friend, and she loves you so much. She couldn't *not* be here. She was the one who ran around and made the abusive phone calls demanding immediate flights for everyone to get here."

He moved me down the line and spoke about Linda, George, Tara, Lyla, Aaron, Mum, Dad, and finally, Melody.

"Little Melody," he said softly. "You saved her life. You brought her into bed with you and shielded her with your own body. She still needs you to protect her and raise her, now more than ever."

My tears streamed down my face. "But how can I do it without Austin? He was my rock. He kept me going, and she loved him more than anything. How can she grow up without her daddy?"

He didn't answer. I turned to him and saw him crying. "Why are you crying?"

He swallowed his emotions and stood taller. "Ask me why your husband's death was a fixed point in time."

"What?"

"You asked me once, but I wasn't allowed to answer." He stared into my eyes, and I was struck by how familiar his dark eyes looked.

"Why was his death a fixed point in time?"

The corners of his mouth curled up, and he nodded down to Melody. "In the first timeline, he tried to save both you and Melody, but he didn't save her. When he saw how lonely and bereaved you were, he begged for a chance to help you, and to somehow save his daughter so you wouldn't lose everything.

"A deal was made that you would be given the rare gift of a second chance. Certain events in your life were evaluated, and you were sent back to an appropriate time to create a better, happier life for yourself and those around you, while also giving you the chance to save your child.

"But there was one clincher in the deal: Austin would still have to die . . . so he could be your guardian angel."

My heart hit my stomach. "Austin?"

He smiled at me, and his face started to change. His white hair and beard darkened, and his face grew younger. "Yes, sweet Cadence, I've been with you all along."

I almost collapsed as tears overcame me. He caught me and held me tightly in his arms as he wept into my hair.

"I'm sorry I couldn't tell you," he said gently. "But if you'd known, you wouldn't have made certain choices that were needed. I meant it when I said you weren't supposed to choose me again. Things were aligned so you could be with James, and have Melody with James. That's how you were supposed to save her. Her spirit is bound to you, not me. That's why she looks like you. But I'm so glad you picked me again. It was strange having two sets of memories being built side by side, but oh, how wonderful it is to know I had those extra few years with you."

I clung to him, desperate to never let him go. "Don't leave me again, Austin. Stay with me."

"Cadence, you know as well as I do that death isn't the end. Look at me. I'll always be watching over you, but from now on, since my part of the bargain has been fulfilled, I'll be watching you the same way others who have passed do. I will visit you in your dreams, and when you need me, I will rest an invisible hand on your shoulder and whisper words of comfort in your ear. But visits like this will be no more."

"No!" I wept, clinging tighter to him. "No! Take me with you then."

He sighed. "Oh, Cadence." He released his arms around me and looked into my face. "There is one more person here whose life you changed, probably the person whose life you changed the most."

He wrapped his arm around my shoulders and guided me away from the gravesite.

"Where are we going?" I asked.

He didn't answer, just squeezed my shoulder. Then, as we approached a tree, a tall man dressed in black appeared out of obscurity. He wore a hat and dark sunglasses to hide his face, and from the angle he stood, he could see the funeral, but we wouldn't be able to see him. As we approached, I froze. "James!"

Austin smiled. "Yes, James. Despite how much you hurt him, he could never forget how you changed his life. He's been watching you from afar all this time. He'd go to football games to chance a glance at you. He'd take trips to the lab out here and drive by our home in hopes that he might just get one look at you."

"But I know he's moved on. I know he's been seeing someone for a while."

"That may be so," Austin said with a smile. "But he still feels he owes you his gratitude for where he is in life. You know more than he does where his life would have gone. He can only guess."

"Should I talk to him?" I asked, meeting Austin's gaze. "Should I explain everything so that he knows and can move forward with his life? I don't want him holding on to me and feeling pain."

Austin ran his fingers through my hair. "I'm sure he'd appreciate that."

He sighed and looked James over. "You never stopped loving him; I always knew that. I was never jealous by any means—you chose to be with me, after all—but I knew it was there."

My stomach flipped as I gasped.

He smiled down at me. "Don't look so alarmed. I want you to be happy, and if he's willing to forgive you, I want you to be with him. After all those years of watching you with him, I know if anyone could love you as much as I do, it would be him. Cadence, you've fought a good fight, but it's time for you to let me go."

"But . . ." Tears ran down my face. "You've always been in my heart."

"And I always will be. But hasn't James always been in there along with me?"

I stared up at him, startled, but he didn't notice. He turned me around, and we returned to the gravesite. He paused in front of Linda and gave her a kiss on the forehead before he bent down and caressed Melody's face.

"Look after Mummy, baby girl," he said. "I'll always be here with you." He kissed her head and stroked her hair before returning to face me. "I love you so much, Cadence. I'm so grateful you chose me again."

I threw my arms around him and kissed him as tears streamed down my face. His tears soon mingled with mine, before our lips parted.

"Don't ever let me go," I said softly.

"I'll never let you go," he replied. "I'll always be right here with you. But you need to live now, Cadence. The rest of your life awaits, and you need to live it. No more second chances—this is your time to shine."

I nodded, and slowly, his arms released me. He guided me into the arms of Dusty and Dad. As time faded back into motion, he spoke in a whisper: "I love you, sweet Cadence."

Dad and Dusty's arms tightened around me as they held me on my feet. But I'd gained control of myself, and the tears turned into a silent stream down my face. My legs took my weight, and I stepped toward the casket.

"I love you too, Austin." I set a red rose over where his heart would be.

Harper wrapped her arm through mine as the casket lowered into the grave, and I quietly sobbed. Soon, the family dispersed, leaving me with silent embraces of love. I remained by the side of the grave with Harper's arm through mine.

"Cadence?" she said gently.

"Mmm?"

"Would you like a few moments? We can go down and grab a bite to eat and come back in about an hour if you want?"

My glance darted toward the tree, wondering if James was still there. "Thanks, Harper."

She kissed my cheek and walked away with Melody in tow. Once they had gone, I wove my way slowly through the graves toward the tree. As I approached it, I saw James duck behind it so I wouldn't see him. I walked straight toward it and leaned against the trunk. "James?"

He took a sharp breath before he stepped out and stood in front of me. "Hello, Cadence."

He slipped off his hat and sunglasses, and I was dazzled by how attractive he still looked. His clean-cut chestnut hair and his mesmerizing gray-blue eyes were as striking as I remembered. He met my gaze and our eyes locked.

"I don't know what to say."

I smiled. "You don't need to say anything."

He rubbed the back of his neck and looked away. "I kind of remember you being more attractive."

Ouch. A knife straight into the heart. But I nodded, knowing I deserved it. "I feel like I owe you an explanation for everything."

He scoffed and turned away. "You owe me nothing."

"James, please." I caught his arm.

He glanced at it, but pulled free. "Don't think, because he died, I will automatically take you back. How desperate do you think I am? I've moved on. I'm living a good life and have a girlfriend I really care about. I'm thinking about marrying her."

"I don't expect you to take me back. I just want you to know the truth, all of it."

He pursed his lips and looked into my eyes. He gazed down at me for a long moment while he contemplated my request. "Okay, Cadence. Explain your life away."

I took a deep breath, trying to work out where to start. "This is all going to sound completely insane."

I gestured to a bench at the edge of the graveyard, under some trees. He sighed and walked over with me trailing behind. He sat and stared ahead, waiting for me to speak.

I took a deep breath and cleared my throat. "You know how you always said I seemed to just know things?"

He scoffed. "Yeah, it was really irritating."

I pursed my lips, remembering how he had enjoyed making bets on it. "Well, you see, this isn't the first time Austin has died . . ."

I went on to explain everything, in great detail. I told him about the first timeline, and what happened differently with all the people we knew. I told him about Geri and how I'd lost her, but how, this time, I'd saved our friendship. I told him about Dusty, Harper, Melanie, and then I told him about Austin and Melody. Last of all, I told him about himself. As he listened to what would have happened, he sat back and stared at me with wide, alarmed eyes.

Finally, I finished by saying, "So now, my contract has expired and I can tell you everything. I know it all sounds completely crazy, but I feel I owe it to you. My decision to be with Austin was already made before we got together, before you even noticed me. You made it so hard for me to keep that decision. But I owe him everything. It was never about whether or not I loved you."

He flinched at my words, but remained silent. He stared across the graveyard toward the grave that had been filled while I talked. He stood and walked slowly toward it. I followed him, and we both stopped at the graveside.

"You realize you sound completely insane," he said.

"I'm aware of that."

He rested his hand on his hip and ruffled his hair. "Geez, Cadence. How can you just lay all that on me like that? I was a druggy slut and ended up a vegetable? That's awful." He rubbed his eyes. "I think you need help."

"James, I'm not lying to you!" I said pleadingly.

He swung around and pointed at my chest angrily, but when our eyes met, he froze. He searched my face, his expression softening as he saw I was telling him the truth. He pulled back and grabbed his hair, swearing loudly.

"James, I don't expect anything from you. I know I hurt you, and I'm sorry." I faced the grave. "I just wanted you to know the truth."

He pursed his lips and watched me out of the corner of his eye. "Cadence?"

"Yeah?"

He huffed. "I can still read you like a book, and it pisses me off."

I suppressed a smirk. "Sorry."

He groaned. "I hate that you're not lying." He faced me directly. "Thank you for telling me. It really does make sense, as completely mad as it is."

I smiled with relief. "You believe me?"

"Of course I do." He locked eyes with me. He opened his mouth to speak.

"James?" James stepped back at the sound of Dusty's voice. "What are you doing here?"

"I'm just . . ." He flushed, uncomfortable about being caught. "I'm just leaving."

He hurried away, and I called out, "Thank you, James."

He glanced back over his shoulder, but kept walking.

Chapter Twenty-Eight

Five weeks later, I moved back in with my parents so they would help me with Melody after I found out I was pregnant. I fell violently ill with morning sickness the first day, and it went on for several weeks. My heart still felt so heavy from loss, and wondering how I would raise two small children on my own didn't help. I spent days curled up in bed or over the toilet. I didn't even take a shower.

Mum came in one day after she'd put Melody to bed and stroked my hair. "Cadence?"

I groaned.

"Did you need anything?"

I sighed and sat up on my bed. "Mum, it still hurts."

"I know it does, sweetie." A tear ran down her cheek. "But he wanted you to live. So grieve, and then let yourself move on."

I nodded, not sure what I could move on to. I curled up again under the blankets to enjoy the quiet time while Melody slept.

A tap at the front door woke me. I tried to ignore it until I heard James talking to Dad. I was mortified. What was he doing here while I looked like death? They moved through the house, so I closed the curtains and hid under my blankets to pretend I was asleep. But, to my dismay, he came in and sat on the bed beside me. "Cadence?"

He shook my shoulder and I grunted.

"Hello to you too, beautiful."

My breath caught, and I peered out from under the blanket. "What did you say?"

His fingers ran over my forehead. "I know that, right now, you're still grieving and dealing with being pregnant, quitting your job, and changing schools, but I just want you to know that I'm here for you. I'm sorry I stepped out of your life for a while."

"James, you don't need to be sorry for anything."

He sighed and ran his fingers down my cheek. "I do. For the longest time, I was so angry at you, when I should have been there for you. We were always best friends as well as a couple, so I should have put that first."

I couldn't say anything to that. My brain was muddled from all the pregnancy hormones, so I knew anything I said would sound stupid.

He reached over and turned on the lamp on my bed-side table. I pulled the blankets back over my head so he couldn't see me.

"Hey," he said gently, as his hand rested on my shoulder. "Come out and look at me."

I shook my head. "If you thought I looked bad at the funeral, I'll look like a freaking ogre to you now."

"Oh . . ." He wrapped his arm around me and leaned down to whisper, "I was lying. I hated that you looked so amazing when I wanted you to look terrible."

My heart skipped a beat, daring to hope that maybe . . . but that would be selfish. He had a girlfriend. "Well, congratulations. After two weeks of puking, your wish has come true."

He laughed softly and peeled the blankets back from my ear. "Do you remember when those girls tried to beat you up, and your braces cut your mouth really bad, and the school nurse stuck all those wads in your mouth?"

"Oh, good heavens!"

He laughed. "I thought even then that you were beautiful."

I turned to face him. "I was a size ten with C-cup boobs—which is large for a fourteen-year-old—and tight little abs."

"Well, yes, that did help," he said teasingly.

I tried to hide back under the blankets.

He caught them and pulled them down so he could see my whole face. "But you're even more beautiful now."

We gazed into each other's eyes for several moments before he sighed and leaned back. "Cadence, I'm going to leave you my number. If you need anything, anything at all, just call me, okay?"

I nodded, watching him program his number into my phone. "Thank you, James."

I sat in bed after he left, stunned. As he made his way back through the house, I crept to the door and watched him as he shook Dad's hand in the hallway. "Thanks, Dave."

"No worries. Thank you for seeing her. She hasn't been coping well."

James sighed and ruffled his hair, making my heart skip. "I'm not surprised. That was a pretty shocking death. I can't even imagine . . ." He sighed again. "And to be pregnant and alone like this . . ." He met Dad's gaze. "If she needs anything, let me know, okay?"

"I will. You're a good man."

James grasped his shoulder, and then stepped out the door.

I rushed to the front window to watch him leave. I wished he would stay and tell me everything would be all right, that my pain from losing Austin again would fade.

"Cadence?"

I jumped at the sound of Dad's voice. "Dad."

"How are you feeling, sweetheart?" He tilted his head, his brows furrowed.

"I'm . . ." I sank onto the armchair. "I want to feel . . ." I covered my mouth as a wave of nausea hit me again and sprinted to the bathroom.

It took me a few weeks to build up the courage to call James. I felt stupid every time I thought about him, knowing I had no right to want him back in my life. But after my morning sickness subsided and I started to show, I wanted to get out of the house. Mum and Dad had gone, and everyone else was working.

I looked down at Melody as she babbled to her doll on the floor, and the haze over my mind began to clear. As much as I missed Austin, I had to think about Melody first and foremost. She needed me now, and more than anything, I wanted her to have a daddy in her life. A daddy who would love and protect her like mine did for me.

I lifted my phone and stared at James's name. Would it be too presumptuous to ask that of him? I stewed over it for quite some time before finally biting the bullet and calling him.

"Hello?" His voice startled me, and I froze. "Hello?"

"Ah . . . James?"

"Cadence?"

My cheeks burned. "I, ah . . . mmm . . ."

"Hey, what's up?" His voice sounded gentle and understanding, and I felt myself trusting him like I always had.

"James, don't feel like you need to say yes or anything, but . . ." The words got stuck in my throat. He would think I was an idiot.

"Do you need me to come over?"

"No . . . yes . . . I . . ."

"I'll be over in a few."

"No, you don't have to go out of your way—"

"It's not out of the way. I'm at my parents' house."

My face felt hot. "Oh . . . I shouldn't have called."

He laughed. "Cadence, it's fine. I know what you're thinking. You think they hate you and are pissed that you're calling me."

He nailed it. "James . . ."

"My parents don't hate you. Here, say hi to Mum."

"No! James—"

"Hi, Cadence!" Karen's cheery voice came down the line. "It's been such a long time. How are you feeling, dear? You've had a bit of a rough spell recently."

"Yeah," I managed to say.

"Well, things can only get better. Don't be a stranger, okay? I'd really love to see your little one. Her name is Melody, right?"

I smiled as Melody gave her dolly a bottle. "Yes, she's two in October."

"My, how time flies. It feels like just yesterday I met the little ninth grade girl that my son had a giant crush on, and now she's grown with a little one of her own and another on the way."

"Mum," James groaned in the background.

"James, we're just chatting."

"Give me my phone. I have to go."

"Okay, okay." She turned her attention back to me. "It seems I must say goodbye. Come by sometime, okay?"

"Okay," I answered.

There were shuffling sounds as James took the phone back. "Cadence? I'll be there soon."

When he arrived, I couldn't even look at him. He was so handsome, while I grew fatter and felt bloated. What was I even thinking?

"So, what did you need?" he asked as he sat on the sectional.

I sat forward, pressing my hands between my knees as I stared at Melody. "Melody needs a father figure in her life, but now that I'm saying it, I realize how ridiculous it sounds. I don't know why I thought you'd—"

"Of course I'll do it," he said abruptly. "Do you wanna do like a godfather thing, or what?"

"I don't know exactly."

He smiled and shuffled closer to me. "Why don't we go out to get something to eat and talk about it?"

I raised my eyebrows. "Melody doesn't do well in restaurants."

"Then we'll have a picnic. I can go pick up Canis. He needs a good run."

"I struggle to get back off the ground right now."

"Then we'll find a picnic table."

My gaze fell on his lips and I looked away, hoping he hadn't noticed.

"Cadence, we'll pick up something on the way, and then Melody can play with Cane while we talk."

I nodded, trying to avoid looking directly at him.

At the park, we ate together and he charmed me like he always had. He had me laughing for the first time in months, which came as such a relief. My heart felt lighter as a glimmer of hope slipped in. I *could* live without Austin. He had wanted me to go on without him.

While Melody played with the aging Canis, James turned serious. "So, I would very much like to be a father figure for Melody, and this next one, but what I'm also thinking might be a little ways off yet."

My stomach did somersaults. I didn't dare look at him. "What do you mean?"

"Well, I guess . . ." He sighed and ruffled his hair. "It's only been about three months since Austin died, so I know you're still grieving, but . . ."

As he hesitated, I looked across at him hopefully. "But what?"

He bit his lip, but when his eyes lifted and met mine, he saw my hope and gained confidence. "But I'm still in love with you."

My jaw fell, and I stared at him for a moment before bursting into tears.

It obviously wasn't the reaction he'd hoped for and he swore. "I . . . it's too soon. I'm sorry. I'll take you home."

But I grabbed his hand and he froze. "James, I'm crying because I'm relieved. I was sure you'd moved on, and I didn't want to dare hope you could still feel something for me. But I've never stopped loving you."

He let out a sharp breath before rushing around to sit beside me. He grabbed my hands and turned me to face him. "Cadence, you love me?"

I nodded.

He caressed my face as tears filled his eyes. "I'd almost lost hope."

He pressed his forehead against mine, and I caught a whiff of his familiar scent. I breathed it in deeply as he said softly, "How do you want this to work?"

"I'm still grieving for Austin, so for now, we should just keep it a promise. When the time is right, we'll start dating again."

He nodded, his eyes locked on mine. "And then, we'll get married, like you promised me."

A tear ran down my cheek. "James, I'm so sorry I broke that promise."

"You haven't yet," he said firmly. "You promised to marry me one day. That 'one day' just didn't exactly come the way I expected."

I started to weep, but he grabbed my face and kissed me. The kiss sent chills through my body, and I wrapped my arms around his neck to kiss him back. He pulled me closer, his kiss deepening as I gave myself up to him completely. Austin had wanted me to be with James—to let him love me, and to let myself love him in return. So now, knowing Austin was happy, I finally let my heart go fully to James.

The kiss felt so warm and loving, as perfect as his kisses had always been. I'd missed him so much, and climbed up onto his lap just to be closer. He chuckled as his hand ran down my cheek, making me shudder.

"Mumma!" Melody shrieked with delight.

I pulled away and looked across at her. The old dog licked her face as she lay on the ground. James laughed and set me on the bench, then rushed over to pull off Canis.

When he dropped us at home, Dusty burst out of the house, staring at us with his jaw hanging. "What . . . where . . . ?"

"What are you doing here?" I asked as James pulled Melody out of the car.

"Geri wanted to see you. Why's he here?"

James propped Melody on his hip. "I thought Cadence needed to get out of the house, and after breaking up with Emily—"

I spun to face him. Dusty gasped. "What? Dude, she was *hot*!"

James's gaze darted to me. "Hot isn't my thing. I prefer beautiful women."

Dusty grabbed my shoulders and shook me. "No freaking way, Cadence! How . . . no, I'm not going to ask."

He rushed back into the house.

James dropped by regularly over the next few months, for all the family events and just to spend time with me. When Melody's birthday came, he dragged Melanie along, to her disgust. She glared at me, her gaze falling to my pregnant belly as she scowled.

Linda and George were there too. They'd arrived a month or so earlier. They wanted to be close to me and the children, so they'd sold everything out west and moved to Sydney. It surprised me that they took an instant liking to James, and Linda even dropped hints for me to date him.

Melanie hung back in the corner while everyone sang "Happy Birthday," and James moved in to help me give Melody the cupcake. He laughed as she dug in and covered herself with icing, and then nudged me. "Hey look, she's a mummy's girl."

I glared at him before he shoved a cake into my face. "See?"

"James, you're lucky I'm the size of a house, or I'd whoop you."

He grinned. "I don't doubt it for one second."

"Daddy!" Melody reached for James.

My heart skipped a beat as I watched him lean over and pluck her out of the chair. I turned away and hurried out of the room as tears ran down my cheeks. I hid in my bedroom. Only a year earlier, she'd been laughing and reaching for Austin. It seared my heart.

"So . . ."

I swung around as Melanie walked through the door, her arms folded around her slender frame in a fashionable dress.

"Melanie . . ."

"You, Cadence, oh you . . ." She leaned closer and glared at me. "James told me everything. I have no idea how he believes your insane story, but he does." She scowled. "So, how'd you do it? Offer him sexual favors?"

I rolled my eyes and wiped away my tears. "We're not dating, if that's what you mean. Plus, look at me."

"Yes, look at you, all knocked up with your dead husband's child and trying to snag the guy you dumped for him."

I huffed. "I never expected James to come back. I know I hurt him."

"But he did, didn't he?"

"We're not dating, Melanie," I said firmly. "I'm not ready to—"

"Oh, here we go again. James is forever waiting around for you!"

I dropped my gaze.

She grasped my chin and lifted my face so she could look me in the eyes. "No more games, Cadence. Promise me, if you're going to do this, you will stick to it. You crushed him before, and I won't stand by and let you do it again."

I gazed steadily into her eyes before taking a deep breath. "No more games."

She released my chin and stepped back. "Good. Then what are you going to do?"

"I . . ." A tear ran down my face. "I want to marry him."

She let out a long breath. "Really? No messing around this time?"

"No messing around."

She nodded. "Well then, I expect to see you around at our family dinners, first Sundays of the month."

I smiled. "I'd like that."

She rolled her eyes, but a smile curled at the corners of her mouth. My baby moved inside me, and her hand shot out to feel it.

"You were there for me when I was pregnant," she said quietly. "And when I miscarried. I remember you . . ." Her gaze lifted to my face. "Melody . . ."

She pulled her hand back. "You've always been teetering on crazy."

She rushed out of the room.

The following first Sunday, James picked up me and Melody for their family dinner. We pulled up in front of the house, and he shot out to help with Melody. I climbed out, staring at the familiar home. It had been so long . . .

"What's up, Barbie doll?" Melanie stepped up beside me, looking up at the house. "Wait, I can't really call you that any more, can I? You definitely don't have the waist."

I frowned, raising my eyebrows.

She smirked, looking back to the house. "It's been a while. You used to come here all the time. I hated it back then."

"I know. And you made sure I knew it too."

She chuckled as a guy stepped up beside her. He had a similar look to Brian—tall, lean, brown hair—except better-looking, probably because he was looking at her and not me. She wrapped her arm through his, motioning to me. "This is Cadence, that airhead I told you about."

James punched her shoulder. "Shut your mouth."

The guy glared at James, shuffling between him and Melanie before he spoke to me. "I'm Trent, Mel's fiancé."

"Fiancé?" I wiggled my eyebrows at her. "This is news to me."

Melanie glared at James.

He ignored her as he adjusted Melody on his hip. "I'm hungry. Let's go."

James and I entered after Melanie and Trent. Karen rushed at us, kissing my cheek before she snatched Melody from James. He shrugged as she took Melody into the next room to give her toys.

John approached me, looking me over, his face cold. I took a step back. "Cadence."

"Mr. Gordon." Although I'd always called him John, it didn't feel right at that moment.

"Dad." James shook his head, resting his hand on his shoulder.

John met James's gaze, and then stepped back. "Do you plan on being here every month?"

"If you'll have me," I replied.

John opened his mouth to respond, but Karen dropped Melody in his arms. "*Of course* we will! Look at this gorgeous little girl, and this one's a boy, right?"

She rested her hand on my belly.

"Yes." I smiled as we both rubbed my bump.

"I love when he kicks," James said with a grin. "He's gonna be a soccer player, I just know it."

John gave him a cool glance, then looked down at Melody. She stared up at him, wide-eyed. Then she reached up and touched his chin. "Prickles."

He cracked a grin, and then cleared his throat. "Let's eat."

Dinner went fairly well, and although John made it clear he was watching me, everyone enjoyed the company.

Just before dessert, I leaned over to James. "So, care to explain the fiancé?"

His arm slid around the back of my chair. "He thinks it's a good idea to marry Mel?"

I nudged him. "Why didn't you mention it?"

"I dunno." He brushed my hair back from my shoulder. "It didn't seem important."

"It's pretty important."

He smirked. "Nah."

"Yeah." I play-slapped his chest.

He caught my hand, holding it over his heart. "They've been engaged for ten months or so, and are getting married in February. It's just a quiet thing, but I'm sure she wouldn't mind if you came as my plus one."

I grinned, my heart skipping. "I'd like that."

"I'd like that too." His hand tightened around mine.

"Mummy?"

I started, turning to Melody. "Yes, sweetie?"

"I need to go pee pee."

"Oh, ah . . ." I glanced at James, and he smiled. "Of course."

As I stood, I caught everyone looking away. My heart raced as I led Melody to the bathroom to change her trainer pants. I'd gotten lost in James's eyes, just like I used to, and had forgotten everything else. I couldn't believe how easily I'd slipped back into my old ways with him.

Over the next few weeks, James seemed nervous around me. It made me wonder if the conversation I'd had with Melanie had gotten back to him, as she most likely would have told him all about it.

Then, my birthday arrived.

I was thirty-seven weeks pregnant, and every inch of me ached. When James arrived at our house after work, I was wearing a worn-out maxi dress with my hair everywhere. I tried to hide from him, but he followed me into my bedroom. "Your parents agreed to watch Melody for us tonight."

"You want me to go somewhere?" I moaned. "James, I feel terrible."

The front door banged open, and three boys came screaming through the house. A moment later, Harper burst in, looking frazzled as she stroked her own pregnant belly. "Cadence, *what* happened to your hair? Stand up. I promised to make you feel pretty."

As she did my hair, she grumbled as she heard Melody scream while one of her boys laughed. "At least yours is a boy this time, too. I feel a little justice knowing that I'm not the only one who will be tortured by them."

Finally, she declared me ready. Despite how awful I felt, James's face lit up when I stepped into the living room wearing my maternity jeans, white blouse, and tan jacket. "Wow, you're beautiful."

I covered my face. "I . . . no, not really."

He scoffed. "I'm always right about these things, and guess what? *You* don't have the advantage anymore."

He offered me his arm, and I took it.

In the car, my stomach filled with butterflies. We were on our first date . . . sort of. He kept glancing at me with a goofy smirk across his face, which didn't help my nervous feeling. When we pulled up to Bicentennial Park, I thought I'd be sick. Was he going to cut me off?

I sat frozen as he dashed around and opened my door for me before opening the back. "I brought a blanket and grape juice, so we can pretend we're having wine and . . ." He paused and straightened. "What's wrong?"

"You want to end it?"

"Huh?" He glanced around and grabbed his hair. "Oh! I was actually thinking this is a nice place, and we

shouldn't have such a negative memory associated with it."
He grinned and offered me his hand. "New beginnings?"

My heart fluttered as my hand rested in his and he
helped me out.

It amazed me how easily I felt comfortable with
James. We talked like we'd never been apart, and while we
ate our picnic dinner under the summer sunset, I rested
my head back on his shoulder.

He sighed and set down his food. "Cadence, I want
to show you something."

He dug into his pocket and pulled out . . .

"The ring!"

He smiled sheepishly. "I almost pawned it, but something stopped me. It's been at the bottom of my sock
drawer for a while now. Dusty brought it to me about a
year after you married, and I just about ate him alive."

He turned it over between his fingers. "It still hurt,
so much. I started going to Fremantle games and traveling
to the Perth lab . . ." He lowered his hand. "I just couldn't
let you go. No matter how hard I tried, something inside
me told me there was still hope. I thought it was stupid,
until . . ."

He paused and looked into my eyes. "Is it selfish of
me to feel like he was meant to die so we could be together?
I feel terrible even thinking it, and even worse saying it."

My heart raced. "James, please don't—"

He pressed his fingers against my lips. "When you told me about your second chance, it all made sense. Seeing you stirred up so many feelings, and I knew that you'd given me a chance at a life I'd lost. You never should have loved me in the first place, but despite everything, you did. I remember how hard you fought me when I was pursuing you, and I'm amazed you gave in knowing what you stood to lose."

He stared down at the ring as I held my breath, sensing where he was going. "I bought this the same time I bought that sapphire ring. Your dad let us continue dating because I showed it to him and asked to marry you once you graduated.

"Cadence, I've loved you with every breath I've taken since high school. You're always on my mind, and even when we were apart, everything I did was for you, to impress you and make you happy. But now I have you back, I won't . . . I can't . . ." He gnawed on his lip as a single tear fell down his cheek.

"James," I whispered, my heart swelling as every inch of me begged him to say the words. I rested my left hand over his, silently offering myself to him.

He caught my hand and turned the ring over. "I love you so much, Cadence."

"Then ask me." I sat forward, and with my free hand, brushed his hair back from his face. "This time, I will say yes."

He let out a gush of air as he slid the ring on halfway and chuckled. "Ah, well, you've swollen up a bit, so this will have to do."

I laughed and slapped his shoulder. "You killed the moment."

"No, I didn't." He laughed and touched my face. "Cadence, my beautiful, wonderful Cadence, will you marry me?"

Tears burst from my eyes. "Yes, James, oh yes!"

He grabbed my face and pulled me in to kiss me. Excitement shot through me, and I clung to him. Never again would I let anything come between us. I pushed into him, brushing his lips with my tongue, making him moan.

He broke away. "If you weren't so pregnant, I'd bang your brains out."

I burst out laughing before I kissed him again.

And so, Austin was born in January, and that June, James and I finally married. We had a small wedding, with just our families present. I worked out hard to be as beautiful as I was for Austin's wedding, but I still wasn't happy with my wider hips and stretched belly.

But as I walked down the aisle of the small country church, James's eyes lit up and a wide smile spread from ear to ear. My stomach filled with butterflies, and as he took my hand from Dad, he said, "You've never been more beautiful."

I melted.

James held tightly to my hand as the ceremony proceeded. When we were pronounced husband and wife, Dusty grumbled, "Finally!" before James planted his lips firmly against mine.

James drew back, and I touched his face. "I can't believe you still love me."

He chuckled. "I can't believe you *ever* loved me."

"I'll never let you go again."

He squeezed my waist. "No more running?"

I leaned forward and kissed him. "Never again. I love you too much."

He grinned, clasped my face, and kissed me again.

At the reception, I scanned the faces of my family and friends. My parents sat with James's, as well as Linda and George. I smiled as Linda passed Austin to Karen, and Melody wedged herself between Dad and John to lap up their attention.

James stroked my back. "They're lucky kids. I wish I'd had three sets of grandparents to spoil me growing up."

I chuckled, relieved everyone had so willingly opened up to each other.

That night, as we unpacked in the hotel room, I pulled out the worn old scrapbook.

James leaned over, tilting his head. "What's that?"

I opened the tired pages, finding them blank. "It used to show me my first timeline, but it's been blank since

Austin died. I think, when my contract expired, it stopped working."

"Or," he said, brushing my hair away from my neck. "It's telling you that the time has come to look to the future rather than the past. Clean slate."

I smiled, taking a deep breath as his fingers worked on unzipping my dress. "My future with you."

"You better believe it."

I giggled as he slid off my dress and tossed me on the bed.

Six months later, I sat in the bathroom holding a cup and pregnancy test. James hovered in the bathroom, watching me.

"Seriously, this is gross having you watch me so closely," I said.

"Just hurry up."

A crash came from the living room, and Austin wailed. James didn't even flinch.

"James!"

He huffed and finally left me to see to the children.

When he returned, I set the test on the countertop. He stared at it as the result slowly faded into view. "Is that . . . ?"

I stared at his face, wanting to take in his reaction. "Positive."

His hand lifted and he ruffled his hair. Slowly, a grin spread from ear to ear. "We're having a baby."

Epilogue

The contraction hit me hard. "Geri!"

She rushed back to my side. "Just keep breathing, Cay-Cay."

"You're supposed to be my nurse! Where's my damn epidural?"

"Cadence." She grabbed my arm and squeezed my hand until the contraction passed.

"Why is this one so much bigger?" I sobbed as I tried to relax.

She chuckled. "The anesthesiologist won't be long."

I lay back and stared up at the ceiling while she checked my progress again. She sighed and shifted her scrubs around her own pregnant belly.

Mum dashed back into the room with a wide smile. "The kids are all with your father and Dusty, and Harper's on her way."

"Thanks," Geri and I said in unison.

James burst into the room, looking frantic. "What's going on? Is it coming out?"

Geri rolled her eyes. "You're so dramatic. She's only five centimeters dilated."

"This is your fault!" I said fiercely to him. "The other two weren't anywhere near this big. Your stupid genetics made a monster."

"Wow, you get mean when you're in labor." He shuffled up beside me and grabbed my hand. "But I'll forgive you, since you're giving me a baby and all."

I groaned as another contraction hit.

Finally, the anesthesiologist arrived, and James held me still while she inserted my epidural. Within seconds, the pain subsided and I relaxed. James stood beside me and stroked my hair back from my face. "Feel better now?"

I nodded.

He leaned forward and gave me a quick kiss. His hand rested on my belly, and he raised an eyebrow. "I can feel it tightening."

"Yeah, I'm glad I can't." I rested my head back and shut my eyes.

Harper came into the room and rushed to my side. "Cadence! Oh, look at you. Melody and Austin want to see you. Are you up to them coming in?"

I nodded.

She grinned and dashed back out the door.

James grabbed a chair and pulled it up beside me. "Everyone's out there, so expect a mad rush."

Melody and Austin came running in, and James lifted them up one by one beside me on the bed.

"Mummy, is the baby coming?" Melody asked, her dark eyes wide and excited.

"Yes, sweetie, the baby will be here in a few hours."

She grinned and nuzzled into my shoulder. "Can I hold it first?"

I laughed. "Maybe after me and Daddy."

Austin's little dark head of hair launched up into my face. "Mummy?"

"Yes, son?"

"Baby?"

I chuckled. "Soon."

James reached out and threw Melody and Austin over his shoulders. "All right, you two! Who wants an ice cream?"

"Me!" Melody replied loudly, and Austin followed suit.

Linda and George came to the door with smiles across their faces.

"Do you need us to take them?" she asked.

"Yes, please." James set them both down, and they charged at their grandparents. He took them out to the hallway, and while he was gone, I glanced down and saw my ring on the chain around my neck. I still couldn't believe he'd kept it for all that time.

James returned to the hospital room with his parents and Melanie right behind him. Melanie pulled a face at me and Geri. "Look at you two!" she groaned. "Seriously, this breeding thing is so overrated."

"Melanie!" Geri scowled. "You're just jealous because your husband doesn't want any yet."

"Actually . . ." She smirked. "I'm the one who doesn't want any yet." She ran her hands over her slim waist. "I like to keep this body to flaunt in front of you two stretched out—"

"Good heavens, Melanie!" Karen said sharply.

Melanie laughed.

James brushed by her and punched her shoulder. "You're such a loser."

"How mature, Jimmy," she sneered.

He rolled his eyes. "How did you get so obnoxious?"

John stepped forward and stared at my monitors. "So, how far away is my grandbaby?"

Geri rushed forward, glad for the diversion. "A few hours yet. These lines show her contractions, and this here is the baby's heart rate."

John leaned closer. "That's a little high, isn't it?"

Geri smiled. "Not at all. Babies have faster heart rates than adults. That's actually a perfect figure."

"I'm bored," Melanie groaned. "Where's Melody and Austin?"

"With their grandparents," James answered.

She rolled her eyes. "Which ones, genius?"

"Linda and George."

"Sweet. I'm gonna go kidnap them."

She left, and Karen and John followed.

Finally, Geri told me to push. With James grasping my hand tightly, watching the whole event with great interest, and my best friend assisting the doctor, I pushed with all my might.

What a big sucker! Melody and Austin had been much smaller, and came out after only a few pushes, but this one was almost ten pounds. Mum rushed into the room as I pushed to help give me encouragement and an extra pair of hands to crush.

Then, I heard the cries.

"What is it?" I asked.

"It's a girl!" James's whole face lit up.

He rushed around to Geri so he could cut the cord. She rested our daughter in his arms, and he rushed over to me, tears streaming down his face.

Harper burst in. "What is it?"

"It's a girl." Mum smiled with tears rolling down her face.

"Don't you dare give her another musical name," Harper groaned.

James ignored her and met my gaze. "Are we still going with Belle?"

I nodded as he rested her on my chest. "I'm so glad I couldn't predict this!"

He chuckled and kissed my head.

"James?"

"Yes, beautiful?"

"Thank you for giving me a second chance. This is so wonderful."

He smiled. "We all deserve second chances."

About Katie

Born and raised in Australia, Katie's early years of day dreaming in the "bush", and having her father tell her wild bedtime stories, inspired her passion for writing.

After graduating High School, she became a foreign exchange student where she met a young man who several years later she married. Now she lives in Arizona with her husband, daughter and their dogs.

She has a diploma in travel and tourism which helps inspire her writing. Katie loves to out sing her friends and family, play sports and be a good wife and mother. She now works as an Acquisitions Editor to help support her family. She loves to write, and takes the few spare moments in her day to work on her novels.

Acknowledgements

As with *Deceptive Cadence*, I'd like to thank my husband, **Landon** for all his support and patience through the entire writing and editing process. He may not read my "girly" books often, but he's my biggest advocate and probably does more to sell my books than I do! I love you, Landon!

Thank you to the REUTS team, especially as I grew more and more pregnant, and more scatterbrained as a result, throughout the editing period. **Kisa** and **Michelle's** patience with me was incredible, and I'm pretty sure they had some good laughs along the way at my random confusion.

Thanks again to **Ashley** for the beautiful covers, and **Summer** for getting the books into REUTS's hands.

There are so many people out there who have helped and supported me along the way that I cannot list them all, but I do want them to know I can't do any of this without them. Cadence's story was an absolute pleasure to write, as each character came to life on their own, and I'm so grateful for all those who saw the potential and power of this story and have given it a chance. So, thank you to you as well, for reading. Without readers, writers don't have much of a purpose.